I0758178

ALSO BY OMARI BAYI

Michael II – *The Sundarbans Park*

Michael III – *Pimps and Poachers*

Esmeralda – *A Harlem Creole Madam*

Esmeralda II – *Assault on a Mambo*

Short Shorts - *A Collection of Very
Short Tales of Fantasy-Fiction*

VISIT WWW.BIKOBOOKS.COM

MICHAEL

A DETROIT SAGA

OMARI BAYI

Preface

MICHAEL is a novel about a mid-western couple attempting to raise their children in an urban setting, with limited resources at their disposal. The story's timeline begins in an auspicious way in 1962, with a highly dramatic ending in the late summer of 1978.

The history of a midwestern urban city is examined under a microscope during the saga.

The family's odyssey covers the urban reformation of the sixties, the Vietnam War, rioting, vigilantism, gangsterism, higher education, drug wars, wealth disparity, classism, organized crime, love, and street violence. The rivalry between an innocent family and a major drug kingpin is the major focus of the tale. As with most wars, only one side can win.

Above and beyond these external forces, and the obvious financial issues of raising a large family, the parents of the family have only one internal problem—they have eight children but only enough room in their hearts for seven.

Introduction

This historically-versed novel is strictly fiction. Some may call it fantasy/fiction. Yet it draws heavily from a real urban setting, with street names, institutions, and communities that are real. The historical references did indeed occur, but the social commentary is strictly derived from literary reimagining. Understandably, the reader may agree or disagree with these opinions.

Michael is my third book; however, I've chosen to publish it first before the previous two. I fashion myself as a storyteller first and a writer second. Those who know me may see similarities of some characters with my real world, but these are mere coincidences. My love for my city, however, is no coincidence. I did cross paths with many of the institutions included in the book. I even shared an education and occupation with some of the characters. I will state up front that I do not have any military or medical experience and I am marveled at what those that do are able to accomplish.

I come from a family of loving parents and grandparents, uncles, aunts, and first, second, and third cousins living all over the United States, with a few growing up in Europe and the Philippines. So, my family tree differs dramatically from this fictionalized family. I borrowed numerous names from my tree to supply the characters with their names. Genealogy is a family endeavor, and I am aware of 13 of my 16 great-great-grandparents. My maternal grandmother was raised in a house with her maternal grandmother, who was also raised in a house with her parents and grandmothers. Oral history was their passion, and I experienced it as an adolescent. Seeing pictures taken in the 1850s of my maternal grandmother's great-grandmother was both fascinating and mesmerizing. Pictures of one multi-great-grandfather who was born around Abraham Lincoln's birth. Hearing stories of ancient relatives receiving their freedom papers just after the American Revolution leaves me with great pride. I still, however, am very proud of other branches of my family who endured enslavement right through the Civil War.

My parent's families migrated to Detroit in 1927, unbeknownst to each other. Both of my parents were born in the city in August 1931. I still have second, third, and fourth cousins living in the same small town of Thomaston, Georgia, where our great-greats were enslaved, working tobacco fields. And I am aware of my British roots as well, with plenty of indentured Irish fruit hanging from my branches. So, whether my people were getting off a ship from Ireland in the 1680s, working plantations in Georgia or Mississippi in the 1860s, or surviving in the borderline northern States with their freedom papers tucked in their back pockets, the final outcome was me continuing to water my Tree in this great northern city.

I hope you enjoy *Michael.* Throughout the writing process, I found myself getting very emotional, with tears flowing numerous times. Perhaps you'll experience similar emotions as you read *Michael.*

Omari H. Bayi
Author

Prologue

November 1969
2:00 A.M.

The shiny burgundy 1970 Cadillac Deville was speeding southbound on the John C. Lodge Freeway, traveling in excess of 100 MPH. On its bumper, driving equally as fast, was a twin Cadillac. The lead car, stolen just minutes before, weaved in and out of traffic, attempting to peel its tail, which caused the second car to brake hard to avoid crashing. The trailing driver maneuvered around the sparse traffic, then floored his accelerator to regain his position to the lead car. As the cars entered the sharp Wyoming Avenue curve, the trailing car broke hard, fearful of the extreme leftward redirection of the freeway, allowing the burgundy car to pull away. The lead Caddie hit 120 mph and was down to the next extreme right Linwood Avenue curve in one minute. The pursuing car was unable to catch up but did not lose sight of the burgundy Deville.

The stolen car entered the left lane exit of an adjoining freeway, braking just enough to avoid crashing, and entered the lightly traveled eastbound traffic. The driver then floored the accelerator again, taking the speedometer to 120 mph for the next sixty seconds, then exited the eastward traffic toward the southbound Interstate-75 Freeway. Once the car was onto the freeway, it again sped up to 120 mph until it reached the downtown I-75 right curve for westbound travel. Again, it sped up and immediately reached the Grand River Avenue exit. The trailing car eventually lost sight of the pursued vehicle.

The driver of the stolen car slammed on his brakes at the top of the exit ramp, turned hard right, drove north on Second Avenue passed Cass Technical High School and the school's track, then around the one-block of Cass Park, located on the north side of the school. Once around the park, he turned left, passing The Masonic Temple, then right up Fourth Street. Finally, the driver pulled into the first parking lot of the Jeffries Housing Projects. He then slammed the Deville between two giant trash containers, severely damaging both sides of the luxury car, then jammed on the brakes. The driver had to roll down a back window to escape the vehicle.

The thief ran west through the housing project, onto Grand River Avenue, then southeast towards downtown Detroit.

The thief, in his fourth year of hustling, was known by only one name.

The seventeen-year-old was called Michael.

CHAPTER ONE

A Meet and Greet

The strikingly handsome Black teen was enamored by the petite girl working at the counter of the burger-joint on Woodward Avenue in Ferndale, Michigan. The city bordered Detroit at the Eight Mile Road county line. Students were rushing off buses along Woodward Avenue and Nine Mile Road, but the teen was not in a hurry that morning since he had an hour before his first class. Heavy traffic moved southward on Woodward, as northern residents rushed into the city to get to work. The trees lining the center of Woodward had already begun the fall foliage, with some of the green leaves resisting the change, while others were already turning red and yellow, or falling from their branches and gathering on the ground. The mild wind hardly stirred the fallen dew-moistened leaves.

It was not his style to be attracted to White girls, but this lady had an aura he could not resist. She was dressed, as all the servers were dressed, in a light blue skirt hanging just below her knees, and a white button-up blouse. Her long dark hair was pulled back into a ponytail, hanging almost to her waist. He could not take his eyes off of her. It did not help that she was returning his gaze.

There were plenty of White people in the eatery, and he definitely did not want any trouble, so he turned to leave. The young lady noticed his departure, so she stopped wiping the counter and rushed out to get his attention, which worked. However, strangely enough, none of the patrons seemed to care. Even the police cruiser, which had just pulled into the parking lot, glanced over at them, then continued on its way.

"Hello," she said, with an east-coast accent. "Why are you leaving? Didn't you come here to eat?"

He was stymied and did not know how to respond to such an aggressive approach.

"Hello," he stammered. "How are you? Yes, I did come in to get a bite but changed my mine. You have a good day." He tried to rush off, understanding the potentially harsh consequences of their interaction.

She interjected, "Well, alright. But I'm new here and have yet to meet any of my people. Actually, you're the first. Can I at least get your name? And please don't make any assumptions about me until you get to know me. The folks inside already did, and I had to set them straight."

The young man's brain kicked into high gear.

He thought, *"Oh my Lord! This is a Colored girl! She could easily pass for White, but obviously chooses not to."*

He said, "I understand. That's the last problem I'll ever have, making an assumption about you."

He paused, then began to laugh. She joined his laughter, reached out her hand, and gave him a slip of paper and pencil. He opened it. It was blank.

"I don't give out my number to strangers, but if you do, I'd like to have yours. My name is Martha. You'll learn my last name after we get to know each other. And maybe you won't need to learn it if eventually you let me use yours."

She winked at him, waited for him to fill out the paper and return it, placed it into her white apron, and returned to the diner, smiling back at him one last time. He tripped over each rise in the sidewalk all the way to school.

Two years later, at the young age of eighteen, Martha and Frank were married. Twelve months later, on December 15, 1950, one day before their first anniversary, they had their first child, a boy they named Mack. Eleven years later, in September 1962 they had their last child, and named him Ervin. Now their teen years were gone. Their home was packed with enough people to field a basketball team with backup players. They were a mere thirty-one years old.

As Martha was leaving the hospital with the newborn, Frank touched her hand. She pulled sharply away and said, "Listen Mr. McCants. I know you love me, and you mean well. But you ain't touching me again until you get something fixed. You pay for your fix, or you pay for my fix. But something is getting fixed." Ervin was indeed the last.

Frank was the second of seven brothers. Martha was an only child by her mother. Both wanted a handful of children, but they just did not expect them to come so quickly. After her second delivery she tried birth control, but every method they tried failed. Both of them were terrible at planning and finance, so they found themselves struggling from day one. They understood the importance of keeping a roof over their heads and food on the table. Beyond that, they were always in debt. Frank's job at Chevrolet Gear and Axle did not pay much, which was a problem for all union workers. After the second delivery Frank decided he needed transportation. Martha advised him to wait before he bought his first car, but Frank could not resist.

He said, "Every man wants his own car. How do I look working at an auto supplier plant and not having my own car?" That purchase pushed an already fragile budget overboard.

Every home they rented quickly became too small. They moved frequently, about every three to four years, even relying on public housing. Their first home was an all-Black project in Royal Oak Township, a small community just west of Ferndale and bordering Detroit on the north at Eight Mile Road. It was temporary government housing, built to accommodate the Black migration to Detroit to help with the war effort. Their next move, in '58, was to 12th Street and Elmhurst Street in the center of the city. Then in '61 the family moved to Detroit's east side, gaining housing in a predominately White public housing project on Mound Road. The children had lived their entire young lives in all-Black neighborhoods, playing in the projects on Eight Mile Road, or running the streets and alleys on 12th Street. They were unprepared to experience the cultural shock of being a minority in an all-White working-class east-side community.

. . . .

Mack, the eldest son, was a very mature, polite, and responsible boy. However, before his parents could get all the way into the house from Martha's last hospital stop, he asked his mother, "Mom, where is this one going to sleep?"

She thought, *"This one?"*

Robert, born ten days before Mack's first birthday, said, "Mom. Really? Eight boys? I already share my bed with Michael and Jack. Richard and Louis sleep together. Mack has Horace in his bed. Where is Ervin going to sleep?"

Martha heard both questions and said, "You'd better not let your daddy hear you complaining, or he might get that strap out again.

And I didn't know you'd already named him. But I guess Ervin will do just fine. Sounds better than 'this one'."

As Frank entered the home he noticed the two boys discussing the newborn with their mother. He asked, "Where are the rest of the kids? They should be here in the house while both your mom and I are away."

Robert said, "Richard and Louis are on the playground, and Jack and Horace are in the bedroom. And you know Michael. Who knows where he might be at any moment. He may be my twin, but I don't try to keep up with him anymore. I gave that up long ago."

Frank did not like that last remark from Robert but let it slide. *"Yeah. Michael,"* he thought.

Frank had managed to get a job at an auto supply plant in Hamtramck the month Martha and he were married. Chevrolet Gear and Axle, on Holbrook, provided work for hundreds throughout the city and suburbs. So, except for the housing, they were never on public assistance.

With a houseful of boys, Martha had no choice but to be a homemaker. She loved her husband and sons but found an alternate lover as well; televised soap operas.

The boys were a bright but rough bunch. They fought a lot, either the neighborhood kids or each other. Each one was slightly bigger than the other, based on their births. Ervin got home in the fall of '62. The winter season came and went. When the family went to buy new spring clothes for the older boys at the new K-Mart, Frank had an unpleasant surprise.

"What in the hell is going on? Mack is almost as big as me! When did that happen? Now I have to shop for him in the men's section. That's really going to cost. What happened to that boy this winter?"

The movie theaters in Hamtramck gave Frank and Martha a much-needed reprieve on the weekends. They merely sent the older boys to the two-feature showings at the Martha Washington theater, which kept them away from home for at least four hours. The cost was perfect, just twenty cents per kid under the age of twelve. Then Mack grew to man-size and required an entire dollar for himself. He ate man-sized meals, drank man-sized drinks, needed man-sized ice cream cones, and he would only play with teenagers. He was gifted in sports, so the White boys in the neighborhood loved him. He was an eleven-year-old kid who could compete with teenagers.

When the family moved to the east side projects, the older boys had to enroll themselves in school, so they walked to White Elementary together. Robert had the most difficult time adjusting to his new surroundings and always carried a small satchel of books with him. He would disappear for hours then reappear as if nothing was wrong. At times, he played with Richard and Louis but usually he was alone. When Mack would ask Robert where he had been, he would merely blame Michael.

"I was trying to find him. Pops makes me keep an eye on him, which isn't fair. He's going to get all of us in trouble. He's such a wanderer. These White people are not going to tolerate his behavior. He leaves early and heads to Joseph Campau to hustle. He sometimes shoplifts. They've even caught him, but he gets away each time. That's why you haven't heard about it. And he's not going to admit it either. He thinks it's a joke. I'm always having to cover for him. He gets in trouble in school, fighting and skipping classes and they come to ask me about him. I don't know how he keeps getting all 'A's. He's hardly ever in his class. The counselor thinks there's something wrong with him, but she's afraid to say anything to Mom because we're Colored. Mom really freaks the counselor out with her pale face, Negro voice and New York attitude."

During the fall of '63 Robert was selected to join the school choir. They performed at most school functions and spent plenty of hours preparing for this year's Christmas play. Mack had already graduated to Cleveland Jr. High, just a few blocks north of the elementary school. He, however, decided to help his mother with the three little ones, instead of hanging out with his friends. She did not concern herself with the other boys, trusting they would behave themselves sitting with their friends.

The play required assistance from some of the older students to handle the curtain. Robert had been given this responsibility but was unable to help during this performance because he was in the choir.

He approached his friend James and asked, "Would you mind taking control of the curtains? I will have Michael help you."

James did not care for Michael but accepted. Robert then walked to the back of the stage to find Michael.

He said, "I need you to help James with the curtains. I have it tied properly to prevent it from falling during the acts. You relieve it this way," and begun demonstrating how to untie the rope.

Michael responded, "I don't need you to show me how to lower a dumb curtain. I've got this. It's easy."

After the choir performed, Robert went to the back of the stage to hang up his choir robe. He had a bad feeling something might go wrong so he went to join James and Michael at the curtain controls. A moment later Mack noticed the curtain shaking violently, then crashed down on the active students.

James came from under the curtain and yelled, "Michael did it!"

Mack ran to the back looking for Robert, whom he knew was responsible for the curtain. He found him looking confused.

Robert said to him, "See what he did! Then he ran off! I thought he could handle this simple task, but I was wrong. Now I'm in big trouble. Perhaps Pops is right about Michael. Perhaps he's right."

Mack just went back behind the stage to help with the confusion and reset the curtain. The play continued with only this minor interruption. Martha just ignored the frowns on the faces of the school staff.

She thought, *"That's my boy. Mack to the rescue."*

． ． ． ． ． ． ． ． ． ． ． ． ．

The Principal from Cleveland called the McCants house in February '64. Robert and Michael had just enrolled in Cleveland, after graduating from White Elementary, and were trying to adjust to their new surroundings. Martha hated getting calls from the schools. She worried about two things: one of her children being injured or someone complaining about Michael. This call was the latter. It was always the latter.

The Principal, a Dr. Washington, said, "Mrs. McCants, can you come up to the school. I need to discuss your son Michael. His twin brother Robert is doing fine, although he's occasionally absent. But Michael is rarely in class and is always getting in fights after school, even on days that he doesn't come to school. He's a little guy, but he's beating up bigger, older boys. Mrs. McCants, some of these boys from the Conant Gardens neighborhood and Sojourner Truth projects are rough boys, but they cannot handle your son. I need to see you tomorrow, or I will have to expel him."

That evening Martha told Frank she would have to get a babysitter so she could go up to the school. He did not have to ask why.

The next morning, Martha appeared in the principal's office.

He asked her, "Ma'am, where is your son? I assumed you understood he needed to be here with you."

Martha was a very astute woman and knew when to fight and when to accept defeat. She took the verbal reprimand without responding back, which was very difficult for her. Dr. Washington was right. Her son was difficult, and it was her responsibility to reign him in. Frank could not do it. She must, or she could lose more than a son. She could lose a marriage. She had the secretary to send for Robert to come to see the office. When Robert arrived, she asked him where Michael was.

He replied, "I'm not sure. He may be in his classroom."

In a very stern voice, she told him to go get him.

"He is your responsibility, remember?"

Robert left the room and Martha explained to the shocked principal, "Sir, I have eight children. The older ones are responsible for the younger ones. Except the twins. They are responsible for each other."

Minutes later Michael arrived. The principal, somewhat dismayed by the way Martha addressed Robert, proceeded to discuss Michael's behavior issues. With Martha present, Michael was on his best behavior. He knew she would deal with him later if he became belligerent in the principal's office.

That evening, she told Robert to meet her in the backyard so they could discuss Michael.

"Robert, I don't know what we're going to do about Michael. You don't seem to be able to handle him. And if you can't, no one can. I need you to get him to start behaving. I surely can't. You two are getting older, and it frightens me to think where he's headed. Do you understand me son?"

Robert merely stared ahead, feeling the same pressure placed upon him as usual.

Later, she decided to inform Frank.

"It's time, Frank. We can't avoid this issue any longer. We're going to have to go to the State and have them find us a child psychologist. The boy is twelve and not getting any better. I don't care that your family is proud, and you've never had to go this route before. My brother William still suffers from the stress of his childhood, so I've seen what can happen when a child is not given the proper mental counseling. That's where we are now. Since you are incapable of addressing this, I'll, as always, take it from here."

Frank did his usual maneuvering when faced with a situation, pertaining to his children, that he could not handle—he walked slowly into his bedroom, closed the door, and laid on his bed.

The following day, Martha called the Wayne County Health Department, and they referred her to a service in Hamtramck, a city within Detroit's boundaries, just west of the Mound Road projects. She wrote down the name and address of the doctor assigned to her case. She discussed the appointment that evening with Frank. The psychologist, a Dr. Woodamire, would initially meet them at their home Friday morning.

The next day, Dr. Woodamire's car caught fire, so he was unable to make the appointment. The Hamtramck Fire Department believed the fire was arson. Martha never called the county back to reschedule.

· · · · · · · · · · ·

The first day of summer vacation, Martha took inventory of her older boys and noticed that she had not seen Robert or Michael all day. When Robert got home after dark, Frank asked, "Boy, where have you been? You know you're supposed to be home before it gets dark."

Robert replied, "Michael and I walked to Belle Isle and worked at the Detroit Yacht Club. We took Mt. Elliot Avenue down to Jefferson Avenue. They gave us jobs, so we'll be there all summer. It was still light out when we headed home, but it's quite a long walk."

Then he looked at his dad and said, somewhat defiantly, "Michael just walked in ahead of me. Why didn't you get on him for getting home after dark?"

Frank was dumbstruck and almost struck the boy.

Robert continued, "You don't like Michael. I know it, and he knows it too. But he's my twin. You've got to care about both of us, not just …."

Robert started to cry, yet he was still able to speak: "The school system has always tried to separate us, placing us in different classrooms. They did that when we enrolled in Longfellow as first graders. Then again at White Elementary as fourth graders, and now at Cleveland as seventh graders. We even thought if we walked in separately, they might not realize we're brothers and put us together, but they always figured it out. They give the silly excuse that siblings should not be in class together. You and Mom never fight them over this. But if Michael was in my class, I could control him better. You're supposed to be his parent, but you always leave that responsibility on me. Michael's always down the hall or on the next floor. Well, keep us together and he won't get into trouble. I promise. You should have seen him today. He does excellent work, and those White folks on those boats loved him!"

Robert continued to cry as he walked away, preventing his father from retaliating with his belt. Frank understood the time for whippings was over.

He could only think, "*What's there to love?*"

Robert went into the lone bathroom, the only room that any of the children had for privacy. Michael was sitting on the side of the tub, wanting to be alone.

He said, "You didn't have to say those things to Pops. I know I'm a handful. I'm the elder of us two, so do what I say. Don't press him or he may send me away."

"If you go, I go. Now shut up Mr. Elder and get out of here so I can use it."

Frank heard the conversation through the bathroom door, then walked into his bedroom. The crowded room with a bassinet, chest-of-drawers, and full-size bed did not leave room for much maneuvering. He and Martha had learned how to dance around the room, so when she followed him in, he naturally slid into a corner to allow her to pass by him.

She closed the door and said, "I know you love that boy, but you've got to give him time to mature. Just give him time."

"I don't hate any of my kids. I'm hurting over this just like you," Frank replied earnestly. Then they settled in for the night.

. . . .

By the spring of '65, Frank had had enough with the extremely crowded conditions of their home. He told Martha that it was time to move again.

He said, "Ervin is now two and a half and can no longer sleep in the bassinet. Two bedrooms for all these boys, especially considering how big Mack has gotten, just isn't enough space. One bathroom. No dining room. No basement. We've got to move. Baby, we've been here for almost four years, the longest we've ever stayed anywhere. Only this time we've got to buy a house. No more renting in the projects or flats."

Martha replied, "I agree we need to move. But shouldn't we wait until after Richard graduates this June?"

He said, "Sure, but it has to be no later than this coming summer."

Martha felt her husband's pain and reflected on his plans as a young man. He was once ambitious.

She thought, *"This is not what he had in mind before that fateful day we met. He was heading to college the next year. Then he meets me, and eighteen years later he is feeling the compression of life."*

She said, "I understand you and totally agree. What do you have in mind? I don't want to have to rob a bank."

Michael overheard this conversation while walking by their room, and thought, *"Why not rob a bank? According to Pops, things can't get any worse."*

The family had noticed the rapid exodus of their neighbors over the previous year. The boys had plenty of White friends at their elementary school, but hardly any of those kids continued to the junior high school. They almost always transferred to the private Catholic school or moved out of the projects. White families were following any new freeway routed out of the city. Sub-divisions were going up in most suburban communities. Frank did not want to buy in the suburbs, but he did consider the west side of town where there was more modern housing.

He said, "I'm going to ask my foreman to be reassigned to a higher paying position. Perhaps even apply for a foreman's position. If I get a raise, we can apply for a mortgage."

Martha smiled at his new-found motivation.

She thought, *"Hardship is a great motivator."*

The next day, Frank approached his foreman at Chevrolet Gear and Axle and asked to be reassigned. He had a good relationship with Dombrowski but did not know if the foreman would support his request. As it turned out, he did not. So, Frank went to the personnel department and applied for a foreman's position. He was informed by a personnel rep that he had to have a recommendation from his foreman to apply for the position. When he got home, his motivation was zapped.

Frank said, "I spoke to Dombrowski today."

Martha, feeling a little excited, said, "Well, what did he say?"

Frank turned to face her, and she knew the answer without his reply.

He said, "I asked him to be reassigned, and he turned me down. I've watched several others get reassigned and I have more seniority than they have. I've been there sixteen years, working in the same area. Hell, I'm still driving a forklift. I went to personnel to apply for a foreman's position, and they told me I had to get a recommendation from Dombrowski. Fat lot of good that'll do. I could go to the Union, but those guys play cards every day with who? Dombrowski!"

Exasperated, he walked into his room and laid horizontally across the bed. He was unaware of prying ears.

A week later, Frank came home from work with great news. Dombrowski had been seriously injured in the parking lot. They needed a replacement since he would be out on sick leave for at least six weeks. Since Frank had already approached personnel for an advancement, and personnel knew he had seniority over all the other workers, the job was given to him.

Martha said, "Oh my Lord! This is such wonderful news! I mean, I'm sorry to hear about Dombrowski, but...with your new salary bump we can now apply for a mortgage!"

Martha had not told Frank, but she had already found a home for the family. She dreamed of it: *It is on the west side, a mixed neighborhood, with grass and trees, and a backyard, and garage, and a supermarket down the street.*

Martha dropped Frank off at his plant the next day and went down to the plant's credit union to apply for a mortgage. She had spoken to several of her neighbors who were successful in getting a government sponsored mortgage. This loan required a smaller down payment and lower interest rate. She took Mack and Robert with her. She felt Richard and Louis were old enough to watch the three youngest. She discussed her desires with a Miss Tominski and completed the forms.

Miss Tominski reviewed the application, then told Martha she did not qualify for the VA Loan. They were reserved for veterans only, and Frank had never been in the military. She would have to apply for a standard mortgage. Miss Tominski would still submit the application for a standard mortgage and Martha would get a response in a few weeks. Martha knew that even with Frank's new position it would take years to save up enough for a standard mortgage down payment. She went home feeling dejected.

The following week she received a letter from the credit union. She opened it and read it aloud.

> *"Dear Mrs. McCants:*
>
> *Your application for a VA Loan has been approved. Please call to schedule time that you and your husband can come to our office on Conant Avenue to complete the application."*

. . . .

Dombrowski pulled into the parking lot at Plant-2 of Chevrolet Gear and Axle. It was just before dawn. The parking area was secured with a chain-link fence and a security guard at the gate, so intruders could not steal the employee's vehicles. He got out of his car and was struck immediately in the back of the head, sending him crashing to the asphalt. When he awoke, his knee was seriously injured. A note was penned to his chest. "Fuck with my wife again and it'll get worse." He could not think of who would want to harm him, then he reflected back several years. "That blond was married?"

An hour later, Jack saw one of his older brothers climb into the open window and back into his bunk.

. . . .

A dark shadow climbed upon the roof of the Credit Union. A skylight was open to help circulate the air. The intruder climbed through the small opening and dropped to the floor. He jogged to the desk of Miss Tominski, opened her desk drawer, found the keys to the file cabinets in the back of the room, and opened the file cabinet marked 'New Applications'. He found two folders, one marked 'coloreds', the other marked 'Whites'. He searched through the folder marked 'coloreds' until he found the application from Martha McCants. He removed it, erased the standard mortgage application box, and placed a check mark in the VA Mortgage application box. He then erased the ethnic box for Colored, marked the one for 'White', then replaced it in the folder marked 'White'. After placing the folders back in the drawer and locking the cabinet, he placed the keys back in Miss Tominski's drawer. He then climbed up on the desk but could not reach the skylight. So, he placed a chair onto the desk, stepped up onto the chair, held onto the skylight, kicked the chair onto the floor, then climbed out of the skylight, onto the roof. In another minute he was back on the street. Thirty minutes later Jack saw one of his older brothers, still fully dressed, climb back into bed.

CHAPTER TWO

A New School

During the Easter week of '65, in mid-April, the McCants clan moved from the Charles Terrance Projects on Mound Road to the Fenkell-Livernois community located in northwest Detroit. Frank, Martha, and the boys had purchased their first home, and they were extremely eager to move in. Martha wanted to wait until June so Richard could graduate from White Elementary, but the house might not be available by then. The house was a white, two-story mid-sized frame home, around 1,500 square feet with a full basement and a detached two-car garage. It had two bedrooms and full baths on each floor. There was a back exit door on the second floor with back exterior stairs leading to the small back yard. They had to share their driveway with the neighbor to their north, so parking in the driveway was not permitted.

Once all the boxes, appliances, and furniture were moved into the house, Martha showed Frank a local ad from *The Detroit News*, an evening daily newspaper. A retired couple in a nearby neighborhood was relocating to Florida and needed to sell most of their furnishings. The McCants wanted to get new living room, dining room, and kitchen furniture, but did not want to create any new bills. So, Martha convinced Frank the best choice was for them to purchase the used furnishings advertised in the ad. Martha contacted the family and made an appointment to visit them the following day. The next morning, the McCants climbed into their 1960 beige Ford Country Squire station wagon and visited the family in the University of Detroit District. They left most of the older boys at home but took Robert and the three younger children with them.

Even though this neighborhood was only two miles from their new home, it may as well have been a universe away. The homes in this community were a collection of English and French Tudors three stories high with extremely steep rooftops and over 3,000 square feet. The community was built during the '20s, mostly by the college professors from Wayne State University and the University of Detroit. The streets were lined with tall trees whose branches canopied the streets. They ran north from Six Mile Road to Seven Mile Road, and a half mile east to west, ending at Livernois Avenue: a huge nine-lane throughfare. The community bordered the University of Detroit, a posh private Catholic school resembling a miniature version of the University of Michigan. To the east was the private Detroit Golf Club, which was encircled by various shaped small and mid-sized mansions and 6,000 to 12,000 square foot Colonials and Tudors, making the segregated golf course nearly invisible to the public.

As they entered the home, neither Frank nor Martha noticed the extreme discomfort that Robert was experiencing.

He thought, *"Why are they buying these people's used furniture? I hate that they always buy used stuff. When I'm grown, I will never find myself in a position where I have to buy someone else's old stuff. And this couple's move to Florida is another example of Whites moving out of the city, just as they're moving out of our projects. Even these rich Whites are moving out of the city."*

He was too young to appreciate that some retired couples moved to Florida for the weather. However, he continued to be polite but never smiled while interacting with the nice Jewish couple.

Frank and Martha agreed to furnish their living room and dining room with furniture from this retired couple. They continued to use the bedroom furniture and appliances they already had.

After the McCants were comfortably settled, 'new furniture' and all, the three youngest boys began rumbling through their brothers' boxes, looking for toys. Ervin, just two-and-a-half years old, found his brothers' report cards from their previous schools.

He looked at Jack and said, "Hey Jack, who does this belong to? What does it say?"

Jack, a few weeks from his fifth birthday, replied, "It doesn't 'say' anything. It can't talk. And how do I know what it says. I can't read yet."

Horace, the middle child, almost four years old, said, "let me see it," and took it from Ervin. Horace, who taught himself how to read during the previous year, looked at the card and said, "This is Robert's report card. See, this is his name. It's from his school, Cleveland Junior High. Looks like he got an 'A' in all these classes."

He dragged his finger down the list of courses.

Ervin then asked, "What's an 'A' mean?"

Horace replied, "It means he's good in this class. They are all 'A's so he is really good in all of his classes. I'm going to get all 'A's too when I start school next year."

Jack, not to be undone, said, "Let me see it. I start school this year, before you," and took the report card from Horace.

"What are these 'A's for?' Jack asked. "Which classes?"

Horace pointed to the list of classes and said, "These 'A's are for English, history, social studies, music, and math. Like in the spelling of your name, stupid. The second letter in your name is an 'A', remember."

Jack balled his little fist up, thrusted it toward Horace and replied, "I know how to spell my name and don't call me stupid again."

Ervin took the card back from Jack and asked, "Jack, what grade will you be in when you start school?"

Jack replied, "I will be in the kentergarten."

Horace corrected him saying "It's kindergarten, not kentergarten," then laughed.

Ervin said, "Well then, what grade is Robert in?"

Jack looked over at the card and shrugged his shoulders.

Horace again took the card from Ervin, glanced over the card, then put his finger on the grade and said, "See this number. It's an eight. This letter is a 'B'. So, Robert's in the 8-B. I think this fall he will be in the 8-A. According to Mom, when Jack starts in September there will no longer be semester grades, just annual grades. Now put that pen down before you write on those cards."

The Michigan school authorities changed the admissions policy, only allowing students born after 1959 to start school in the fall, which effectively ended the January semester enrollment.

Jack drifted away for a moment then said, "Michael will also be going to this school with Mack and Robert, if he stays out of trouble. But we'd better not mess with his report card. He's my favorite big brother, but I still don't want him thumping his finger against my head for ruining his card, like Richard likes to do."

. . . .

The following Monday, Mack and Robert walked to Post Junior High to enroll in school.

As they crossed the Lodge Freeway overpass on Greenlawn Street, Mack said, "Man, you don't need to carry that dumb bag everywhere you go, and you didn't need to bring all those books. We don't know which classes they're going to put us in, and I hope you didn't bring that silly truant letter for your 'twin' with you."

Robert replied, "We should have waited for him. He was only a few minutes behind us, and I didn't trust that he would bring it."

Mack frowned but did not reply. They walked into the building, found the office, and entered. Mack approached the front desk and informed the secretary that his family had just moved into the neighborhood and he and his brothers needed to enroll into the various schools. The secretary, dressed in a bright yellow dress, didn't bother to look up. She asked for Mack's report card from his previous school.

She examined the card and said, "Mack McCants. Nice grades. You really shouldn't have scribbled on this."

She returned the card with a routing slip, indicating which 9-B room the fourteen-year-old should report to.

Mack took the slip, and said, "Yeah. Sorry. My baby brother got into our things."

He then said to Robert, "See you later. I'll meet you on the Greenlawn corner after school." He then exited the office.

Robert approached the counter and handed his report card to the secretary.

"I have a truant letter for my twin…", he hesitated, remembering what Mack had said.

This forced her to look at him. She asked him to speak up. He merely looked at her, so she continued with her examination of his report card. She noticed the similarity between the boys and assumed they were brothers. When she glanced at his report-card, she noticed it had been scribbled on with a pen as well.

She thought, *"Baby brother too, huh."*

The grade was barely readable. She examined the card and noticed the grades were all 'A's.

She said to herself, "This kid is really smart. He's got all 'A's."

Not noticing the half-foot height difference, she thought, *"Since he mentioned something about his twin, we don't want them in the same room so…"*

She handed Robert his report card and a routing slip, sending him to a different 9-B classroom than Mack, not the 8-B classroom he belonged in, but the 'Honors 9-B'. She informed him where to find his classroom. Upon hearing the directive, Robert proceeded to his new class.

Michael walked into the school ten minutes later and bumped into the principal as he entered the office.

He mumbled, "Watch where you're going, dude."

The principal, dressed in a dark blue suit with a pink handkerchief in the welt breast pocket, was an excellent interpreter of mumble.

He replied, "Young man, why aren't you in class. What room do you belong in?"

"How do I know? I just got here," he said as he thrusted his report card toward the principal.

The principal, unamused, examined the card and said, "You shouldn't have written all over this card. I can barely make out your name. McCants, what's your first name? What do they call you?"

Michael dryly replied, "Well, everyone knows I hate being called Mike!"

The principal walked over to the secretary and said, "Miss Smith, send this young man, Michael McCants, to Honors 8-B."

He then walked away thinking, *"Another Michael. Such a common name. Guess it could have been Leroy. But this one's going to be a problem. His responses to my simple questions were belligerent at best. And addressing me as 'dude'? Well, I never!"*

Michael took the routing slip, exited the office, proceeded down the hall, and out the back door onto the playground.

When the bell rang at the end of the school day, Mack exited the building and walked to the Greenlawn corner. He had heard a rumor that some boys named Banyon might be looking for him, but he was not too concerned. He heard clamor from a crowd of kids on the playground but hesitated to drift toward it, instead looked for Robert, who had not arrived on the corner yet.

As he slowly walked toward the commotion on the playground a kid who lived next door to them, called Butch, approached him.

"Hey Mack! Your brother Michael just fought two Banyon boys at once and whipped both of them! Man, can he duke!"

Mack, alarmed, said, "What happened?"

"I didn't see what started it, but you know the Banyons. They always pick on the new kid, but they sure made a mistake messing with your brother Michael. He had all of the kids laughing at those bullies."

Mack looked at the dispersing crowd and asked, "Where did Michael go after the fight?"

Butch replied, "He saw the principal coming out of the building and took off that-a-way toward Puritan. Heck, he's probably half-way home by now. He can really move!"

Mack thought, *"Here we go again. The first day of school and he couldn't maintain himself. Pops is going to explode when he hears about this."*

Instead of walking directly home, however, he walked through the streets near the school hoping to find Robert. He eventually arrived at Livernois Avenue, but since he never saw his brother, he headed home.

When Mack arrived home, he waited for Robert in the front yard but saw Butch first.

Mack said, "Butch, don't say anything to your parents about what happened. I don't want my father to get wind of a fight. Especially if my brother finds out it was you who squealed on him."

Butch frowned and nodded in agreement.

"Mack, can you take Michael?"

Mack replied, "That's a dumb question. What do you think?" and walked up the driveway and into the back door.

He found Robert sitting in the kitchen and said, "I thought I told you to wait for me on the corner."

Robert replied, "Yeah, well you weren't there. Then a fight broke out, so I split. By the way, have you seen Michael yet?"

Mack just stared at his brother, then went upstairs to his room.

He thought, *"I was hoping we wouldn't continue with this silly drama. How am I going to keep Pops from finding out about this? Unlike Mom, Pops doesn't handle this situation well. He may try to use the belt again, and I know that won't work anymore. We're getting too old for that abuse."*

After dinner, Robert remained downstairs studying in the kitchen while Mack went to his room for the rest of the evening. He wanted to be sure he was up to date with the material the school assigned him. Mack suspected he was ahead of his classes since he was an honor student at Cleveland Junior High, and Post only placed him in regular 9-B classes. Since he had not talked to Robert about their class placement, he was unaware that the school had placed Robert ahead a year in the honors 9-B.

Robert, however, had indeed noticed Post had moved him up a year. He assumed it was because of his grades and the level of study Cleveland's honors 8-B was offering. He felt that his being in the same grade as Mack, however, would need to be kept quiet. Mack may not appreciate it and Pops might not allow it.

Over the past three years, Robert and Mack had been pulling apart. Mack was hanging out with older kids, more his size. They were still close, just not as close as they were when they were in grade school. That first year that Mack spent in Cleveland Junior High away from him may have contributed to his maturing quickly. Mack and Michael had never been close. They just could not get along.

The older boys had agreed to set up the two bedrooms as one bedroom and one games/study room. They had their bunkbeds along the walls, with the front wooden window in between. They also set up pallets for the younger brothers if they wished to spend the night in their room. Sharing their bedroom space was the norm for these brothers, since they were used to sleeping in homes with only two or three bedrooms.

At 9:30 p.m., Mack climbed slowly into his bed and promptly fell asleep. Richard and Louis had already gone to sleep, and Robert was still downstairs. Fifteen minutes later, Mack only dreamed he saw Michael climbing into the front second floor window, which was only accessible by climbing over the roof from the second-floor backstairs.

As Michael drifted off to sleep, he contemplated his day. "*Those Banyon brothers were a handful. My shoulder is still aching. But they should never have spread the word that they were going to stomp Mack and Robert after school. I knew we would be in a fight today since we're new to the neighborhood. So far, the kids on our block have been laid-back, amazed at our numbers and strength. Who wants to mess with five dudes at once? But in school we get separated, and those kids in the classes did not know we were together. It didn't help that the girls were talking about us McCants. Mostly they checked out Mack, since he is so big for his age. Don't know why I didn't see Robert in school even if I did only go to one class today.*

"It might be wise for me to stay away from school for a day or two, just in case that Principal might be looking for me. He's not a bad White dude, but why chance it? And I really don't want to get into another argument with Pops. He's whipped me for the last time. I'm not going to put up with such childishness anymore. But I know if I raise my hand to him to defend myself, then it's over for me here. I can't fight my dad. None of my McCants' cousins would ever understand, and Mack and Robert? Oh man, they would destroy me. I might be able to handle Robert, but I'm still not able to handle Mack. Besides, how in the heck am I going to fight either of them, especially my twin? I need to stop thinking about this before I go mad! Need to fall asleep. Please, God, let me sleep these thoughts away. Please God. Help me end these thoughts."

Frank was still up when Martha headed to their bedroom.

She said, "This first day of school enrollment is finally over. I was able to get Richard and Louis into Clinton Elementary, but the older boys had to continue to walk to Post without me. They're old enough. I didn't go to Cleveland Junior High when they enrolled there. They definitely have matured."

Frank added, "You're not concerned with our 'twin' situation? That Michael will eventually prove to be a problem?"

"It is what it is."

Frank said, "Well, they got that first 'new neighborhood' fight over with. Seems they kicked some kids' butt pretty good. I didn't notice anything unusual about Mack, so he may have hung back, since he's so big, and let Robert do the fighting. Hell, that boy is almost as tall as me."

Martha, having grown up in New York's Harlem, replied, "Hell, it was probably Michael who was fighting. I know the importance of establishing yourself in a new neighborhood. That was Mack's mistake when we moved from the Eight Mile projects to Elmhurst when he was only seven. He was bullied a lot, and it took too long for him to begin fighting back. Those were miserable times for him. He was able to start all over once we moved to the Mound Road projects. Those White kids loved him. Don't want to ever go through that 'new kid on the block' shit again. But don't get too excited about Mack's size. I believe he may have peaked at five foot eight. My brothers never reached my dad's height of six foot two. My grandmother was really short, which is why I'm so short. Yeah, Mack may have peaked. We'll see."

. . . .

Martha had had enough seeing her first born come home with tears in his eyes and clothes torn. The family had only lived on Elmhurst Street and 12th Street for just three weeks. She took seven-year-old Mack by the hand and walked him into the shared basement of the four-family flat. She told Robert to keep his brothers upstairs. The basement was cluttered and dusty, and she did not feel there was enough room for all the boys. Nor did they need to see what was coming next.

When Martha was sure no one else was in the basement, she got down on one knee, looked a frightened Mack in his eyes, and said, "I am fucking tired of seeing you coming home all bruised up. This is the last time this is going to happen. Your brothers fight back and so will you. Put your hands up! Not like that, like this. Okay, now, every time you pull away, I'm going to smack you in the face. When I strike, you had better strike me back. And you had better not start crying. Either you kick those boys' asses who are fighting you on the block, or I'm going to kick your ass. Do you understand me boy? And you'd better not tell your dad!"

. . . .

Meanwhile, across Fenkell Avenue, east of Livernois Avenue, Randy Banyon, the sixteen-year-old brother of Sam and Tommy Banyon, was discussing the fight his younger brothers had that day. Randy, a high-school student at Mumford, was furious his brothers were ganged up on by these new kids. His brother Sam told Randy that he and Tommy had been jumped by the McCants boys in an alley near the school. The fact that Sam was fifteen years old, and Tommy was fourteen years old, the same age as Mack, never crossed his mind since he knew little about the McCants. He called the Walker boys, who lived across the street, and told them to join him and his brothers after school the next day. The five of them would make sure the McCants never messed with the Banyons again. Randy said aloud for anyone to hear, "Tomorrow I'm goan mess doez punkasses up! Dae goan learn not to mess with my brothers ever again."

CHAPTER THREE

Rumble in the Alley

News of the pending rumble spread throughout the neighborhood, north and south of Fenkell Avenue, and east and west of Livernois Avenue. Clinton Elementary and Post Junior High were abuzz with the gossip. It even reached the teaching staff of both schools, but the authorities were not summoned.

"It's just street-talk," said Clinton's Principal Smith. "Playground gossip. I've spoken to Principal Johnson at Post, and he's not concerned about it. The students involved are mostly from his school. I will call Mumford High and Custer Elementary as well, just in case their students are involved." Mumford was the well sought-after high school that almost all of the junior high students in the community wanted to attend. Custer was the elementary school for the students living east of Livernois.

The fact that the school administrators did not want to involve the police did not stop certain parents from contacting them. Calls such as, "Officer, there's a new family of hooligans in the neighborhood. They're called McCants and they live on Santa Rosa, near Lyndon. They're bullies and they're beating up the kids on the block. Please come check them out." These types of calls were frequent enough to get the Tenth Precinct involved.

Before noon, a patrol car visited the McCants home. A White male officer climbed the stairs to the porch but did not need to ring the doorbell. Martha knew of his presence the moment the squad car parked in front of her home. The officer was surprised when a White woman came to the door.

"I'm here to speak to a Mrs. McCants. There's a complaint filed at our precinct that her boys have been beating up the neighborhood kids for the past month or so. Would you mind getting her for me."

Martha did not particularly care for the police, especially White officers.

She dropped her prep-school accent and spoke in her Harlem accent, "I'm Mrs. McCants. These are my boys." indicating the three young children standing behind her.

She continued, "That's interesting, Officer, considering my family moved here last week."

The officer, still confused by her appearance, asked, "Ma'am, where are your older sons at present?"

Martha responded, "They're in school, of course. I enrolled them in school just yesterday. They attend Clinton and Post. As I said, we moved in last week. So how could we have been terrorizing this block for months? My boys have only been in school for two days. And these little fellows are not allowed outside the backyard until their older brothers get home."

The confusion the officer felt in realizing Martha was married to a Black man was betrayed by his facial expression. He did not approve of inter-racial marriages and could not hide his disdain. He did not hear any of the remarks Martha made about the children. Martha witnessed it, and her arrogant smile really bothered him.

Before he could speak, however, she said, "Officer, I know what you're thinking. But you can relax. I'm not White, just have a lot of White ancestors. Please tell your partner, so he can relax as well."

The cop was now really discombobulated. He stammered his apology for disrupting her morning and left the porch.

His partner said, "Was that a White woman answering that door? Some Black nigger married that pretty white girl?"

His partner responded, "Just get in the car. False alarm. And the woman ain't White, just an uppity high-yellow bitch. Let's go."

Even though the police dismissed the complaint about the bullying, after confirming the family had just moved in, they still put out a bulletin to watch out for a pending brawl. They did not escalate their patrol of the area, but monitored the kids walking home, looking for any signs of trouble. The few skirmishes they did witness at Clinton were ignored.

The kids coming from Clinton were mostly Black. The White kids went to Saint Gregory, a Catholic school east of Livernois, so their walk home was in the opposite direction. The school district arranged to have the Saint Gregory kids get out thirty minutes before the Clinton kids to avoid any potential conflict, even though many of the kids played together after school.

．．．．．．．．．．．．

Samuel Banyon approached Mack in the lunchroom and informed him of his intentions.

He said, "My brothers and I will be waiting for you. Name the place."

Mack responded, "What the heck happened to your face?" and smiled.

Samuel angrily stammered, "We'll see whose face is messed up after tonight. Just be there."

They agreed on a time and place in an alley off the south-side surface drive of the Lodge Freeway, one block west of Livernois Avenue. Mack had only one request.

"Don't spread this around. We don't need an audience. That will only alert the police. Besides, you had an audience yesterday and they're still laughing at you. Keep it to just your brothers and mine."

. . . .

Robert, Richard, and Louis were waiting on the corner of Livernois and Fenkell when Mack arrived. Robert said, "I found Richard and Louis, but I could not find Michael." No one responded to Robert, as Mack began the march toward the alley. When they arrived, the Banyons were already there. However, they also brought along the Walker boys.

Robert's fighting style was different from Michael's. Robert was far more controlled, not furious like Michael. The effects, however, were the same and the Banyons would soon find out. Mack was just power and being the size of the older Banyon boy made Randy pause to reconsider what he had gotten himself into. He noticed that there were only four boys here, and the other three were small. Mack, however, was very muscular, which gave Randy reason to hesitate. He also noticed how his brothers looked as they stared at the second boy, Robert. They looked scared even though they were noticeably bigger than he was. Finally, he saw that the other two younger boys looked extremely eager, moving from side to side, standing on one foot, then switching to the other. It made the Walker boys nervous. No smiles, just Frank-like stares.

Mack said, "I thought we'd agreed to only bring relatives. These two don't look anything like you."

Randy said, "Just to even the odds, I can have one of them sit out if necessary. Either way, you're going to get your ass kicked for jumping my brothers."

Mack smiled, then said, "We didn't jump your brothers. Just one of us kicked their butts. But let's have less talk and get this over with. I've got homework to do."

Samuel asked, "So where's Michael? Why ain't he here?" Robert replied, "To even the odds", and hit Samuel with a left jab that drew blood. The rumble was on!

The rules of a street rumble were simple. No weapons. Weapons bring the police, a terror in the neighborhood. Nothing else mattered. All sounds from the freeway and Livernois Avenue ceased, a complete vacuum of silence. Just the sound of the boys.

Unfortunately, the Banyons did not have any real experience with gang fighting. They had always over-powered other kids with their superior size. They really did not know how to fight.

Samuel drew back from the unexpected punch from Robert, but his brother Tommy rushed in. That proved to be a big mistake because Robert anticipated this and moved to his left, circling Samuel, so Tommy could not reach him. He punched Samuel in the face three more times, before pulling back right and circling left again, avoiding Tommy. Robert, still free from Tommy, stepped in once more and punched Samuel in the face three more times. Left, right, left combinations again and again. Samuel was unable to begin throwing any punches. Every time he attempted to fight back he was punched in the face. He was now so confused he back peddled to a building wall, allowing Robert freedom to confront Tommy.

Mack rushed Randy, ducked Randy's first punch, reached out to lightly touch Randy's waist, then pivoted around to Randy's back. He then wrapped his arms around Randy's hips, lifted him off the ground, tilted him slightly, then flung him to the ground. Randy landed on his side, having lifted his head to prevent it from impacting the alley rubble. The impact was devastating.

In an unrecognizable voice, he moaned aloud, "Ooohhhh!" as the air in his lungs escaped without being replaced. He belted out, "Oh my God! Oooooohhhhhhhhh!!!" as the final amount of air left his lungs.

It would be a while before he could breathe again. His entire body ached as never before. His eyes glazed as he looked up at Mack, who stood over him ready to pounce. Mack was a clean fighter, never wanting to strike a downed opponent. He was smart enough, however, not to get careless and allow Randy to sweep his feet. He merely stood there with his arms slightly behind his back, palms open and turned backward, slightly bouncing, his eyes surveilling the other action. He could see Robert handling Tommy, as Samuel backed away. He checked on Louis and Richard, which proved to be a wasted moment, for they did not require any assistance. Even though Mack was just fourteen years old he had plenty of experience fighting older boys, thanks to the wars he and his brothers were in at the projects on Mound Road. And he rarely had to intervene in the other's battles.

Louis and Richard rushed in on the older Walker brothers and threw so many punches the Walkers could not counter. They only held up their hands to protect their faces, but it did no good. One Walker boy fell on the ground, and before he could rise, his brother tripped over him and was on the ground beside him. When one of them finally got up, he went down again, tripping over his downed brother. Louis and Richard were extremely experienced in their tag-team approach, and the Walkers were finished within sixty seconds. They never landed a punch on either McCants. They just continued to back up, bump into each other, trip and fall, get back up, bump and fall and bump and fall, over and over.

Robert only had to fight Tommy after dispatching Samuel with his initial volley. Tommy kept throwing punches at the shorter Robert, but Robert stayed out of his range, darting in for three-punch combinations, then sliding back out before Tommy could react. Robert hit Tommy with his combinations again and again, circling to his left after each one. It did not concern him that he occasionally had his back to the Walkers because he knew Louis and Richard would not allow anything to happen to him. He noticed that Mack was just standing there watching with the most amused smile on his face, and he knew his older brother was proud of him.

Finally, Samuel, who never actually entered the fight, pleaded for the fight to end. His brother Randy had never gotten off the ground and Tommy was unable to land even a single punch on Robert. The Walkers continued to have to get off the ground only to go back down again. They were offering no resistance.

He leaned against a telephone pole, a bloody nose blocking his breathing, and shouted, "Okay, Okay! Stop! We've had enough. Oh my god!"

He was Mack's size, but not as muscular. Even though he was fifteen years old, and had been a bully his entire life, he had never been crushed like this before. Two days in a row by only one fighter. First Michael, now his twin!

"Okay man, okay, we've had enough. Please stop this shit! Please stop."

Randy continued to lay on the ground, barely able to breathe, too afraid to rise in front of the huge-looking Mack. So, Mack backed away allowing him to stand up. Once Randy was standing, he realized that he was still bigger than Mack.

He thought, *"This guy looked so much bigger when I was on the ground! What the fuck?"*

The Walker boys had backed up, all the way to an abandoned garage. Louis and Richard had already stopped hitting them but kept them corralled between the pole and the garage.

Mack said, "Okay. They've had enough. Stop fighting guys. Robert… I said stop!" Robert heard his brother and held back his final volley. Tommy continued to hold his ground and tried to look brave, bloodied face and all.

Mack said, "Alright. This is over. We will see you guys in school tomorrow. This does not have to get out, unless one of you guys mentions it. And remember, no more messing with my family." He walked over to Randy and said, "You heard what I said. No more messing with my brothers. You do understand, don't you?" Randy could only stare at the shorter boy, but offered no response.

Mack walked out of the alley onto Fenkell Avenue, looked both ways to ensure no police patrol cars were in the area, then summoned his brothers. They avoided walking down Livernois Avenue, instead walking two blocks west to Monica Street, then south through the neighborhood streets.

When the boys got home Richard and Louis went upstairs, while Mack went into the basement to get clean clothes for school tomorrow. When he returned, he said to Robert, "You're going to need some peroxide for your knuckles. I'll get the bottle from upstairs." Robert asked, "Anyone else in the basement?"

Mack shook his head and headed upstairs. Robert proceeded into the basement only to find Michael sitting in a corner by the storage boxes, out of view of the basement sink.

Robert yelled, "I thought no one was down here."

Before he could ask Michael about his whereabouts Michael said, "What happened to you? Your sleeve is torn. And your hand is bleeding."

Robert dryly said, "So where were you? We had a rumble, but you weren't around. We could have used you today."

Michael retorted, "Well, you shouldn't schedule stuff without asking me first. I heard about the rumble but…besides, I did my share when I kicked those Banyon boys' butts yesterday. That was for you and Mack. They were looking for the two of you when I got to them on the playground."

Robert said, "Well, that's why we were fighting today! Because of your fight yesterday!"

Michael said, "You would have had to fight them anyway. They were threatening you, and I couldn't take it. I was definitely coming today, but Pops came home a little early and I couldn't get pass him. He would have stopped me because of yesterday's fight, and I didn't want to hear it. So I stayed down here. He and mom stayed in the kitchen like…forever. I had to shush the little-kids, who came down here to play. They almost gave me away."

Robert looked incredulously at Michael and said, "Likely story. Pops doesn't even allow them down here yet. Anyway, the war is over for now. They won't be bothering us for a while, but I told Richard and Louis to stay together for the next few days and to walk home from school using Lyndon for the remainder of the week. Perhaps you should meet up with them, just in case."

Michael paused for a moment, then said, "Are you suggesting you don't trust the Banyons?"

Robert replied, "I don't trust Randy, the older boy. He did not like getting his butt handed to him. He wasn't even in the fight! He laid on the ground the whole time! He may want to take it out on Richard and Louis. So no, I don't trust him at all. Mack really humiliated him in front of his brothers and those Walker boys. And Mack also cautioned him on attempting to retaliate against us. He was really serious, too. However, Randy's not going to take this humiliation lightly."

. . . .

Michael waited until bedtime, when everyone was asleep, then began climbing out of the bedroom window. He could have used the upstairs backdoor, but he did not trust the noise it made when opened. Louis saw him leaving, even though he was half asleep, and said, "Michael, where are you going?", then fell back to sleep.

Once he was in the alley, he began running north to Chalfonte Street, then over to Livernois Avenue. He was headed for the Banyons. He had followed them the previous day and knew where they lived. He also found a way to get into their house. He climbed a tree to their roof, armed only with a Louisville Slugger baseball bat. He peeked into the bedroom window and saw Randy get up and head out of the bedroom.

He thought, *"Punkass is probably going to the bathroom."*

He climbed through the window and walked by Tommy, who was in a deep sleep. Randy was indeed in the bathroom sitting on the toilet. Michael walked in on him and raised the bat over his head, placing his index finger to his lips. Randy froze in utter fear.

Michael whispered, "You see what I can do to you, motherfucker. You see how I can kill yo ass at any time. Don't you come near me or my brothers ever again, or I will fuck you up and all your brothers. I'll burn this fucking house down, you hear me! And don't think you can get your 'boys' to take us on. I'll bring 50,000 McCants cousins over here, and we will tear this whole neighborhood apart. And if you yell when I leave, I will crush Tommy's skull. You got me? You punkass motherfucker!"

Randy, noticeably bigger than Michael, remained petrified. Sitting on the toilet with his underwear down and his head at Michaels chest-level left him feeling extremely vulnerable. Michael walked out of the bathroom, not bothering to close the door. He walked pass Tommy, climbed out of the window, down the tree, and out of the yard. He was back home fifteen minutes after he left. Fifteen minutes to run to the Banyon's home, climb into their window, accost Randy, climb back out the window, set the Banyon's trash cans on fire, and run back home. No one in the McCants home noticed he was gone. No one except little Jack.

. . . .

The school was silent the remainder of the week pertaining to the rumble. It seemed the results were too frightening to imagine. There was talk about it but nothing boisterous or exciting. Kids were just going about their affairs.

The following Monday Principal Johnson stopped by the cafeteria to speak with Robert. He found him sitting in a corner eating his sandwich and reading a book.

"Hello young man," said the principal. "How are you adjusting to your new school?"

Robert replied very politely, "Just fine, sir. My family moves around a lot so new schools are not uncommon to me."

Johnson smiled and said, "I was speaking to Miss Brown, the secretary in the office, when you enrolled last Monday. She said you mentioned a truancy letter. Do you still have it? Is it for your twin brother Mack?"

Robert was caught off guard by this question and responded, "No, sir. That was a mistake. Mack did not have any letters from our old school. If he had, he would have presented it himself." Michael thought, *"He knows Mack is not my twin."*

Principal Johnson said, "You seem to have an unusual vocabulary, as do your brothers. Is your mother a teacher?"

Robert became irritated by this remark. He did not know if the principal was setting him up with this insulting question or just plain ignorant.

He replied, "My mother is a homemaker. My dad works in the plant in Hamtramck. Both are educated and come from educated parents. My mother does not tolerate poor grammar in our home."

Principal Johnson continued probing. "Is that the case with your brother Michael? I notice he uses a lot of slang. In fact, he is actually your twin, isn't he? Wasn't the letter of truancy for him? He has not been to class much last week."

Robert almost fell into Johnson's trap.

He thought, *"He doesn't want to discuss me. He's trying to get info on Michael. He probably has already called Cleveland's administrator to get a status on the three of us. He knows I belong in the 8-B!"*

Robert said, "Sir, I cannot speak for Michael. Only Michael can speak for Michael. I don't know if he's been to his classes since we don't discuss school."

Johnson was disappointed this young kid did not give him the answers he was looking for.

He continued. "It seems you are in the wrong grade. Cleveland has you in the 8-B. Why did you tell Miss Brown you were in the 9-B?" Robert had been practicing a response for this question since last Monday.

Without missing a beat, he said, "I'm sorry, sir, if there was any confusion on my part about which grade I belong in. I assumed you were impressed with my grades and advanced me to the level I truly belong. The classes you offer your 9-B students were the very same classes I was taking at Cleveland. I never intimated I was in the 9-B. If you wish for me to repeat all those classes offered in the honors

8-B I can, but I will be extremely bored. I am already at the head of your honors 9-B class, which I'm sure you've checked out. I will do as you wish."

Johnson was not prepared for such an eloquent diatribe with a thirteen-year-old but did not want to appear so.

"No son, I do not intend on moving you back to the honors 8-B class. Besides, your brother Michael is in that program, even though he never seems to attend classes. What I want from you is to have your mother come up to the school so I can discuss Michael and his truancy. You and I can talk again later."

Robert said, "Sir, I will make her aware of your need to speak to her. You could call her but we are still waiting for the phone company to respond to our request for a new phone line. However, we only have one car in the family. My dad uses it to drive to work. We live over a mile away, and my mother watches my three little brothers who have yet to start school. So, I'm not sure if she will be able to make it up here."

Johnson replied, "Well, perhaps I should arrange to meet your mom at your home. Please make her aware that I will be paying her a visit. Have a nice day."

He smiled, and turned to leave thinking, *"This little shit! He thinks he's bested me. But I will get back at him by expelling his brother Michael."*

After school that day, Principal Johnson locked his office and proceeded down the hall to the exit door. After holding the door for a few students, he walked to his car, swinging his briefcase along his side. He was in a good mood since he had figured out how to deal with this McCants kid.

He thought, *"I will bring up the rumble! There was no need to discuss it with Robert. He obviously was not there, but his brother Michael surely was! Even though the Banyon boys did not report any fighting, their faces revealed there was a serious fight.*

"I don't know why those boys' parents didn't report their son's abuse. These people…what are you going to do."

He approached the passenger side door of his car to place his briefcase inside. That is when he noticed that all four of his tires where flat.

CHAPTER FOUR

Cass Tech

The school year ended with Robert getting all 'A's, as usual. As he was leaving the building, Principal Johnson called him into his office. Johnson was unconsciously nervous of Robert and consciously afraid of Michael.

"Yes, sir?" Robert said, as he entered Principal Johnson's office.

"You wanted to see me?"

"Yes, Robert," Johnson said.

"I wanted to speak to your brother Michael, but I can never find him in class. It seems he only goes to class for his tests. How he is able to ace all of his classes is beyond me, since he hardly ever attends them. Anyway, how would you like to attend summer school?"

Robert immediately knew where Johnson was going with this offer but played along.

"Sir, if you recall, Michael and I have already taken all of the classes you offer in the 8B. Therefore, they are repeats so of course he's going to ace them again. As far as me attending summer school,

I never gave it consideration. I'm not behind in any of my classes, so I don't know what I'd study. Plus, the cost of summer-school is beyond my family's finances."

Johnson said, "That's not of any concern. I thought this would be an excellent opportunity for you to advance to high school early. You can attend Mumford or even go back to your old east side neighborhood school of Pershing. All you have to do is take the remaining three classes of your 9-A semester. If you're interested, I can arrange for you to graduate this summer. You won't be the only one graduating."

Robert knew a lot of the other students would be those who were supposed to graduate last week but failed. The summer program for them will keep them from having to repeat the 9-A courses at Post.

He said, "But sir, I really don't think I should be asking my father for money just so I can advance early. Thank you for the opportunity, but I must decline."

Johnson, not to be outdone, said, "Son, I will excuse your payment requirement."

. . . .

Mr. Johnson finally arrived home, in the University of Detroit District, an hour later than normal. His friend looked out of their window to see him climb out of a yellow Checker cab. Once he was inside, Johnson flopped down on the couch in front of his usual martini on the cocktail table.

"Why did you ride home in a cab?" was the obvious question. "Where is your car?"

Mr. Johnson drained the drink then said, "Someone slashed all my tires. I had the car towed to the nearest service-station near the school. Maybe you can give me a ride in the morning?"

His friend said, "What are you talking about? Who would do such a thing? You love those little brats, so why would they do that to you of all people? Negros! Sometimes I just don't understand them."

Johnson got up with his empty glass and walked over to the table and poured another drink. He said, "I know who did it. He's a little guy, but he terrifies me. I've got to find a way to get him out of my school. And by the way, they don't like being called Negroes anymore. They are Afro-Americans now."

His lover walked over to him, stroked his temple, then said, "Oh baby. Sometimes I am sorry you have to deal with those little shits." The two lightly kissed then his lover said, "Okay. I know what you need. Come upstairs and stroke my pet. It will make you feel better."

. . . .

As Robert walked home, he thought about Principal Johnson's offer. He was bored with junior high and was really looking forward to high school in January. It would be great if he could start early. He must, however, not share this with anyone until the proper time. Mack and Michael will know what Principal Johnson is planning. So would Mom and Pops, who are still mad that he was advanced to Mack's level prematurely.

He thought, *"I'm going to do this. I just won't tell anyone. Mack won't be attending school this summer, so no one needs to know where I am in the morning. I'll just say I'm hanging out with friends in the neighborhood."*

He walked into his room, not expecting anyone to be there. Richard and Louis were cleaning up their side of the room and making their beds, a chore they both dreaded.

Louis said, "Hey Robert, can you get Michael out here to help clean this room?"

Robert replied, "Where is he?"

Louis said, "He was in the study, but then he left. I asked him to help, but he just smiled and said, 'ta-ta', whatever that means. He's probably in the basement."

Richard looked at Louis and shook his head.

He said, "Hey dude. Too bad you couldn't attend my graduation from Clinton. Mom was there with the little-kids. Looking forward to finally being in the same school with you again this fall." Robert could hear the sincerity in his voice.

He thought, *"Richard is genuinely happy to be graduating and starting Junior High. It was very unfair that he had to leave his friends at White Elementary because we couldn't wait to move. In less than three months, he would have graduated. Now he will be leaving Louis behind, but joining Mack, Michael, and me. How do I tell him that I might not be there?"*

Robert understood that if he did decide to go to summer school and advance to high school, Mack will be alone in the 9-A, Michael will be in the 8-A, Richard will be in the 7-B, and Louis will be left behind at Clinton in the 5-A.

He said to Richard, "I'm glad you'll be joining us too. And Louis, I'm glad you're staying behind for the next year and a half. Jack this year and Horace next year will need you to get them adjusted to school."

Louis' response was expected. "Why does it always have to be me hanging with the little-kids?"

Mack, having overheard the conversation as he climbed the stairs, walked in, and said, "Birth order, little fellow. It's just birth order. Your time will come. I guess being a middle child can be difficult. But look at it this way, you're going to be able to rule Clinton with Richard gone. Even the sixth graders know who you are after the spring we had."

Robert was now beginning to feel selfish. If he goes to summer school, the big brother role will be all on Mack. He knew that Michael could not be relied upon. If he succeeded, he would leave Mack alone to watch over Michael and Richard. He also understood that for the first time ever he would not have a brother in his school.

· · · · · · · · · · · · · ·

When the boys finished cleaning the room, they went downstairs to hangout. As they were walking down the stairs, Robert heard a noise in the study room and went back up to see who was there. He saw Michael, just lounging around, doing nothing.

"Hell man, how long have you been in here? Why didn't you come help clean the room? You sleep there too, you know."

Michael smiled and said, "Now did you really want all five of us in that tiny room, bumping into each other? Since Pops nailed the window close, we can't even get any air!"

Robert replied, "He wouldn't have nailed it shut if you wouldn't sneak out so much."

Michael said, "I saw you go into the principal's office after school. What did he want?"

Robert replied, "None of your business. He just thanked me for having a good report card."

Michael smirked and said, "Sure he did. He didn't thank me, and I had the same grades as you. Are you sure he doesn't have designs for you?" and laughed.

Robert never liked to fight Michael because Michael always goes crazy when he fights, even with Mack. Before he could step up to him, however, Michael said, "I know what he wants. He's going to offer you summer school, isn't he? You snuck into the ninth grade, and this gives him a chance to get rid of you early. With you gone, he thinks he can keep a closer eye on me!"

Robert was dumbstruck. He thought, "*How in the world does he know this? I know he's my twin, but he shouldn't be able to read my mind!*"

He said, "You don't know what you're talking about. Mr. Johnson is not gay, just a liberal racist. And what we discussed is between him and me. And you'd better not tell Mack, Richard, and especially Mom that I spoke to him. You would really upset Richard if you told him. Leave it alone."

Michael replied, "Sure baby brother. Sure."

. . . .

The following morning Martha rose at 5:30 a.m. to converse with Frank before he left for work. Frank's job was only fifteen minutes away, but he preferred to get there early to set up, so he only had a moment to spare. He looked up when she entered the kitchen.

"We need to talk," she said impatiently. "I had to visit Post yesterday to discuss Michael. The principal was nervous just talking about him. And Michael just smirked, like he has a secret that only he and the principal know. How would you have me handle this?"

Frank looked at his wife, placed his coffee cup on the table, then walked out the back door to his car. A minute later he was on Livernois Avenue, heading north to the Lodge Freeway.

. . . .

The first summer in the new neighborhood was interesting, since they were no longer in the projects. No playground to romp around on. Traffic on streets instead of mere parking lots. Barking dogs in fenced-in areas and fruit trees to raid. Mack, as usual, found an older set of boys to hang out with. Michael was nowhere to be found. Richard and Louis stayed around the immediate blocks, playing with friends they met in school. And the younger three found plenty of pre-school kids to play with along the block. They could not cross the street, of course, but the alley was a haven for them, offering almost as much freedom as the projects provided. Ervin was not quite three years old, but he could keep up with his older two brothers fairly well. Martha made sure to keep an eye on the three small ones, a very difficult task. Especially with all the soaps on the television. Finding Ervin walking on the roof of the garage freaked her out the first few times, but she got used to it. The boys would climb the telephone pole behind the garage, walk out onto the roof of the garage, then jump to the ground in the alley, some seven feet down. Only Ervin was bold enough to climb over the top of the garage to the other side and look down over the concreate driveway.

"Whose idea was it to put a telephone pole next to a garage?" she often said.

The younger McCants boys knew they had to be home by 3:00 p.m. when Frank arrived home from work. Then they could go back out to their respective locations. The older boys, however, had stopped this practice years ago.

With all this activity going on around the home, no one noticed that Robert was never home and Michael only showed up for lunch. Robert was in school in the morning and in the library in the afternoon and early evening. He would walk up to the Seven Mile Road library on school days, which was 1 ½ miles north of the school, and the Ewald Circle library, which was closer to his home, on weekends. The staff at both libraries knew him and quite often had books on reserve for him. He would get home in time for his dinner, crash for an hour or two watching 'Man from Uncle', 'Bonanza', or 'Combat!', then off to bed. One evening in particular there was no dinner left.

When he went into the little boy's room to inquire, Ervin said, "Talk to Michael. I saw him eating two plates full!"

He never wasted time playing with the neighborhood kids.

Mack was now hanging out with an older crowd, which worried Frank. The older crowd meant girls, and Frank had no intentions of becoming a grandfather anytime soon. He hated to admit it, but his eldest was not a boy anymore, but a full-grown man-child, mustache, chin hair and all. He was very mature but still not ready for the adult world. He had not had to whip Mack in a couple of years, and those whippings were probably not warranted, as Martha loved to point out. He had to restrain himself, however, when one day, on his way home from work, he spotted Mack in the block north of their home, with a do-rag on his head. He pulled over immediately and embarrassed Mack in front of the crowd of older teens, girls and all, by snatching the rag off of his head.

When he got home, he blurted out, "Do you know what I just saw your oldest boy doing?!" The kids were always her kids when they were bad. They were his kids when they handed in their excellent report cards.

"The boy had a pimp rag on his head. He's even shaping his mustache like Clark Gable!"

Martha, having grown up in Harlem, knew about Black men and do-rags, and she definitely did not want any of her sons associated with that style of living. Mack was beginning to look like her father, and hearing about the do-rag did indeed trouble her.

She, however, did not act alarmed, but instead calmly said, "Relax. It's probably just a faze he's going through. You can't expect him to act like a fourteen-year-old when he looks sixteen. He's already shaving. You barely have to shave weekly, but he's going to have to shave daily."

Frank responded, "Yeah, all that Irish blood in you is ruining my boys! First that high-yellow color of yours, now the facial hair growth," and laughed heartily. Martha had a way of relaxing Frank, especially after a hard day's work in the plant.

She said, "Okay, get out of those smelly clothes and meet this high-yellow Irish bitch in the bedroom before those brats of yours get in here. I'll lock the doors."

. . . .

In the final week of summer school, a counselor approached the class of 9-A students and passed out forms for admission to high school. The forms were stamped with Mumford High on them. Before the counselor left, however, he approached Robert and asked him not to fill his form out. Instead, he wanted Robert to come to his office after school. Robert acknowledged the request and walked to the counselor's office after the school bell rang. He was not concerned with the request because, as usual, he finished at the top of his class.

The Counselor, Mr. James, an older Black man, said, "Robert, I've noticed your progress since you arrived here in April. As you can see, I'm one of the few Negro males in this school. I take pride in my ability to mentor young men. As a Negro male, I want you to imagine all the possibilities the world has to offer you. With that in mind, I want you to consider your high-school choices. Mumford is an excellent school, especially for athletics. But they only have two curriculums to offer you, college prep and business. I want you to consider Cass Tech. The school has over thirty curriculums, including science focused studies, so your choices are endless."

Robert was always trying to anticipate what adults would say to him so he could have a prepared response. He, however, did not realize that Mr. James knew he existed. So, he did not know what he might want with him. He had never had any teacher reach out to him before, and now he has two adult males advising him.

"Sir, I appreciate your attention to my progress here at Post. I have been considering Cass Tech, even though the Principal, Mr. Johnson, has advised me to attend Mumford or even Pershing. I don't know how he plans to keep me out of Cooley. Cass Tech never came up. I will have to think about it. Can I get back to you tomorrow?"

Mr. James said, "Sure young man. Tomorrow is the last day to submit these applications, so please get it to me as soon as possible. Otherwise, I will submit your application to Mumford. Have a good day."

Mr. James had kept Robert after class for ten minutes so when he walked out of the school all the other students had departed the grounds. What he did not expect was to see Michael standing there waiting for him.

Michael said, "So this guy wants you too, huh?" and laughed again. Robert just shook his head and punched Michael in the shoulder.

Michael said, "So let me guess. You are a Black kid, and he wants to be sure you get a good start in life."

Robert stumbled on the sidewalk, not expecting Michael to say that. Even calling him 'Black' was startling. Michael continued, "He thinks you're special, so he does not want you to go to Mumford. He wants you to consider going to the high school Harvard of the Midwest, Cass Technical High School."

Robert stopped walking and just stared at Michael. He thought, *"This sucker was hiding in the hall and heard the entire conversation. Except, Mr. James' office is within the school's administrative office. Michael could not get in there without being seen by the office staff. And he does not have a school pass to enter the building. And how did he know I was even going to summer school? I kept that to myself. God, sometimes I hate that he's my twin. Why couldn't he trade places with Richard or Louis."*

Robert said to Michael, "So you know my business. Big deal. And yes, that is what he offered me. I know I'm only thirteen years old, but

I want to get away from these immature teens. I'm ready for the older group, just like Mack is hanging with. You're going to still have Mack here in the fall, and Richard is going to need you to get him on track as well since Mack will be gone in January."

Michael got quiet, and they walked silently for a few blocks. When Robert looked at Michael, he could swear his eyes were moist.

Then his voice quivered as he said, "So you really wish Richard or Louis were your twin instead of me? You really don't enjoy being my twin? Well, I guess I asked for that. Sorry I disappoint you. Take it easy."

He turned and walked, then ran, back up the street toward the corner. Seconds later he was gone.

. . . .

That night, Robert was lying in bed unable to sleep. It was already 11:00 p.m., and Michael had not returned. Mack was asleep, as were Louis and Richard. The little-kids were sleeping downstairs, as they had been since the weather had gotten warmer. Robert sat up and shook Mack.

He asked Mack, "Have you seen Michael this evening?"

Mack, still asleep, ignored the question and instead said, "Leave me alone and go to sleep." Mack turned back over and was gone in seconds. Robert considered waking up Richard but decided against it. Instead, he got out of bed, pulled on his jeans, checked the study room and the bathroom, then walked downstairs. He looked into the younger children's room to see if Michael was sleeping with them, but he was not there. He checked the basement, but Michael was not down there either. He opened the back door and walked outside into the cooler night air. He walked around the house, looking for his brother. He checked the garage and the upper back porch. He walked, still barefoot, to the corner of Lyndon Street to see if anyone was walking up the street. No luck. He then walked two blocks east to Livernois Avenue to look around the two corner gas stations and liquor store. He could not find Michael anywhere.

He returned home and checked the entire house one final time. Then he did something he had not done since he was four years old. He knocked on his parents' door. When the door opened, he could see his mom sitting up in the bed, with an anxious look on her face. He pushed pass his startled father and climbed onto his parent's bed, crawled on his hands and knees to his mother, and dropped his head onto her lap, an experience he had never had before. He was suddenly a four-year-old.

He sobbed and said, "Mom, I can't find Michael. He's gone, and I'm afraid he may never return. I hurt him, Ma. I really hurt him today. I wished him away and now he's gone. Please help me Ma! Please help me find my brother!"

. . . .

Unfortunately for Robert, his parents were not equipped to handle his emotions. Frank's father had been ostracized by his family for an unapproved marriage. At the age of sixteen Martha's mother moved her away from her half-brothers and half-sisters a few years after their father was killed in a tragic accident. Neither of Robert's parents were comforted as children, so Frank and Martha were only capable of comforting each other or their babies. By the time the children were school age the potential comforting ended.

Frank went out of the room to allow Robert time with his wife. He was troubled by his thoughts that it may be time for Robert to take care of himself and not concern himself with Michael. Maybe his household could return to normal. At no time did he admit his son needed psychological help for his depression, as his wife had been suggesting for both twins.

Frank was wise enough to allow Robert the time he needed with his mother. Maybe this will give him a chance to get closer to the boy. He had watched enough family TV, like 'My Three Sons' and 'Father Knows Best', to know there are other means of relating to one's children than whippings. This may be why he was not whipping the younger children. He thought about the possibilities until he finally drifted off to sleep on the couch.

. . . .

The following morning Robert woke up in his own bed. He thought that perhaps he had been dreaming but soon realized it was not a dream. Michael was truly gone. He could feel him but knew he may not return any time soon. This, of course, saddened him, but it gave him the direction he knew he must take. His mother, as much as she tried, could not understand his pain. She treated him as a baby who had lost his toy. His father was of no use, just the non-emotional man he had always known. He may be wrong, but from his perspective neither parent ever loved Michael. In fact, Michael was such a handful that none of his brothers seemed to care for him either. Michael and Mack used to fight a lot. He occasionally smacked Richard if he could not have his way, and Louis seemed to avoid him. Only the little ones ever played with him.

Robert also felt that Mack had been drifting away from him, since Mack started Junior High back in '63 and began hanging out with the older teens. Richard and Louis had always been a pair, assuming Robert had Mack and Michael. So, with Mack spending all of his time with the older crowd and Michael gone for the first time in their young lives, Robert felt he had no reason to share his life with anyone. From this point forward, his life was his business, and his alone.

CHAPTER FIVE

Stash House Rip-off

"Hey Mack!" said Pookie. "Yo brother Michael got a contract out on him. He's been hitting drug dealers. Crazy MF been stealin they rides! Been going on for a few months now. Since the riot. He waits til they go visit they lady then when they get busy, he's got em. Joy rides for a while then burns the suckers. He's only working the eastside so far, and those fuckers are smoken!" "How they know it's Michael?" said Mack. "Cause he's so loud, man!" replied Pookie. "It's like he don't care if they know. Act like he ain't scared of nobody! Word out he's got a screw loose." "Watch it man." replied Mack. "That's my brother you're talking about. I don't believe that shit anyway. I see him every day. No way he's on the eastside. I see him in school." "You lying, man. Everyone knows Michael dropped out back in '65. Dude, he only went to Post for a few months! Nobody's seen him over here in a couple of years. They see Robert and Richard and Louis. But nobody's seen Michael. Wearing all black like he do." Mack never liked Pookie, but he was able to tolerate him. That was until now. "Are you

calling me a liar, punkass?" said Mack. "Say one more thing about my
brother! Pookie, I think you better move on."

. . . .

After Michael left home, near the end of August '65, Robert began
distancing himself from his entire family, including Martha. At first,
no one seemed to notice him pulling away, since he had always been
quiet. It was Mack who first began to sense the change. He never
saw Robert in school or hanging out with any of the kids in the
neighborhood. Mack would ask Robert's honors classmates about him,
but none of them reported seeing him either. They barely knew him
since he had only arrived in April and was so quiet.

One group of female students replied, "We haven't seen either of
your brothers, Robert or Michael." Therefore, neither of them were
missed at school, since the students barely knew them.

Mack began to notice that Robert left home very early and did not
return until well after dark. Some nights he did not come home at all.
When Mack would see Robert, he would attempt to engage him in
conversation, but Robert was not very responsive. Mack also noticed
that Robert stopped talking about Michael since the night he informed
his parents that Michael had run away. From Mack's perspective, his
parents did not seem to notice the change in him. So, being the only
responsible adult in the house, he reluctantly informed his parents that
it appeared their son had dropped out of school and would not finish
the '65 fall semester nor graduate along with him.

His parents were actually alarmed by his change in behavior and
knew it was because Michael was gone. Martha, however, had to keep
her focus on her youngest and not concern herself with Robert or
Michael. Frank had always been distant with his children, always
playing his 'cop-parent' role. Mack felt that his parents believed that

the older children were now mature enough to be responsible for themselves and that was fine with him. They stopped asking for report cards, checking up on them when they got home, and who they were hanging out with. From the younger ones' perspective, however, two of their brothers were gone.

. . . .

Racial segregation had always been the norm in the United States: in the job market, housing, and especially the public and private school systems. The 1896 Plessy versus Ferguson Supreme Court ruling made segregation legal throughout the United States. However, almost sixty years later, the 1954 Brown versus Board of Education Supreme Court ruling ended legal segregation in the public schools.

Tension was extremely high all over the country due to attempts to integrate various school districts. In 1962 the governor of Alabama, George Wallace, in an effort to prevent Black students from attending classes at the University of Alabama, personally blocked the entrance to the school. Federal troops were required to protect Black students attempting to enter segregated schools in various sections of the country. Most of the neighborhood schools in Michigan's Wayne County were still mostly segregated, primarily due to segregated housing. By 1966, however, with the mostly White exodus from Detroit to the suburbs, most of the high schools in predominately White neighborhoods had lost significant student population. Therefore, the Detroit Public School administration decided to balance out the student populations in some of these high schools.

Frank and Martha moved their family onto Santa Rosa Drive for better housing. They, however, enjoyed the side benefit of living in a mixed neighborhood. What they did not realize was that most of their White neighbors were sending their children to private Catholic schools. So, Clinton and Post had predominately Black student bodies. Their children interacted with the White children in the neighborhood after school but did not attend the same schools.

Cooley High School, located approximately two miles west of Post, was selected as one of the high schools that required redistribution. So, in 1966, all graduating students from Post Junior High that lived south of the school and west of Livernois Avenue lost their opportunity to attend the coveted Mumford High School. Their only choice was now Cooley, situated in a predominately White neighborhood. The Post Junior High graduating class of January '66 was now fish-bait.

For the McCants family the nearest bus stop to Cooley was a half-mile away. So, a lot of the students in the neighborhood chose to walk the nearly three miles to and from school rather than wait on the public buses. The unfriendly crowd of neighboring students made attending the school difficult at best. Fighting before and after school became the norm. This tension continued for the next two years until the ethnic composition of the student population balanced out.

. . . .

Fort Pontchartrain du Detroit was founded in 1701 by Antoine de la Mothe Cadillac, a French explorer. The French surrendered the Fort in 1760 to the British as reparations after the French and Indian War. The fort became American property after the American Revolution.

The city had a history of aiding in the Underground Railroad, a secretly protected effort of assisting enslaved Blacks with escape from southern slave states. Detroit's demographics to Windsor, Canada was ideal as a final drop-off point, since Canada was a refuge for the enslaved.

The city had several racially tense social disturbances during its long history. In 1863, during the civil war, a riot broke out due to immigrants not wanting to be drafted into the military. The Blacks in the city paid a heavy toll from this riot in death and destruction of their homes. In 1943, during the middle of the Second World War, the social tensions in the city culminated in a race riot. Black and White picnickers on Belle Isle fought on the MacArthur Bridge leading to the island, which spilled into the city. The rioting lasted for two days and was the deadliest riot to date in America. In 1967, a riot began when the police department attempted to close a popular after-hours nightclub. Over forty people were killed during that disturbance, and the city suffered extreme commercial and residential property damage due to looting and arson fires. The following year, Martin Luther King Jr. was assassinated resulting in rioting throughout the country. Detroit was no exception.

The city housing had always been segregated. Newly built public housing, authorized by the Federal Government in the 1940s, was designated as White projects or Black projects, with the city, working with the U. S Department of Housing and Urban Development, enforcing the segregation. Of the seven projects built in the '40s, three were reserved for Black residency. The first project was completed in 1941 in a predominately White neighborhood on the east side of the city. The city governing body, however, alarmed at the severity of the housing shortage for the Black residents, had the designation of the project switched from White to Black, even though the project was in a White neighborhood. The authorities had to escort the first residents into the Sojourner Truth Homes due to the White protest that erupted over the decision. The city resolved that situation by opening the Charles Terrace Homes for White residents a couple of miles south on Mound Road.

The U.S. government created the Servicemen's Readjustment Act in 1944. This bill, commonly referred to as the GI Bill, gave returning servicemen access to funding previously unavailable to them. This included low interest home mortgages. Unfortunately, due to the segregation laws of the United States Military, Blacks were hindered from serving in the military and thus had very limited access to the GI Bill.

The federal government, at the urging of President Franklin Roosevelt, began construction on interstate highways that tore through the center of Detroit, allowing a gradual exodus to the suburbs for the city residents. America's third largest city had established a reputation as the Arsenal of Democracy, with the automotive industry switching from car production to aiding in the war effort. The President of the United States was concerned that the Germans might attempt to bomb the city. Therefore, he believed it was in everyone's best interest to create evacuation routes running north, west, and south. Interstate-94, locally named the Ford Freeway, cut through the center of the city east to west. M-10, named John C. Lodge Freeway, traveled north to south just west of the central artery of Woodward Avenue. The Davison Freeway, reputed to be the first freeway built in America, traveled a short two miles connecting the Lodge to the eastside city of Hamtramck, and eventually the Interstate-75. The city was never bombed but a different, unanticipated, evacuation still occurred.

After the war, Detroit began to lose scores of White residents, now that they had easy access to travel back and forth from the suburbs. In the 1950s entire neighborhoods turned from predominately White communities to predominately Black communities. A study by a local newspaper found that on January 1, 1951, the block of Elmhurst Street, between 12th Street and 14th Street was one-hundred percent White. Every home, flat and apartment was occupied by a White resident. Seven years later, on January 1, 1958, that same block of Elmhurst was one hundred percent Black. Every home, flat and apartment was now occupied by a Black resident.

One of the freeways, Interstate-75, locally named the Chrysler Freeway, traveled northward through Ohio into Michigan all the way to the Mackinaw Bridge. It was constructed along the western side of the Detroit River until it entered the city of Detroit. It then traveled east through the northern edge of the downtown district. Then north to the Mackinaw Bridge, which connects Michigan's lower and upper peninsulas. The construction for the curve coming out of the downtown district of Detroit required the complete destruction of Hastings Street south of the Ford Freeway.

Hastings Street was the main artery for the Black community. It was known locally as Paradise Valley and Black Bottom, referencing the color of the rich soil of farmland during the nineteenth century. Paradise Valley was the location of the city's Black business district. The Black residents lived just south of the business district in Black Bottom. The Valley included pharmacies, barber shops, bakeries, doctor and dental offices, grocery stores, and auto repair shops. The community was located just west of the famed Eastern Market, where tristate farmers came weekly to sell their produce. These two communities were predominately Black, with over ninety percent of Detroit's Black citizens living there.

The east to north curve of I-75, just east of the downtown district, was so dramatic that traffic had to slow to 25 mph or drivers would risk losing control of their vehicles. Traffic jams were common because trucks were constantly flipping over in the two-lane curve. All of I-75's curves that switched directions remained the standard four-lanes wide, from Ohio to Mackinaw, excluding the curve exiting the downtown district. By expanding the curvature of the freeway, moving the curve lanes further northward, the Black business district's destruction would have been avoided. The interstate planners even built a completely useless three-quarters of a mile Interstate-375, just south of the curve, to Jefferson Avenue, causing the demolition of the remainder of the Black Bottom.

The condemnation by the city government of the remaining residential properties east of the freeway to create the large Lafayette Park condominium complex completed the death of Paradise Valley and the Black Bottom. The destruction of the housing and business district forced the Black residents westward and eastward. The westward migration found new residences in the 12th Street-Clairmount-Davison community on the city's west side. 12th street, Linwood Avenue and Davison Avenue became the new Hastings.

Twenty years later that community would erupt in the worse riot in American history.

. . . .

In the summer of '67, the Black urban areas in America were very tense due to racial tensions throughout the country. A riot broke out in Harlem in 1964 due to complaints of police brutality. Los Angeles erupted in '65, also due to police brutality complaints. The CIA and FBI warned their respective officials of the potential for civil discord during the coming summer of '67. Detroit did not let them down.

On a hot Saturday night in July '67, the Detroit police planned a raid on an after-hours blind-pig on 12th Street and Clairmount Avenue. Twelfth Street, a one-way, northbound three-lane road, was one of the busiest thoroughfares in the community. This community was a collection of densely populated Black neighborhoods that stretched for miles in all directions. The city was so segregated that one would have to drive three miles north from Clairmount to find White residences. There were very few White residents south of Clairmount to Grand River Avenue, a two-mile drive. One would have to travel east of 12th Street to the city of Hamtramck to find substantial White residents.

The insurance company's redlining of the city's west side was at Schaefer Highway, almost four miles west of 12th Street. Automobile insurance rates reflected the racism, as agents would ask residents if they lived east or west of Schaefer.

This central enclave of the city was almost completely Black, a turnover that began in the early 50s, after the destruction of Hastings Street. Its population density was double that of the city's average. The housing conditions were poor in some areas, with plenty of four-family flats, large homes built on thirty-foot lots, designed for four families. The houses were initially developed to manage the Eastern European immigration influx that began at the end of the nineteenth century. The standard lot in Detroit was forty feet for each individual house. These flats, however, built on thirty feet of property, were so close together that they could not have driveways, leaving the residents no choice but to park their vehicles on the street. Four families in one building with no parking created a lot of tension. Especially with multiple four-family-flats all along the block, on both sides of the street.

This 'city within a city' was hardly an impoverished community. Plenty of the area's neighborhoods, where the houses were single family brick dwellings, resembled suburban communities, including the presence of manicured lawns and shrubbery, flower gardens and elm and maple trees on most lots. Children played on the sidewalks and cars parked in driveways. The Boston-Edison District, with its huge mansions and 5,000-7,000 square foot homes, stretching one-and-a-half miles from Linwood to Woodward Avenue, was centrally located in the community. It was also just a few blocks north of Clairmount Street, site of the '67 summer eruption.

The business district that used to exist in Paradise Valley relocated itself within this enclave. Almost any service the residents required could be found within it. Grocery stores, prescription drugs, liquor stores, candy stores. Doctors, dentist, pediatricians, auto mechanics, shop repairs, clothiers, ice cream parlors, movie theaters, Conyers Ford auto dealership, even the Red Wings Hockey arena. Northern, Mackenzie, and Central High Schools, St. Martin de Porres High School, Sacred Heart Major Seminar, a huge Catholic complex. Hostess Bakery, Carling Black Label beer manufacturer and Heinz Catsup factory. Even a Sear's department store in Highland Park. Woodward Avenue, south of the Davison Freeway, had over a dozen huge major Christian churches built before the depression. Henry Ford Hospital, a behemoth collection of medical and administrative buildings, serviced the entire city. Herman Kiefer Hospital was located north of Henry Ford Hospital. This internal city was also filled with hundreds of small business operations that employed the original residents of the area but not the present residents.

Overall, the community was a mixture of upper-class, middle-class, and working-class Black residences. The currency earned in the community was spent in the community. It was a Black city within a major American city, but with no control over its destiny.

A major issue within the city was the complaints by the Black community of extremely poor treatment by the predominantly White police force. The community was being patrolled by a squadron of police units notoriously called the 'Big-4' and the Tactical Mobile Units, a militarized squad often carrying automatic weapons in their vehicles. Stop and Frisk was the norm for the TMU, stopping residents without cause.

The late Saturday night, early Sunday morning of the 23rd of July 1967 was a typical warm night in the middle of the summer. Plenty of young people were out and about when just after 3:30 a.m. the police raided an after-hours joint, arresting over eighty participants celebrating the return of two soldiers from Vietnam. The community exploded, and for the next five days the city burned. It was a civil eruption, quite different from the racial conflict of the '43 riot.

Snipers mounted the rooftop of buildings around the tenth precinct at Elmhurst and Livernois, raining bullets down upon the station. It was one of several stations fired upon over the coming days. Dozens of people were killed, making this riot the deadliest one to date in American history.

The police murdered three young men staying at a motel off of Woodward Avenue. The officers were placed on trial, but the trial was moved out of Wayne County to Mason Michigan, a city south of Lansing and nearly 100 miles northwest of Detroit. The officers were found not guilty by an all-White jury.

The city police, knowing the tense situation that existed in the city, were reckless in making an arrest that evening on the twenty-third of July. It took the National Guard and U.S. Army with their military tactics, tanks, and automatic weapons to end the 5-day disturbance.

This riot would prove to be career-ending for Jerome P. Cavanaugh, the young Mayor of the city. After winning the mayor's seat in 1961 with a grass-roots effort and plenty of support from the Black community, then being reelected in '65, he was accused of bungling the handling of the riot by delaying a request for national guard support. His bright future was over. He would not run again for re-election in '69.

Frank McCants, who witnessed the terrible race riots in Detroit in 1943, made sure his sons did not leave the yard on Sunday. They could not travel off the block for the remainder of the week. He did not concern himself, however, with Michael.

. . . .

By the fall of '67 Mack had not seen Michael in two years. Robert very rarely saw him either. Robert informed Mack that Michael had taken up residence in their old neighborhood in the east side Mound Road projects. Robert noticed that at the mention of Michael, Mack would freeze up and change the subject, so he stopped discussing him altogether. The two brothers rarely talked, so Mack did not know that Robert had not dropped out of school, but instead was attending Cass Technical High School in the downtown district. Since very few students from the neighborhood attended Cass, no one shared Robert's secret. He was always quiet and private, but now, being so much younger than the other Cass students, he was further withdrawn from his older classmates. He often isolated himself and felt most comfortable being introspective and alone.

He relied on Michael far more than he realized and now that Michael was gone, he felt completely alone. Richard and Louis were together again at Post Jr. High, and Mack had become Mr. Popular at Cooley High. The three younger brothers were all in Clinton Elementary, so Martha could truly enjoy her soaps in private. Robert usually left home at 6:00 a.m., and did not return until after 9:00 p.m. From his perspective, no one noticed or seemed to care. Then he met Carol.

· · · · · · · · · · · ·

In November 1967, a month before his sixteenth birthday, Robert enrolled and was accepted into Wayne State University on a full scholarship, starting in January. The University was located two miles north of his high school on Cass Avenue. It was the third largest university in Michigan. Robert skipped his final semester at Cass by going to summer school each year.

His very first class at Wayne had another sixteen-year-old student in it. She was the daughter of a prominent Black lawyer. She lived in a near-mansion along the Detroit Golf Club, housing so exclusive most city residents did not know the golf course existed. Her name was Carol Bordeaux, and she quickly became the love of his life.

After the class, she approached him and said, "Hello. You look familiar. You resemble a guy my brother Pierre knows named Mack. I've seen him around our neighborhood. Any relations?"

Robert responded, "Hey. How are you? Yeah, Mack's my older brother. My name's Robert. Robert McCants."

"Yeah," she said, "I thought so. And I know your last name. You guys are famous over on the west side. News of that fight you guys had with that weirdo family reached the entire northwest side. The McCants Boys, they call you guys. Your brother hangs out with guys my brother hangs with. So, you're one of them dudes, huh? But Mack is my older brother's age so you must just be sixteen too!"

Robert was not expecting this development. He went through over two years of high school, and no one ever mentioned the brawl.

"Hell!" he thought. *"That was almost three years ago."*

He said, "And your name is…?"

She laughed and said, "Carol Jennings. You attended Cooley while I was at Immaculata." She lied about her last name of Bordeaux, not wanting to immediately be connected to her famous attorney father. It was not necessary since Robert had never heard of him.

"No, I attended Cass Tech, not Cooley. Immaculata is an all-girls school. That must have been interesting. I cannot imagine not having both genders in my classroom. I have only brothers and male cousins, so not having any girls around is normal for me, just not in school."

Carol responded, "Well, I sometimes wish I didn't have any brothers. They can really get on your nerves. Pierre is now finishing U of D Jesuit on Seven Mile, then going to University of Michigan. Like you, I've passed my brother in school due to double promotions. I wanted to go to U of M, but my dad thinks I'm too young so…I'm stuck here."

Robert was sensing a little bit of elitism from her but ignored it. She was extremely attractive but was completely different from his mother. Instead of long flowing hair, she was wearing a large afro. Her complexion was the shade of cinnamon, similar to his. She wore her skirt in the new-fashioned mini skirt with plenty of thigh showing.

She noticed that he was staring at her legs and said, "We used to have to fold our waist bands a couple of times to hike up our skirts. Now I don't have to. Boy would the Catholic nuns be mad at me. They would just freak out! My parents are not crazy about this new style either, but I love it! I guess you do too, huh?" She just smiled so exuberant of her freedom and confidence.

Neither of them had a class the next period, so they talked the hour away and exchanged phone numbers. Having to give Carol his family's number was difficult for Robert, so he told her he was rarely home, since he studied late. Not that she would ever call him. The third period was about to begin, so they parted ways.

"I'll see you tomorrow, Carol. It was a pleasure meeting you."

Carol responded, "You are so proper. Relax. I don't bite. Not on the first meeting."

Then she laughed the most beautiful laugh he had ever heard, threw her head back like a girl used to long straight hair, and walked away. Robert could not help but just stare at the most beautiful girl he had ever seen. He barely remembered anything said in the following classes.

. . . .

Robert knew he had to prepare his mother just in case Carol happened to call, so he told her he had taken a job at the University.

Martha responded, "Oh, you've got a job at U of D. That's nice. Perhaps maybe you'll start back to school someday."

Robert said, "Not U of D, Ma. I'm working at Wayne State, on Woodward Avenue. I work in the cafeteria during the day and janitorial during the evening. I'm saving up to buy a car. I'll be able to help you guys out financially now that I'm working."

"That's awful nice of you son. Things have been getting a little tight around here now that you guys have gotten older. The price of clothing is outrageous."

Robert said, "Sure, Ma. Anything to help. Have a nice night," and walked upstairs to his bedroom. Once he got into his room, he realized that now he needed to start bringing home money, so he really would have to get a job on campus.

Frank came into the living room, having overheard his son. He said to Martha, "I think that boy's met a girl."

Martha responded, "Yes, I can tell. He hasn't had that happy tone in his voice in quite a while."

Frank said, "Yeah, since Michael left."

Martha's mood suddenly darkened, and she said, "Don't go there. Not tonight."

. . . .

Robert went into the basement before he crashed for the night. The house was quiet. He walked in the dark, not needing a light. Until he bumped into someone.

"What the…" he said.

"Ssh. Keep it down. I don't need anyone to know I'm here. I needed a place to lay low for a while." Robert was dumbstruck. It was Michael!

He said, "Where the hell have you been?"

"Keep your voice down. I'm only staying the night. I'll be gone in the morning before anyone gets up."

Robert could barely speak so they sat in silence for a while. Then Michael said, "You've met a girl, haven't you? Is she nice lookin? Bet she's high-yellow, like mom! You need to get you a girl with a natural tan."

Robert, no longer surprised by Michael's gift, said, "Stay out of my head, will you? Yeah, she's nice. First girl I've really liked. And she does have a natural tan, stupid."

Michael said, "You should come over to the east side. That's where the girls are really hot! Project girls, Conant Garden girls around Pershing. Really nice-looking soul sisters on the east side. Girls with color, light, brown and black! And asses…" Robert interrupted him. "Okay. I get the message. Since when did you become a ladies' man, anyway?"

"Well, we're not kids anymore, are we? How do you think Pops met Mom?"

Robert interrupted him again, uncomfortable with the direction the conversation was heading.

"So, the grapevine is you've been getting into trouble. You've been gone for over two years! I freaked out for weeks! Why can't you just come back home and avoid all that stuff? The eastside has to be too hot for you right now. Some dude told Mack that you've been ripping off drug dealers. Why are you getting so wild?"

Michael paused before responding and then said, "Robert, when have you not known me to be wild. Come on, now. You're the quiet one. I'm your alter-ego."

Robert said, "You've been reading too many comic books. Seriously. Why don't you contact Uncle Horace or Uncle Herb or any of Dad's other brothers, and see if you can move in with either of them?"

Michael replied, "Don't kid yourself. I wouldn't be able to get along with either of them any more than I do with Pops. Don't worry. I've got something cooking that will put me over for a while. I've got things under control. Look, it's getting late. You've got school, and I've got late night research to do. I won't be coming back here for a while. Don't get that new girl pregnant, you hear?"

Then he did something strange. He hugged Robert, went up the stairs and out the back door.

Robert waited a while before coming out of the basement. He turned the corner and bumped into another figure. It was his father.

"Boy, who were you talking to downstairs?"

"Oh, no one Dad. I was just mumbling to myself. Good night, Pops."

He then turned and walked up the stairs to his room. Frank walked back into his bedroom and said to Martha, who was sitting up, staring anxiously.

He said, "Michael's back."

. . . .

Three months later

The Cadillacs were parked four deep in the driveway of a home just north of Fenkell Avenue, near Wyoming Avenue, approximately one-and-a-half miles from the McCants. The card game was loud. The air was full of smoke from tobacco and marijuana. Lines of cocaine were laid on the table with plenty of straws.

"Joker, cop me a beer will ya?" said Busta. "I wants ta keep my buzz. And shut dat fuckin mut of yourn up!"

Joker, very high, replied, "Fuck you mother fucker! Git off yo ass and get yo own beer!"

He looked at the dog and shouted, "Shut up Bitch!" The dog stopped barking, knowing the consequences if she did not.

Busta was thirty-seven years old, and at 6'4" and 260 pounds, was a frighteningly brutal looking man. Joker, however, was even bigger and weighed over 280 pounds. The two of them filled the tiny kitchen and had to rub bellies to pass one another.

Jake saw the two squeezing by each other and said, "You two should just kiss and make up!" and laughed, causing Joker to fake throwing his can of beer at him.

"So whose bet is it now, fool?" said Ray Ray.

The four men were carefully guarding their stash house after word spread of a gang of thieves on the east side ripping off dope dens. Now the rip-offs had begun spreading westward for the past three months, so they were on high alert. The cash they paid certain officers of the law did not make them feel any easier. The large $500,000 stash in the attic belonged to their boss, Shapatilo. He ran his operation from the Mediterranean Boot Social Club, near East Baltimore and John R. Street. It was a monthly collection of payments from multiple sources including prostitution, car theft rings, after-hour joints, strip clubs, porn shops, protection, gambling, scammers, loan sharks, warehouse heist, and drug money. A lot of drug money. All from the northwest quadrant of the city. Busta was personally responsible for the drug money and the collection of the rest. Absolutely nothing can happen to it. Each man was armed with a revolver. Two rifles lay across the couch. A loaded shotgun was in the kitchen corner and the back hallway. In addition, a police cruiser patrolled the area passing by the house every fifteen minutes. The men had no real concerns. No one was dumb enough to rob a mob stash house.

The smoke in the air was so thick they did not notice the shadowy figure just outside the yard, staring over the fence. Besides, it was only there for a few seconds, then it was gone. A moment later there was a shadow on the roof of the adjourning house. Then in the tree behind the 2nd house. Then on their roof. The noise from the stereo was so loud they could not hear the sawing of wood. Nor could they hear the creaking of the rafters in the second-floor ceiling. Or the rafter relaxing as 25% of the weight on it was relieved. In another moment the silence returned. Only Bitch noticed the difference.

The following morning, the first day of April, Jake woke up to a loud howl from the second floor.

"God damn, mudda fucka, som bitch!" Busta yelled.

"Weez bin robbed!"

CHAPTER SIX

MLK

Robert and Carol had been hanging out for almost three months, after meeting during their January '68 freshman English class. Robert was initially hesitant to get closer to Carol, since he knew she dated other guys. He, however, had no intentions of just being a good friend. He wanted more. So, he decided to ask her out the following Monday, the first week of April. They had planned to meet at the campus library. Like his father, he liked to arrive early. Unfortunately, Michael showed up as well.

Robert said, "What are you doing here? I thought you hung out on the eastside. Wait a minute. I heard on the bus ride over that there was a major rip-off on the west side last night. Somebody stole a million dollars from a mafia stash house not far from our home. All the dudes on the bus were talking about it. Please tell me you had nothing to do with it. Please tell me you were nowhere near the west side last night."

Michael laughed and mocked Robert, "Please, please, please! Man, nobody stole no million dollars from no stash house. Ain't that much money in none of them places. If there was, it would be guarded by a couple of squad cars armed to the teeth. You were supposed to say, 'Hey bro, ain't seen you since January!' Not accuse me of robbing Fort Knox!"

Robert paused, then said, "Why are you here? You can't be here. I'm waiting for someone, and you can't be here when she arrives."

Michael said, "I know brother-man. And I do understand. But you don't want to keep hanging out with that square chick. Besides, her pops ain't gonna let her date a ghetto boy like you. You think you've moved up because we've moved out of the projects onto rosy Santa Rosa? Well, my brotha. Look around. The whole projects have moved to the west side! There are more 'hoods' in our hood than White folks. Especially after last summer's revolt."

Robert said, "That wasn't a revolt. It was just chaos. Anyway, don't change the subject. Why are you here?"

Michael said, "You planning on dating that girl, ain't ya? Well, forget it. She ain't our type. Why don't you join me on the east side, and we can double date? There are so many fine sisters over there. I even know some twins! That would be fun, and I know Momma would approve. Pops too. I support your continuing your education after Cass, but you still have to keep your feet on the ground. That girl ain't for ya, I mean 'you.' Ha! Here she comes now. I'll leave before I embarrass you. See ya. And by the way, her last name ain't Jennings. She's the daughter of a big-time…"

Carol turned the corner, saw Robert, and flashed a big welcoming smile. The sun hit her face and it radiated off with golden rays. At least it looked that way to Robert. He looked back at Michael, but he was already blending in with other students, never finishing his final remark. *What did he mean about her last name?*

Michael winked at Robert just as Carol said, "Hey Robert, I thought I'd beat you here, but you're so early. How long have you been waiting?" Robert temporarily forgot about Michael as he reached out to take her hand and pull her to the bench. She was surprised by his action but did not pull away.

"He's never touched me before," she thought.

"Robert, what's going on?"

Robert looked around one last time to be sure Michael was gone, then said, "I want to date. I've been planning this for some time now. I want to get closer to you, friend-wise I mean."

Carol paused, then laughed and said, "Friend-wise? Friend-wise? Robert, are you actually asking me out on a date? Or is this some 'April fools' prank? Seriously, Robert, why would you want to date me? You know I'm seeing other guys, and you're very hesitant to meet my parents or even come into my neighborhood. I don't know what that's all about. Why would we mess up a great friendship? I like our present arrangement just the way it is. Come on. Let's get some donuts and head to the library."

. . . .

On Thursday, Mack was walking to school when he heard the buzz about an assassination. Martin Luther King Jr. was dead. He had been shot in Memphis, Tennessee. Mack's mood dropped immediately. By the time he got to the building, the entire Cooley student body was freaked out. None of the students, Black or White, were able to focus on classes. Just the news that flowed out of Tennessee. The teachers were getting antsy. They saw young men and women their physical size, not little-kids, and they felt the tension in the air. Since the school was bi-racially mixed after two years of diversification, the fear of potential retaliation by the Black students toward the White students was real.

By eleven o'clock students all over the city walked out of classes and wandered through the halls. Thankfully, no skirmishes occurred between the students. The walkouts, however, were happening at all twenty-two high schools throughout the city. Downtown Cass Technical High School was no exception.

Cass Tech was a city-wide invitation-only school located at the north-west edge of the downtown district. The building was eight stories high with gymnasiums located in a sub-floor and on the seventh floor next to the cafeteria. Students had five minutes to transverse the building between classes. Two service elevators operated, but students knew if they did not catch the first trip up not to wait for another. Walking up five or six flights, then through long corridors seemed daunting for freshmen; however, they quickly learned the importance of being on time. It was not unusual to see freshmen running through the halls to prevent being late. Being late to class was not an option.

Students from the suburbs gave false addresses to get admission to the school. The school offered a collection of over thirty curriculums in the sciences, engineering, technology, computer sciences, automotive, business, accounting, drama, and music. The building reached out to the sidewalk on three sides with minimum to no space for lounging. The front of the building faced Second Avenue, a one-way, northbound, five-lane street. Most of the student body traveled by city bus. Parents also dropped off students on various corners in the area to avoid the three-lanes of airport-like parking in the front of the building before and after school. The small college-like atmosphere of the school was unique compared to most high schools, resembling the major college of Wayne State University two miles north.

After classes a lot of the students walked southeast down Grand River Avenue to the downtown shopping district to window shop along Woodward Avenue's Grinnell's music store or Hudson's Department store, intermingling with the business and shopping crowd. They hung out at one of three Dunkin Donut shops within two blocks of each other. Major retailers lined Woodward for over half a mile, as well as all adjacent streets. Hughes and Hatcher, a clothier, had two four-story stores at the far ends of the shopping district. The downtown district was the major shopping center for the city prior to the emergence of the suburban shopping malls. The holiday season required traffic cops to direct foot traffic crossing Woodward Avenue. The district was thriving. The management of the stores welcomed the well-behaved students as they would any other shoppers.

Cass Tech's student body was equally mixed between the White and Black students. Very little tension existed in the school along racial lines primarily because the integration of the Black students into the school had occurred naturally over decades, unlike the sudden integration in the mid-sixties at other schools. There was also a small Asian student body who lived only blocks away in Chinatown.

The principal, sensing the tension within the halls, called for a schoolwide assembly of all 5,500 students. They assembled in the theater-sized four-story auditorium, entering through doors on the first through fourth floors. The principal walked onto the stage and announced to the student body that a tragedy had occurred.

He said, "I have bad news for you today. With a heavy heart, I must inform you that Dr. Martin Luther King Jr. has been assassinated. He is dead. Will you please bow your heads in a moment of silence?"

The troubled students did not react to the announcement since most already knew of his death. They dropped their heads, and thirty seconds later the principal said, "Okay. Please return to your scheduled classes." No discussion on what occurred or what the government was doing about it. Just 'return to class'.

The Black students were now very angry. Some did not understand what 'a moment of silence' meant.

A few questioned, "What the hell was that! Thirty seconds then go back to class?!"

The White students were dejected for their Black friends but did not know how to console them. The students immediately left the auditorium but did not return to their classes. Over 5,500 teenagers were now meandering in the narrow corridors of the school, primarily on the lower four floors. After thirty minutes, the administration understood they would not be able to get the students back to class. Information was coming in about the potential for city-wide disturbances. So, the officials announced that the school day was over, and the students should return home. After another thirty minutes the halls were emptied.

The Black students' frustrations were not directed toward their White classmates, so the dispersal of the student body was normal.

For the next two days the city burned, a repeat of last July. This, however, was the last straw for a lot of the city's White residents. Within the next five years, the White population of the city would drop to just fifty percent and impact the city's political arena for decades to come.

The city schools, however, were spared major vandalism. So was the downtown business district. Within the next decade, however, with the advent of suburban shopping malls to handle the increase of the suburban population, the enjoyment of shopping in the downtown business district along Woodward Avenue would begin to fade away.

· · · · · · · · · · · ·

Robert was with Carol when news came out at the University that classes were cancelled. Now, with time on her hands and no transportation readily available, Carol asked Robert to stay with her on campus. She knew her father, who usually picked her up from Wayne, would not be there for a couple of hours, and she did not want to sit alone. Riding the bus home was out of the question. She had never been on a city bus even though the Hamilton bus route would have lasted only thirty minutes and drop her off across the street from her home. She did not know her father, who worked three miles down Woodward Avenue in the downtown business district, had anticipated the cancelation and was coming early to pick her up.

Robert said, "No problem. I can sit until your ride gets here."

The anxiety on campus was similar to the rest of the student bodies throughout the city. Robert felt the anxiety in the air as well. He thought about his brothers, especially Michael, since he was always in the streets. He, however, felt the need to protect Carol by remaining at her side until she was safe. Then he would catch his bus home.

"You know I was serious about the discussion we had Monday. I want you to be my girlfriend." Carol could not stop him quick enough.

She said, "Robert, let's not ruin this. I was hoping you were playing an April Fool's joke on me."

She was not being truthful because she knew full well how Robert felt about her. She had been collecting boys' hearts since she was a little girl. Robert, as fine as he was to her, was no different. He, however, did not belong to Jack and Jill, a secretive, privileged club for elite Afro American youth. He did not vacation at Idlewild or Inkwell of Martha's Vineyard and possibly had never heard of them. His father did not play golf or tennis or take trips to Europe or the Caribbean. She understood that Robert could be no more than a friend. She had lots of male friends just like Robert, guys hanging around waiting for her to take their friendship to the next level—guys she grew up with in Jack and Jill, whose parents did play golf and tennis, travel to Europe, vacation at Inkwell, and belonged to Plymouth United Church. Was it time to break his heart as she had done to others so many times before?

Before she could respond to Robert, her father appeared. He called out to her then walked up to the couple.

He said, "Hello young man, I'm glad you were able to stay with my daughter until I arrived. I really appreciate it. Carol, come on, let's go. The streets are starting to get a little wild. By the way young man, if you live on the west side, perhaps I can give you a ride home as well?"

The sixteen-year-old, ever the quick analyst, knew the proper response to the question.

He said, "I appreciate your offer sir, but my parents will be here shortly. Thank you for asking. Carol, I will see you next week when classes resume. Have a safe weekend."

Carol stood up, nodded to Robert, and said, "Thanks Robert for waiting with me. Hope to see you next week. Goodbye." She then turned and walked away with her father.

When they got to the car her father said, "Is that the boy your brother mentioned? The one who was in that street fight some years ago? Pierre told me you were taking classes with him and hanging out on campus with him. Why are you still talking to him? I want you to stay away from his kind. Hell, he doesn't even know how to dress on campus. And his parents probably don't even know where this campus is. He'll be riding the bus home, I'm sure. Do you understand me girl? Do you want your friends talking about you dating that hood-rat?"

Carol understood and agreed, but for a different reason. She realized that she really liked Robert. Perhaps too much. He, however, could never fit in with her lifestyle, in her circle. Her friends at the social gatherings would never understand. The fact that she was wearing an afro was still freaking them out.

She reluctantly said to her father, "He's not a hood, Dad, but a kind and considerate young man. I do agree, however, that he's not my type. He was just filling in my empty schedule, but I think it's time for me to transfer to Michigan. I can start all over in the fall."

Robert would never see Carol on the Wayne campus again.

. . . .

By 2:00 p.m. the city was fully ablaze. Looters were hitting the remaining businesses on Fenkell Avenue and Livernois Avenue, the businesses that survived last summer's riot.

Mack was alarmed that his brothers Richard and Louis had not arrived home from school yet. He had left Cooley early and walked up to Post to get them, but they had already left the school. When he arrived home, he found that his mother had already gotten Jack, Horace, and Ervin from Clinton, but Richard and Louis were still not home. So, Mack asked his father, who had arrived home minutes earlier, if he could use the car to find them.

"What about Robert?" his father asked.

Mack paused then said, "I wouldn't know where to begin to look for Robert. I know where Richard and Louis should be. Can I have the keys?"

Jack, having heard his father mention his concern about Robert said, "And what about Michael?"

Frank just looked at Jack, gave Mack the keys, then said, "You drive their route to school. I'll walk up Lyndon just to be sure they didn't walk that way home."

Mack drove the car north up Santa Rosa then followed the boys' normal route to school. He had to look closely because of the number of students still walking along the streets. When he still did not see them, he turned up Greenlawn Street toward Post, but seeing a large crowd of students walking down Fenkell, he turned right onto Fenkell and drove down the busy street toward Livernois. Within a few blocks of Livernois, he encountered looters breaking into businesses and was forced to pull over to avoid a potential traffic jam. He saw a boy who resembled Louis, so he parked the car and ran over to him. He turned the boy around, but it was not Louis. That's when the police arrived and started the arrests.

Mack was unable to get back to his car and was forced to run through an alley to avoid the police, but they saw him and gave chase. He ducked here and there, but a squad car continued through the alley. He was trapped but did not want to give the cops a chance to stomp him. He heard what happened to a lot of guys who were alone with cops during the '67 riot, so he hid under some plywood leaning against a garage.

The cruiser drove up to Mack's hiding spot, and a big burly cop, with his night-stick out, got out and said, "Okay, boy. Come on out. We just want to talk. Get your ass out here, mister!"

The husky cop pulled back the plywood Mack was hiding under while his cautious partner waited behind him, gun drawn. The cop raised his stick, but before he could strike Mack, he heard his partner yell out. He turned around to see a teenager standing over his partner's prone body, face down, in a puddle of water.

He shouted, "You little runt!" and drew his gun.

Before he could fire, however, the runt threw his partner's nightstick at him, striking him in the forehead, causing him to drop his gun and fall to his knees. The 'runt' then leaped over the fallen officer, grabbed the burly cop's gun, and placed it to the cop's forehead.

Mack yelled, "NO! Don't!"

Michael hesitated, then pulled back his arm and struck the cop across the temple, rendering him unconscious. They heard more police cars heading through the alley. Michael wiped off the gun, then the nightstick, grabbed the still crouched Mack, and the two of them ran through the houses and streets until they reached Chalfonte Street, three blocks away. They hit their alley and ran through it, then stopped behind their garage. Mack leaned against the back wall of the garage, turned to Michael, and said, "What the hell were you going to do, shoot that cop? What's wrong with you!"

Mack was no longer bigger than Michael, but the size difference never mattered to him anyway.

He said, "Shut the fuck up, dumbass. He was going to kill you! Don't you get it?! He was going to beat you to death and claim you reached for his gun! Get the fuck into the house and never speak to me like that again!"

Then Michael turned and ran off before his brother could utter another word. Mack would not see him again for many years.

· · · · · · · · · · · ·

Mack entered the house through the back door only to find Louis and Richard sitting in the living room. His father was on the front porch, looking up the street for him.

Mack joined him and asked, "Where did you find them?"

Frank replied, "Those knuckleheads decided to stop for a game of basketball on Clinton's playground. It's like they don't understand the seriousness of this day."

Then Frank paused, realizing that Mack had gotten home without the family car.

He said, "Where did you go? And where is my car…?"

Mack explained what had happened to him, leaving out the part about the cops or Michael. He did not need his father to get shot complaining at the tenth precinct. Frank would not be able to contain himself and, at best, might get arrested.

Mack said, "It's parked on Fenkell, but don't worry. No one wants an old Country Squire. We can get it in the morning. Sorry Pops."

Robert got home a few hours later. His clothes were wet from sweat, and his shoes were scruffy and dirty. He had a depressed look about him as well.

Mack approached him and asked, "Robert, are you alright? Do you feel alright?"

Robert was somewhat confused by the questions. Mack was no longer bigger than Robert, but he was still acting like his big brother.

He gently brushed Mack's hand away and said, "No, I am not alright. I just lost my girlfriend."

· · · · · · · · · · · ·

The police cruiser in the alley off Fenkell Avenue was driven out of the alley and an ambulance pulled in. Both police officers had regained consciousness, but they were still taken to the nearby Grace Hospital on Meyer and Seven Mile Road. When their Lieutenant asked them what happened to them and who was responsible, the one officer said, "I have no idea. One moment I was backing Sumanski up, and the next thing I knew, I was waking up in the mud."

The burly Sumanski said, "I don't know either, Sir. I heard O'Brian yell out, then someone struck me from behind."

The Lieutenant walked up to Sumanski, examined his forehead, and thought, *"Likely story. Attacked from behind with a boomerang, huh?"*

The Lieutenant then asked, "Did either of you get a look at the guys who did this?"

The two cops looked at each other, then both shook their heads. Sumanski lied.

· · · · · · · · · · ·

Weeks after the assassination, Eastern High School's predominately Black student body, having just moved into a new building on the eastern edge of the Lafayette Park condo community near downtown Detroit, staged a walkout, wanting their school's name changed to Malcolm X High. The school board relented but decided on a different name. They felt Malcolm X was too volatile an image for a city school, so they chose Martin Luther King Jr. as the name for the school.

CHAPTER SEVEN

Street Wars

Busta made a phone call to the Mediterranean Boot Social Club and asked for his boss. When Shapatilo took the phone Busta stammered, "Boss, wez got a little problem. Some motha fucka robbed ya last night. Boss, he tooks half the stash, fucken 250 G's. I gots my boys on it. Nobody gets away wit dat kinds of bread. Don't worry Boss, I gots dis handled." Busta was now sweating through his gabardine knit shirt. Shapatilo replied, "Busta, you said I got robbed. But you are mistaken. I didn't get fuckin robbed. Your ass got robbed. Have my money to me before the end of the week. All 500. Period." He hung up the phone.

. . . .

After three long years at Cooley High, Mack was preparing for college. He was looking forward to getting away from the racial tensions in the school even though they had eased up considerably.

He found it was difficult to be in constant racially tense moments in school after having lived with Whites for four years in the Mound Road projects.

He was ready to talk to his mother about his next plans.

Mack said, "Morning, Mother. And how are you today?"

His tone completely got her attention.

Martha thought, *"'Mother?' Not 'ma' or 'mom'? What is this boy up too?"*

She said, "I'm fine. What do you have up your sleeve now?" and laughed. She knew her son was ready to graduate, even though her focus for the past few years had been the younger three.

Mack said, "Mom, I plan to start college next fall. I know you haven't been able to attend my graduations, because of the little-kids, but I'm graduating from Cooley in January. I have already enrolled at Wayne State University and have been accepted. My counselor is working with me to get some financial aid, so I won't be troubling you with finances. Just wanted you to know."

Martha said, "Look boy. If you think I'm not going to your graduation, you've got another think coming! Of course, we're going. I'll pull Jack, Horace, and Ervin out of school for this event. And if it's in the evening, your dad will be there too. Both of us graduated from high school. We both had college plans as well, but you know how life is. Anyway, I know it's not for a couple months, but get me the information needed for the graduation. And get all the information about Wayne State as well. Perhaps we can contribute somewhat toward that. Imagine, a Frank McCants kid graduating from high school. Hallelujah!"

She reached up and hugged Mack, a strange feeling for both of them. Then she started her day. A day of phone gossip and soaps. Now, however, she can gossip about her firstborn child's pending graduation.

That evening, Robert arrived home and heard his younger brothers discussing Mack's future college plans. He was excited for him as well and joined in on the discussion until they mentioned which college Mack had planned to attend. Robert cannot remember why he believed he needed to keep his life so private, but it troubled him that Mack had chosen Wayne.

He walked away and said to no one, "Wow, I didn't see this one coming. I'm glad he wants to go to college, but I still want to keep my affairs private. Now I've got to find a way to get around without bumping into him on campus. That ain't gonna work."

The following week, Mack received a letter from the private Catholic university just north of his home. The University of Detroit, one-and-a-half miles north on Livernois Avenue, is closer to his home than Cooley High. The school, however, had never been an option for the neighborhood working class students, due to its high tuition rates, unless scholarships were involved.

Mack opened the letter which read, "We have received your application for admission to our university for the Fall 1969 semester. We are glad to know of your interest and will be processing your application immediately. The enrollment period ends on the last business day in November 1968, so your application for next fall's 1969 term is on schedule. You will be hearing from us in the coming weeks." It closed with congratulations.

Mack was floored. It never dawned on him to apply to U of D. He might as well have applied to University of Michigan, or Michigan State, or Harvard! Or the private Black colleges in the South. They all cost too much money! At least at Wayne, he could live at home, avoiding dormitory cost, and work near the school for tuition and books. Who, he wondered, sent in this application? Then it came to him. *Mom!*

The last week of November, Mack received another letter from U of D. He read it aloud in the dining room.

"You have been accepted into the University of Detroit and are now a proud member of our student body. In addition, an anonymous donor has contributed one hundred percent tuition cost for you for the next four years. Congratulations Mr. McCants!"

Mack was beside himself. He yelled for his parents. When they arrived, he shoved the letter toward them. Once they were able to digest the letter's contents they were as joyous as he was. Robert, Richard, and Louis entered the room, and soon the entire family was dancing with joy for their son and big brother. Robert was especially joyous. Now he no longer had to be concerned for his privacy.

That night when the entire house was quiet, someone entered the backdoor, closing it quietly. He walked into the living room, making sure no one was sleeping on the couch. He opened the China cabinet door and pulled out an envelope addressed to Mack. After reading the contents of the envelope, he smiled, then placed the envelope back into the cabinet. Then he peeked into the younger children's bedroom, whose door was always left open at night. After a moment, he returned to the back door and exited the house knowing no one saw him. No one except Jack.

．　．　．　．　．　．　．　．　．　．　．　．

The year 1969 arrived in Detroit following a tumultuous '68. The city and business leaders were bracing for another long hot summer, since the previous two years the city burned. The Tigers won the 1968 World Series in October with minor mayhem during the subsequent celebration. This year had to be different. The tension between the Black citizens and the police remained volatile. The White citizens continued to exit the city at a record pace. As they sold their homes, the Black community slowly moved further west and east. The Black community, however, was not able to maintain the city's lost population.

Segregation was still the culture of the city.

. . . .

Busta had not gotten over the hit he took last April '68. For the last 12 months, he had been robbing Peter to pay Paul to get square with Shapatilo. He was finally coming out of the hole having to replace the $125,000 stolen from him, but now he owed his crew. His reputation had taken a hit since he never caught the thief. The eastside boys told him it was probably a dude called Michael, who had been hitting them pretty hard.

Eastside Snake said, "It was Michael. I fuckin' know it! He normally does shit like steal cars from dealers and shit, then torches the suckas. He torches brand new Caddies! If you were home when you were robbed, and you didn't hear nothing, then it was definitely Michael. Most teams steal it all. They come in shootin'. But he works alone when he does that cat-burglar shit. You said the sucker only took half? Yep, that was Michael. I'm surprised he took that much. Hot damn, that's one motha fucka that believes he can walk on water! Or so he thinks. But I gots an ace up my sleeve and it's gonna cost ya, brother, to cop it. See, I knows where the fucker lives."

. . . .

In the fall of '69 Martha became aware of an unusual set of circumstances. She called her friend Delores and bragged, "My older boys are in separate schools. Mack has just started U of D. Richard is in his eleventh-grade year of high school. Louis is still at Post, preparing to graduate this January."

Delores waited for her to finish, but Martha paused. Then she said, "And the little-kids are all together at Clinton!"

Delores said, "Girl, I know you're proud. All boys, and they are doing you so proud."

Delores thought, however, *"She didn't finish. What about Robert and Michael, huh?"*

. . . .

Mack finished his first college classes for the day and began to walk home. It was a warm fall day in September and since he was ahead of schedule, he decided to visit the administration office. He was still puzzled with his admittance to the school and wanted to find out who sent in his application.

He approached the administration desk and said, "Ma'am, my name is Mack McCants. Here is my student ID. If you don't mind, could I see my application for admission to the school?"

The staffer looked at him, smiled, then pulled his application.

"This cannot leave this desk," the young lady said. She thought, *"He's cute. Wonder why he wants to see his application? It has his mother's name on it."*

Mack glanced at the bottom of the application, then passed it back to the flirtatious clerk. She paused for a moment then slipped him a note. He read the note then winked at her and said, "Danke! Ciao!"

She blushed as he walked away and thought, *"Silly boy shouldn't mix his languages. But man is he fine!"*

When he got home, he interrupted his mother's TV program.

"Mom, I saw my school application to U of D. Thanks for submitting it. If only I could find out who the anonymous donor is?"

He smiled at her as he walked upstairs.

Frank got home an hour later. Martha asked him to join her in their private place.

She closed the door and asked, "Did you by any chance send in Mack's application to U of D?"

Frank responded, "No, of course not. Why would I apply for him to attend a school we can't afford?"

Martha said, "Well, he thinks it was me, but I didn't either. Apparently, your Sherlock son decided to find out who did. He must have read the application and saw my name on it. Who could have done that? And now I'm wondering who this anonymous donor is?"

Frank could only shake his head.

However, he was thinking, "*It had to be my dad. Who else could afford it?*"

. . . .

A young man walked into the University of Detroit's Administration office and asked for Admissions. It was late November '68, but the clerk told him he had plenty of time. She was just glad to see an inner-city kid seek admittance to her university. Once inside Admissions he requested an application. He was handed one, thanked the desk clerk, then left the office. An hour later he returned with a completed application, handed it to the clerk, said his goodbyes, then departed. She read the application to ensure it was completed, then placed it in the desk input box for new applicants. She thought, "Mack McCants. Mother's name 'Martha'. Just like my mother's name."

The young man walked to the National Bank of Detroit office on Livernois Avenue and Puritan Street, down the block from the school. He filled out a savings withdrawal slip for $30,000 to be applied to a cashier's check made out to University of Detroit.

A week later, after business hours, an unauthorized entry was made into the admissions office of the University of Detroit. The intruder searched for new applications until he found the one application he was seeking. He reviewed other approved applications in a nearby folder, noticed the notations of approval, then copied this notation onto his sought-after application and placed it with the approved applications.

Three days later, the University of Detroit's tuition office received a letter from an anonymous person. The hand-written letter was accompanied by a cashier's check for $30,000. The letter stated that the funds were to be attributed to an incoming student named Mack McCants, covering all tuition and book fees. He would be starting the fall of '69. Any residual funds should be attributed to any post-graduate work of Mr. McCants. The donation was to be contributed to an anonymous donor.

· · · · · · · · · · ·

Late Fall '69

Busta made a call to Eastside Snake. After he hung up the phone, he called Drither into the room.

He said, "Go fetch 10 G's from my mattress. Place it in dis hare bag. Den takes it to Eastside Snake."

Then he called in Joker.

"Joker, git da boys ready. Both groups. Weez ready ta roll."

Joker realized Busta was not in a teasing mood. He had not been since they were robbed almost eighteen months ago. April of last year and still no payback. So instead of being snide, he said, "Busta, you want us to ride now? It's still broad daylight." Busta looked at Joker, realized he was making him nervous and merely replied, "Yeah. I know."

An hour later, they were turning down Santa Rosa Drive from Chalfonte Street.

．．．．．．．．．．．

Trigger walked onto the porch of the McCants residents and knocked. When Martha answered the door and saw Trigger, she immediately knew Michael had brought trouble to the household. She had been wondering just how long it might be before it came to this, and she had hoped they might escape it. She now wondered if it was time for her to use her 'one-time-call' option. Before she could finish the thought Frank entered the room, still holding his t-shirt, looked at her as she turned to him, and immediately went to the door.

Martha knew to step back.

"Yes, may I help you?" said Frank.

Trigger thought, *"I was all set ta talk to da White bitch, den dis dark-ass motha steps up. Shiiiit! Wonder what day kids looks like?"*

Trigger said, "Lookin foe a dude name Michael."

Frank replied in his low bass voice, "Michael is my son. He doesn't live here anymore, but if you have business with him, then you have business with me."

Trigger thought, *"Proper talkin prick! Must be edumacated. Probably where he meets his bitch."*

He abruptly said, "When did ya seed him last? Me and my boys gots serious bitnez with em."

Frank stepped out onto the porch, forcing Trigger to back up. He kept walking toward him, and Trigger eventually found himself having to step down onto the top step. Now he was looking up at the six-foot, 200-pound mass of pecs and biceps.

Frank calmly replied, "I said my son doesn't live here anymore. And I said if you have business with him, then you have business with me."

His cadence did not change, which was somewhat unsettling to Trigger. Trigger stepped down an additional step.

By now most of the neighbors on the south end of the block were out on their porches. Some of them recognized Busta and knew trouble was brewing. Word spread up the block of a potential problem at the McCants. Four '70 Cadillacs full of thugs parked on the wrong side of the street proved very informative. Mack was at the north end of the block walking down the street from school. Louis and Richard were coming out onto the porch, joining their dad. Both had removed their shirts, something Frank generally did not allow. Martha's radar went out for the little-kids, so she told Louis to bring them in. He ignored her, not leaving his father's side. So, she went out to the backyard and brought them indoors, sending them to their room. They did not stay in there long. Then she joined Frank and her two boys on the front porch.

Trigger opened his mouth to speak, but Martha cut him off, switched to her Harlem tone, and said, "Look son. My husband already told you Michael ain't here, so tell your boss over there to take his shit elsewhere."

Trigger's mouth never closed as he was now shocked by Martha's declaration. He backed down two more steps then turned, jumped the remaining ones, and walked toward Busta's car.

Busta said, "What da fuck is goin on? You let dat factory motha back ya up? And his White bitch sass ya? Well, I'll…"

Busta started to cross the street. Trigger reached out his hand and lightly grabbed Busta's arm.

He said, "Busta, I smells trouble. Dis ain't no 'tap-dance' job. Dat nigga say Michael don't lives dare no-mo. And dat ain't no White bitch. She New York, through and through. A Cotton Club sista. I can tell by her meaner, she's been growed up in the street, I tells ya. She growed up in the life. And I can tell by da way her man looked at her, he don't even kno what I's kno."

Busta stopped and stared at Trigger then at Frank. He took a step toward the house, then stopped.

He thought, *"Shit, Trigger may be on ta sometin. Yeah, sometin ain't rights hare. Smells fishy. We standin hare twelve strong, and he ain't even got no piece on em."*

He yelled across the street, "Ya tells Michael, Busta lookin foe 'em! Busta knos where he lives!" He turned around, got back in his car and drove away. Three Cadillacs followed.

· · · · · · · · · · ·

Mack, having witnessed the cars pulling away, picked up his pace. He could tell they were at his house, so he took the seven-step porch in two bounds. He walked in to see his dad sternly talking to Martha. In all his years he had never seen his father speak to his mother in this manner.

Frank said, "Baby, when I'm doing business like this don't ever walk into it. That was dangerous as hell, and you walked into the middle of it. I can't operate if I've got to keep an eye out for you as well. The boys know what to do, but you can't possibly know."

Martha knew the moment she spoke up she was making a mistake, but she could not resist.

She said, "Honey, you are right as usual. I put my nose where it didn't belong. Excuse my French, but the thought of that motherfucker threating our family just got the better of me. Sorry. It won't happen again."

She then thought, *"The next time that punkass comes on my porch will be his last time on this earth."*

Frank just stared at his wife.

He thought, *"I have never heard her talk this way before. Did she just use the MF word? And in front of the boys."*

Mack interrupted his parents.

He said, "Can I ask what just happened? Does this have anything to do with me or the boys?"

Frank said, "Son, your brothers will fill you in. Martha, please come with me."

The two parents walked into their bedroom and closed the door.

Mack walked over to Richard and asked him, "What just happened?"

Richard motioned for Mack to follow him and Louis upstairs.

When the three of them were gone, nine-year-old Jack said, "This must be about Michael and all those trips he was making in the middle of the night."

Just then, Robert walked into the house and Jack, for a moment, was rattled. Then he calmed down, said hello to Robert, and headed for the backyard.

As he turned the corner he looked back at Robert and said, "I think you may want to go talk to Mom and Pops."

.　.　.　.　.　.　.　.　.　.　.

Dr. Joseph McCants was born in 1906 on his family's horse ranch near Brooklyn Michigan, west of Ann Arbor. He was a professor of history at Eastern University in Ypsilanti, Michigan, just east of the University of Michigan.

He had warned Frank not to marry so young and to enroll in college so he could finish his education.

Dr. McCants married without his father's approval and was disowned by the family. He had seven sons with his wife Willamae, similar to his son Frank. He was forced to drop the family name, since he defied his father. He took her surname and gave it to his sons.

Now Frank had repeated this act of defiance, marrying without his father's approval. Dr. McCants had not disowned him, however, and at times had offered financial assistance. Frank, however, did not want his father's help, nor did he want him around his children unless he could also love his wife. The last time he and Frank spoke was the week Frank's family moved into the projects on Mound Road in October '61. On that fateful day he said to Frank, "Son, I can't believe you live like this!" He shifted his car from park to drive, then drove away. They remained estranged.

. . . .

Around 10:00 p.m. that night, Frank placed a phone call to Ypsilanti. When the phone was answered he said, "Father, we have to talk. I may need the family's help. I've talked to Horace, but he insisted that I call you first."

Dr. McCants replied, "Anything you need son. Anything you need."

. . . .

Busta fumed over the insulting results of his visit to Santa Rosa, so that night he decided to return with his crew. Just before midnight, he got a call from Shapatilo. He was instructed to come to the club. He informed Shapatilo that he already had plans and would be there later. That did not go over very well with his boss. Thirty minutes later Busta was at the club.

Shapatilo was very upset. He had heard that there had been consistent raids on drug houses over the previous year. He understood that he could not control the crime in the city. As long as the houses pay their dues, however, he did not care. Now one of his stash houses was hit. He initially made Busta pay up, which he did. Yet, when he attended a meeting in Grosse Pointe, the big boss was not happy that he allowed this to continue without any retribution.

He said, "Busta, the big boss is not happy you was robbed. He wants to know what you've done about it. That shit happened way back in April last year. Who's balls are hanging from your belt Busta? I don't see any balls hanging from your belt. What's up with that Busta?"

Busta hated to be in Shapatilo's presence. He was a big guy, but not nearly as big as Busta, and he knew he could crush him in a quick moment. He also knew that they would be fishing him out of the Detroit River soon afterward.

Busta said, "Boss, da thief was so quiet dat nobody heard a thang. Even Bitch don't bark." Busta knew this was not true. In fact, the dog did alert them, but they ignored her.

Shapatilo continued, "One of my men was talking to one of your boys about a trip you recently made on the west side. You pulled up twelve strong on a residential block and thought no one would report it? Shit man, there are still White folks living on that street! You can't be bringing heat down on my operation by going into that middle class neighborhood and causing a scene. Don't you know there's a city council member, Tony Wierzbicki, who used to live in the middle of that block! His phone must have been jumping off the hook. Busta, we take our affairs out of sight! Not with the whole fuckin' block watching! Now, maybe you were onto something, I don't know. But you better work it through another angle. Stay the fuck away from Santa Rosa unless I send you over there myself! Capeesh?"

· · · · · · · · · · ·

As Busta was being disciplined by his boss, Michael arrived home and climbed the back stairs. He sat on the top railing of the upper back porch, waiting for Robert to walk by the window. When he did,

Michael tapped on the glass. Robert opened the door and stepped outside, closing the door behind him.

He said, "Michael, you've brought shame to the house. You've brought death to the house. Pops is a good man, but he could have killed a man today. Pops is not a killer. He should be a doctor or lawyer, not a factory worker. But he loves us, so he gave up his future for us. You've got to do better than this, man. You've got to do better than this. Why would you mess with some thug's place this close to home? How did they even know it was you? Has your reputation proceeded you? Or do you have a rat in your midst?"

Michael just sat for a while and listened.

Finally, he said, "Yeah, that 'doctor' sure showed me love when he was whipping my ass! Okay, okay, I know you're right. I brought most of that shit on myself, and he gave as much to you, Mack, Louis, and Richard as me. But he should not have taken his frustrations about his life out on us kids. But…Okay. I did do something to that thug Busta. I'll get this straightened out. Maybe not the way you might want me to, but I'll straighten the whole mess out."

Without waiting for Robert to respond, Michael flipped over the rail, hung for a moment twelve feet off the ground, then dropped down and disappeared. Robert came back indoors to see Jack staring up the stairs at him.

CHAPTER EIGHT

To Steal a Cadillac

"Busta, you knows dat strange feelin youse had when youse was on Santa Rosa? You thought it was da daddy? Cause he don't have no guns on em? Well, I's be thinkin. Could it has been his bitch?" Busta looked at Trigger for a moment then said, "What ya gettin at?" Trigger said, "I spenz some time in Harlem ways back yonder. Gots to kno lots of folks. They's got a part of Harlem where dem mullatoes live, couple of dem blocks between I-tal-yin Harlem and da real Harlem. Shit, youse can hardly tell dem yella niggas from dem dagoes. I's bettin she from dar. And ifn she is, we can git a guy hare who might knos her. I thinks we should git a brotha from dare to come visit us hare. See ifn he recognizes her." Busta thought, "Nigga, you aint never been to Harlem. Youse from Mississippi, same as me." He said, "So you lived in Harlem?" Trigger replied, "Yeah. My ole man sends me dare in '51 for few yars. Gots in some trouble wit some crackers down yonder and had to skedaddle." Busta replied, "Okay. Sets it up."

. . . .

Busta woke up with the bright sunshine illuminating his bedroom, blinding him. He did not recall leaving his curtains open. In fact, he never left them open. He rarely ever opened them. He got up, quite an effort for such a big man, and jerked the curtains closed, then climbed back into bed. An hour later he got a call from Joker.

He answered the phone to hear Joker yelling, "Busta, some motherfucker stole my car!" Busta paused for a moment then said, "What cha mean? Yo ride is gone? Ya didn't give it to dat bitch of yoren? Yeah, she's probably gots it and is kickin it wit some other dude, earning you som dough!"

Joker said, "Busta, I don't play that! And besides, my hoe is laying right here!"

Busta said, "Well, put da word out ta dat car rang ta be on da looksout fo yo ride. Now let me gits back ta sleep."

The following morning Busta woke up again with the bright sunlight shining in his face. This only exacerbated his headache from too much partying.

He got up shouting, "Who's fuckin' with my curtains!" He jerked them so hard they almost fell off the rods, then dropped back onto his bed. The floorboards complained. Before he could close his eyes, however, the phone rang. It was Trigger.

He answered it to hear, "Busta, sums-a-bitches gots my ride! My baby blue!" Busta sat up and thought, "Two Caddies in two nights! What da fuck is goin on? We gots a new car theft rang goin' on and I doesn't have a piece of da action?"

He paused, then said aloud, "But dem guys knows my crew and wouldn't touch our rides…Oh shit! Eastside Snake said dat Michael stole cars! What da fuck?"

He sat on the side of the bed and called Eastside Snake. When the phone was answered he said, "Hey, fool. What was it dat you said Michael did after he stole yo rides?"

Eastside Snake did not appreciate being disturbed before noon, and it was only 8:30 a.m. "Busta, is you crazy man! Calling me in the middle of the night!"

Busta said, "Nigga, it's eight fucking thirty! I ask ya a question! What da fuck do Michael do ta cars he steals?"

Eastside realized something was amiss and quietly responded, "Ah, he burns them. He sets them on fire and burns them up. Check out a vacant lot near your place. You might find them there. Can I go back to sleep now?"

But all Eastside Snake could hear was a dial tone.

Busta looked out his window to check on his car. It was parked where he left it last night. He got up and dressed in yesterday's clothes and was out the door in five minutes.

. . . .

The younger McCants children were settled very well in Clinton Elementary. Ervin was now in the 2nd grade, Horace in the third and Jack in the fourth. They played together with the group of young boys on the playground and rarely, if ever, had to fight. Their family's reputation preceded them. And if it did not, they handled any and all newcomers fairly easily. Growing up watching their older brothers tussle was highly educational.

Louis was a senior at Post Junior High, ready to graduate in a few months. He did not miss his brother Richard, having expanded his own circle of friends. He was one of the more popular boys in the school. He had inherited his mother's straight hair and that drove the girls wild. On occasion a new kid would misinterpret his looks for softness and soon live to regret it.

Louis was the most athletic of the older five with lightning reflexes. At fourteen he could dunk a basketball even though he was only 5' 5" tall. He ran like the wind, had brilliant hand-eye coordination, and could sing and dance exceptionally well. His potential was unlimited. Like Robert and Michael, he was an all 'A' student as well. He never understood why Mr. Johnson, the principal, avoided him, and assumed rightfully so, that it had something to do with Michael. Mr. Brown tried to recruit him to Cass Tech, informing him that he was successful in recruiting Robert to the school, but since Louis knew Robert had dropped out of school, he dismissed the notion.

Richard was not handling being alone at Cooley well. He did not like being in a school without a brother watching his back. He understood, however, that Louis would be attending Cooley soon. At sixteen he was enjoying his second year in high school. He was looking forward to the holiday season. His grades were fine, but he never was an all 'A' student and realized that getting an occasional 'B' was acceptable.

The tension between the Black and White students was over. A lot of the White students had transferred to high schools west of Cooley either because their families had moved further west, or they just gave the school board bogus addresses.

Robert was well entrenched in his studies. He had designed a plan that would allow him to graduate a year from now, a couple of weeks after his nineteenth birthday. Three years was long enough, he reasoned. There was always the possibility that he could be drafted, but he was not concerned since his draft board contact had assured him that he would maintain a college deferment. He rarely went home, staying on campus to save time for studies. He would occasionally call his mother, interrupting her soaps, but she did not seem to mind. After all, the phone was her second hobby, after the soaps.

Michael was Michael. Wheeling and dealing. After his discussion with Robert concerning Busta, he never went back to Santa Rosa. He never saw his older brother, since he was still angry with Mack. He did check on Richard and Louis from afar because he missed them. He was careful, however, about going by Clinton during their recess to see the younger three. It may have been his imagination, but it seemed that Jack always looked in his direction whenever he appeared.

He thought, *"I sure wouldn't want to have him working as a lookout for these dopers. That's for sure."*

.　.　.　.　.　.　.　.　.　.　.　.

Mack was also enjoying his first semester in college.

He thought *"Finally, I'm with adults!"* He was popular with the freshmen students, and the neighborhood kids were mostly proud of him. He had considered joining the freshman track team and attended the basketball games, which boasted a '68 Olympic gold medalist on the squad. The racial stress he experienced from high school hardly existed on the predominately White campus. He did have one experience in his first month while crossing the campus parking lot one late evening. He encountered a student who was a senior at Cooley when he first arrived there in '66. The student was a large football player who liked to intimidate the new Black students at Cooley. When he recognized Mack, he walked up to him, made a snide remark about his curly afro, then reached out to rub his head. Mack walked away after knocking the student unconscious with one punch.

The vast majority of the boys who graduated from Cooley with Mack did not get the opportunity to attend college, either because of finances or poor educational planning. Some of his friends did not graduate at all and just hung around the neighborhood. The neighborhood grapevine implied that Mack was becoming standoffish.

When he heard about the gossip, he realized he needed to spend more time staying in touch with his friends. He understood that he was extremely fortunate to have been admitted to U of D and did not want to be 'that guy' who had forsaken his friends.

Martha was now relaxed. She had gotten over the turmoil of last month. The children were safely in school. The family had gotten no more indications that the trouble Michael had started was returning. Frank was earning more; she was considering asking him to buy a second car, so she could get around. But she was not in a hurry for that. She just wanted to continue to enjoy her solitude in her quiet home.

Frank was a mess. He had spoken to his father and now spent his evenings planning a defense of his home if and when the drug lords returned. His father gave permission for his brothers to assist him, not that they required it. If the old man had said no, they would have come running anyway. Frank's six brothers and he met every Saturday at Horace's home, going over defensive strategies. If war did erupt, Horace still had the pipeline to his cousins, who were more than happy to assist them. They had not grown up together due to the strife with Dr. McCants and his overall family. As adults, however, most of them had looked beyond the older generation's harsh treatment of their uncle and began communicating with Horace and his brothers. Horace believed his cousins would be there for him whenever he needed them. One of Frank's brothers felt they should go on the offensive and eliminate Busta as a problem once and for all. However, Horace kept reminding them that most of the Black gangsters were tied to the Sicilian gangsters. If they wanted to take them on as well, they would have to call their entire extended family. That was not an option.

Frank knew that the situation was not over. He knew it was not over because he knew Michael.

· · · · · · · · · · · ·

For a third night that week Busta woke up with bright sunshine blinding him.

He bellowed, "Whose fuckin' wit my curtains!" and jumped out of bed. He knew instinctively that his phone was going to ring.

He reached for it just as the first ring began. "

Ray Ray, don't ya tells me yo Caddie is missin' too?!"

. . . .

Busta contacted Trigger and asked about the scout he was bringing in from Harlem. Trigger replied, "Man, dat nigga Dillon drove his car off da Pennsylvania turnpike! Had to take da train from Philie. He gits hare inna neck brace and I's takes him over dare to da block. We waits til the queen bee comes outta da house. He tooks one look at da bitch and damn! He cursed me out and catched da next train back to Harlem! Ain't nevva seen sucha scared-lookin nigga befo! Mumbled sometin bout some ole bitches kid or sometin. Say dat why he wreaks his ride. One thang fo sho dough. She Black!"

. . . .

Busta called his boss and told him he had a problem that he needed to fix that might involve the Santa Rosa family. Shapatilo reminded him of what he told him previously and hung up the phone.

"Mada fucckkkkkerrr!" he bellowed and slammed his receiver down.

He jumped into his car and picked up Ray Ray, then drove to the Cadillac graveyard. There was Ray Ray's car, burnt to a crisp.

Ray Ray cried, "Boss, when are we going to get this prick? Why can't we just stake out his block?"

Busta said, "Don't ya think I's already done dat? Jake and Drither are over dare right now stayin' in a rented room on da corner of Chalfontay. If dai had seen him, don't ya thinks day woulda said something by now. I even pays one of da nearby neighbors to watch da house. Every now and den day report seeing 'em, only to finds out its his fuckin' twin! We gets moe sightings on the east side, so dat's wheres we needs be lookin, not way da fuck over hare. He stay on da east side! But I gots a plan. Da next car dis nigga goin foe is mine. I bet yo bottom dolla. So I gots a plan."

The following morning Busta woke up tied to his bed. This was not an unusual position for him since his lady often tied him up to work him over. He closed his eyes to enjoy the noticeable pleasure he was experiencing. It had been a while since Busta's equipment worked and the last thing he wanted to do was interfere with her. The pressure began to mount as he strained on the ropes.

Then he thought, *"Waits a minute! Dat bitch still in da hospital. Dat last ass whuppen I gives her made sho she wouldn't be out too soon."*

His dazed eyes began to focus on a large white container hanging from the ceiling. It was a gallon of milk with a small hole in the bottom of the container, dripping milk on him. He still felt incredible pleasure, but he needed to know its origins. He soon realized the milk was landing on his crouch. His eyes focused more, and he noticed movement on the bed. Then he finally understood the beautiful feeling he was having was not the dripping milk or a new lady, but four little kittens licking the milk off his erect johnson. A newfound fury allowed him to burst the ropes and the bedspring at once. He roared like a madman, then tore through the house and down the stairs in his birthday suit. He looked into the downstairs bedroom and found two of his boys tied to a bed, butt naked, and lying one on top of the other, facing each other in a sixty-nine position.

Busta was stunned for a moment then yelled, "My ride!"

He left the men and ran to the window, ripping the shades down. Parked in the driveway was a shiny Burgundy '70 Cadillac.

He yelled, "Thanks you, Jezus! Nobody messed wit my car. It's still har."

Then he realized that something was still wrong.

"So who da fuck tied me and da boys up?"

It was only then that he realized all the yelling he kept hearing was his crew, still tied up. However, only Ray Ray was yelling. Drither, who was on top, was facing down with his eyes closed. He was actually smiling, since he had released his load.

. . . .

A shadowy figure walked through the neighborhood, crossing streets, walking through yards, crossing alleys, then more yards, until it came upon a new Burgundy 1970 Cadillac. The man boosted the car and drove slowly away. When he reached the intersection, he turned right, not noticing a car up the block had pulled out as well. He drove north up Wyoming to Eight Mile Road, made a Michigan left turn, then went west on Eight Mile. The second car followed the lead car from a distance until the driver crossed Schaefer, then pulled up next to him and pointed a gun through the window. Michael smiled at Ray Ray and Drither then sped off.

Just one mile up the road, he made a left turn at Greenfield Road, then drove onto the southbound Lodge Freeway and hit 100 mph almost immediately. On his bumper was the twin '70 Caddie. Michael weaved in and out of traffic, attempting to lose the trailing car, which caused the chaser to brake hard to avoid crashing. Ray Ray weaved around the remaining traffic and floored his accelerator to regain his position to Michael's. As the cars entered the Wyoming curve, Ray Ray slowed, fearful of the extreme leftward redirection of the freeway, which allowed Michael to pull away. He floored his accelerator, hitting 120 mph, and was down to the next extreme 90-degree right curve near Davison in one minute. Ray Ray was unable to catch up but did not lose sight of Michael.

Michael entered the exit for eastbound Davison Highway, hitting the curve so fast the right tires rose off the ground. When the car settled, he floored the accelerator again to 100 mph, then exited the Davison onto the southbound Chrysler Freeway. Once the car was onto I-75 it again sped up to 120 mph until he reached the downtown Chrysler right curve for westbound travel. Now the pursuing car was nowhere in sight. Again, Michael sped up and immediately reached the Grand River Avenue exit. He slammed on his brakes at the top of the ramp, turned hard right, driving north on Second Avenue by Cass Technical High School and the school's track, then around the one-block of Cass Park, turned left, passed the Masonic Temple, then right up Fourth Street. Finally, he pulled into the first parking lot of the Jeffries Projects, slammed the car between two giant trash containers, severely damaging both sides of the luxury car as he jammed on the brakes. Michael had to roll down the back window to exit the vehicle. Before he left the vehicle, however, he rifled the glove box, taking a small but thick binder with him.

Michael ran west across the housing project quad and parking lot areas, then southeast down Grand River Avenue. He slowed to a jog and continued down the street to Woodward Avenue, then weaved through the downtown streets to Lafayette Street, then east on Lafayette by Martin Luther King High to Jefferson Avenue, then east to Iroquois Street. Then he finally slowed down and entered a yard with a carriage house over the garage. A cross country track coach would have been proud of the seventeen-year-old.

Some of his many hideouts were carriage houses in Indian Village. The Village was a community of massive Romanesque, Tudors and mansions built around the turn of the century. Most of the owners were too busy to notice their property was being intruded upon. He always left no trace of his presence, and even had to clean up a few. Those that did notice merely changed their locks. Their liberalism would not allow them to bring the police in over a minor trespassing incident. Especially after the recent civil disruptions in the city. He never went back to those locations. *"Don't need any trouble from these rich White folks,"* was his creed. He never robbed them, just slept, cleaned up and moved on.

. . . .

The following early morning, an elderly lady of a large French Tudor on Iroquois decided to go clean up her carriage house. She and her husband had just arrived back home from Europe that morning and she was antsy after being waited on for the past three months. She usually had a lady from the neighborhood come in twice a week to do housecleaning. She, however, did not want anyone to see just how unkept the living quarters over her garage might be. So, she gathered up all the cleaning materials she needed, buckets and all, and headed for the carriage house. She entered the garage, climbed the stairs, and opened the door.

Then she yelled, "Oy gevalt! Oh, God! Ezekiel, come quick!" and ran down the stairs and out of the garage. When she returned, her husband in tow, she instructed him to enter the room first. What they found stumped them both. The room, kitchen and bath were immaculate.

CHAPTER NINE

Greektown

December 1969

"Mothafuckin' sombitch! I caint believes you let dat sombitch steals my ride! I planted you dare ta stop his ass, not go on a fuckin' joy ride drag race wit 'em! Now my baby is gone! And dat ain't all! My books gon too! I forgots I left it in da car! I'm gon kills me a nigga ifn it's da last thang I does!"

. . . .

Robert had been doing extremely well on the Wayne campus. He was taking extra classes each quarter semester, including the summer semesters. It had been over a year since Carol had transferred from the university. He found that without her around he was able to completely focus on his classes. He periodically went on dates, but by the third one his interest would fade, and he would move on to another. Apparently, Carol set the bar too high. Every few months, however, Michael would make a surprise visit.

Robert was in a study hall late one evening, studying for fall '69 semester finals, when Michael sat next to him.

"Hey little brother. How are things?"

Robert responded, "You tell me, since you can read me so well."

Robert immediately regretted saying that.

Michael said, "Well, let me see. That uppity bitch is gone out of your life. I don't know where, and I don't care. Neither should you. Join me on the east side and you'll completely forget about her. Our big brother has been accepted into University of Detroit, full scholarship and all. That's better than what you've accomplished here. By the way, I was able to attend his graduation from Cooley in January. Boy, mom and Pops are really having reasons to be proud. Have you told them about your Cass Tech graduation yet? You didn't even go, did you? Or that you've attended this illustrious university for two years now? As a student, not a dishwasher and janitor?"

Robert interrupted him and said, "Alright, Alright. You've made your point. You are keeping up with the family. No one, however, can keep up with you."

Michael uttered, "But I bet mom and Pops are sleeping better! Ha!" It disturbed Robert whenever Michael intimated that their parents don't love him.

"Leave it be, will you?" Robert replied.

"Things are getting better now that Pop's income has improved. The unions are doing great things for the workers, and foremen are benefiting from it as well. By the way, not to change the subject but the other day I was walking up Livernois and saw two of the Banyon brothers. I said hello to them, but the one named Samuel frowned, and they crossed the street, despite the heavy traffic. Are they ever going to get over that silly fight we had? That was over four years ago. We were just kids then."

Michael smiled and said, "No little brother. They are never going to get over that beating you gave them. Just accept that fact."

Students began to enter the room, so Michael said, "See ya later, little brother."

. . . .

The gang leader gathered his boys to let them in on their next hit. He said, "Guys, this is my last job. I'm getting too old for this shit, so we're going to hit them hard tonight. Then I'm calling it quits. Here's the plan."

He explained they were going to rob four after-hours nightclubs before morning. Every hour they would hit another club, starting at 2:00 a.m. on Saturday night. They will rob the first club and tie up the occupants, so no one can make a phone call. The plan was for them to continue through the night until they had hit them all. They would be informed which clubs they would rob the night of the assault. Ken was the only one he trusted with the plan. The four of them will drive separate cars just in case they have to become evasive. They are only to pack automatics since they are easier to reload. Michael concluded with, "And no unnecessary shooting."

"Make sure you don't drive your own cars, just in case we have to ditch them."

In fact, he does not plan on robbing after-hour clubs but new operating drug houses, ones that were just getting their operations started. They had been robbing the drug stash houses so hard over the past two years that the new security at the houses made it very difficult not to have to go in shooting. They were less likely to have heavy security at the new houses.

On Saturday night Michael gave his three partners the location of the first hit. It was a popular nightclub called the Twenty Grand, on 14th Street and West Warren Avenue. They would continue northward, ending at Watt's Club Mozambique, on Fenkell Avenue.

His three partners pulled up at 1:30 a.m. across from the Twenty Grand, only to find him sitting in an old Country Squire station wagon.

Michael said, "Jump in fellas. Change of plans. Leave yo cars on the street. We'll be back for them later."

"Michael, I ain't styling in this piece of shit. Where'd you get this old-ass station wagon?" Kevin joked.

Michael laughed and said, "It's my Pops car!", lying through his laughter. "Besides, a car ain't nothin but four wheels and a radio."

Ken, his closest friend asked, "Michael, what's goin on? I thought we was hitting the 'Twenty' tonight?"

Michael smiled and said, "Ken, has your mama ever gone to the Twenty Grand? Jim, doesn't your sister love to party there? Why would we hit a place that our families attend? Shit, one or more of them is probably in there right now! No, boys. We're going up the street. Get ready."

Michael drove the car up 12th Street into an alley four blocks north of the Twenty Grand, parked and waited. At 1:45 a.m. they pulled out and circled the block, pulling up behind an old dilapidated grey house. The house had no front porch light, but lights were lit on the first floor.

Michael said, "That's our first hit."

Ken was not happy with the change of plans. He thought, "*Why do I care about yo mamas. I don't have no one partying in the Twenty Grand. We should have stuck to our first plan. Everyone knows these podunk little houses ain't got no heavy cash.*"

Twenty minutes later, the boys were back in the alley and in the car. Michael said, "See, no one resisted. They are tied up tight with no telephones. Besides, they are not connected to anyone, so there's no one to yell 'wolf' to. They definitely can't call the cops." Everyone laughed.

Kevin said, "Michael, I think that kid who yelled 'wolf' was yellin about an imaginary event. What we just pulled off was real." All the men continued to laugh. Except Ken.

They pulled off three more robberies without anyone getting hurt.

Jim said, "Michael, it freaks me out how you're able to scale those roofs so easily. Shit, I'd be terrified to climb on these old ass houses."

Michael smiled and said, "Yeah, I was scared of that last one. I didn't realize just how old and decrepit some of those roofs are."

The gang just laughed.

Ken said, "It's still early. We've got time for one more job. But I think it should be a big score. I was counting on a heavy payout tonight. I don't think those little ass stashes are going to do it for me. If you guys want to join me, I want to go over to Fenkell and Livernois, just down the street from Watt's Club. There's a major score there that's never been hit. I've scoped it out, just haven't said anything until now."

Michael did not like Ken changing his plans. He knew Ken was not attentive to fine detail. He would just as soon go in blasting. Besides, it was too close to home. He had promised Robert he would not operate in the neighborhood anymore. He, however, saw that if he did not go along with Ken's plan the others would go without him. It could prove very dangerous and since he gathered them that night, he felt responsible for their safety. So, he let Ken fill them in, while they drove north to Fenkell Avenue.

The drug house Ken picked was a huge mistake, and Michael immediately knew it. It was one of Busta's. Michael believed he had already robbed Busta enough and did not want to aggravate him further. Ken's plan was foolhardy and very dangerous. So, Michael, knowing the boys were going in with or without him, made the necessary adjustments. This did not sit well with Ken.

He said, "Okay, I see your point. But it's getting late so we've gots to get movin."

The plan was for Michael to do his usual scaling to the roof, enter an open window on the third floor of the apartment, then open a back window on the second floor. He would carry a rope with him so the boys could scale the wall. Once inside they would burst in on the security, tie everyone up, lock the street security out, then grab the stash and be out the second-floor window before the crew knew what hit them.

The plan almost worked, but just outside, one of the security guys saw them and began yelling, "Pookie, we're being robbed!" and started shooting.

Ken ran to the car, pulled out a rifle and began blasting. Jim and Kevin opened the squire's hatch, laid down their forty-fives and came out with sawed-off shotguns. Michael just began firing with his forty-five. Bullets were flying everywhere. Then the boys jumped into Michael's country-squire and peeled away. The security guys jumped into their car and sped off after them.

The station wagon was not built for high-speed car races, so they were constantly having to weave in and out of traffic to avoid being overtaken. The car was also not designed for an obstacle course, so they almost flipped over several times. The guys were screaming for their lives throughout the run. All except Michael, who was laughing throughout the chase.

He raced east on Fenkell to Linwood, then turned right onto Linwood, then traveled south on Linwood to Davison, then east on Davison to 12th Street. Finally, he turned right onto the one-way northbound 12th street, heading in the wrong direction. Since the car was slow the security guys managed to stay close behind them. Bullets were glancing off of the squire and smashing the windows. Finally, the security crew lost control of their car, due to their inability to maneuver around the oncoming northbound traffic and crashed into a telephone pole. There was a roar of approval from the gang in the station wagon.

The squire continued south on 12th Street to Clairmount Street, then turned right onto Clairmount for one block, then switched over to southbound 14th street. They traveled down 14th Street until they were a block north of the 20 Grand Club. They ditched the station wagon and ran on foot back to their cars.

Michael had the stash from the previous jobs on him. Ken had the other bag. Michael stole the first car available and pulled away. He would not see the other guys until tomorrow, when he would give them their split. The guys knew Michael had never cheated them before, so they were not concerned. They had noticed that for some reason, Michael rarely showed interest in the stash money. He just seemed to rob for the thrill of it.

Ken eventually got home, with some angry fellas awaiting him. They were a secret crew he had set up for the evening.

He said, "Okay, guys, okay. Relax. I know I said we were hitting the Twenty tonight. But there was an unexpected change of plans. But don't worry, I got the stash from the last job, the one I was telling you about. I already split part of the dough with the other fellas, except that fucker Michael. He got the sack from the first four jobs. But we got so much more from my job that I've plenty to go around. So, you didn't have to rob us afterwards at the Twenty. Besides, this worked out better. You would have had to kill Michael. He wouldn't have let you take the Twenty's money without a fight."

What he did not tell them was he hid a sizable portion of the money before he turned the corner to his block.

Ken thought, *"I've got to get even with Michael for ruining my evening. We almost got killed tonight and all that fool did was laugh. That crazy motherfucker needs to die! I wonder what Snake did with that info I passed to him."*

. . . .

Michael had been living wild since he was thirteen years old. He had built quite a reputation as a dangerous dude. No one knew much about him other than he had a very short fuse. Some of the drug dealers had decided he needed to disappear since he had been hitting their stash houses on a regular basis. However, few were bold enough to go directly at him. He was like a shadow, disappearing for weeks only to pop up for a score, so no one knew when he would appear. Yet he was only seventeen, a fact few knew.

He was walking up Mack Avenue to have dinner at Green's Barbeque on the far east side when he ran into Ken.

Ken said, "Hey Mike? Where are you celebrating tomorrow? I know Friday's the fifth of December, your birthday nigga. I think we should meet up in Greektown. We can get fake IDs and have your first public drink!"

Michael replied, "Thanks Ken. Sounds good to me. And by the way, great work last Saturday night. I don't know how much you cleared from that last job, but I'm happy with mine after I split the loot with the boys. See you tomorrow."

Ken paused, then smiled and said, "Tomorrow will be a great night. We can meet on the corner of Monroe and Randolph at 6:00. You can park in the lot off Monroe, near the freeway. Tell the attendant you're one of my boys. He'll let you in for free. See yah tomorrow."

The following evening, just before 6:00, after taking Ken up on his parking lot suggestion, Michael walked west on Monroe toward the many restaurants in Greektown. This four-block strip in downtown Detroit was a popular tourist haven, with a dozen or more Greek restaurants throughout the district. Michael was feeling pretty good about having turned eighteen that day. The streets were decorated with Christmas ornaments, and the mood of the crowd was festive. The sun had already dipped below the horizon and the sky was clear with the temperature just below freezing, nice weather for a northern city in winter if you are dressed for it. Most of the young people were underdressed in light leather jackets. Michael was no exception. He wore his usual black beret, black t-shirt, black slacks, and a black leather jacket. It was the known Black Panther Party look, even though he was not a member.

He crossed St. Antoine and was approaching Beaubien Boulevard when he sensed trouble. A large man, whom Michael recognized as Sammy the Pincer, was some distance up the block but coming toward him, walking as if he owned the sidewalk. At 6'2" and an easy 250 rotund pounds, Sammy was feared by all. He was as mean as any made-man in the city and demonstrated it often. Everyone was getting out of his path, but that was not Michael's way. When Sammy got in front of Big Papa's restaurant, a popular hangout for the mob, he began turning left into the entrance, noticed Michael not yielding to him, then turned back right, deliberately bumping Michael.

"Watch it nigger!" growled Sammy.

Michael stepped up to him, if only for a brief moment. He completely underestimated the speed of the behemoth who shoved him so hard, the next thing Michael knew he was flying backward toward the sidewalk. Sammy, however, was dead before Michael hit the pavement.

"Pop, pop, pop." was all the guys in the front of the restaurant heard.

Within seconds, they were on their feet, rushing out the door.

They found Sammy in a heap on the sidewalk, not laying either way, just in a 250-pound heap with his head on his chest. Three spots of blood were oozing out of his chest where his heart once beat.

"Oh my God!" yelled Salvatore the Slim.

"Someone just killed Sammy the Pincer!"

The others looked around and saw a black streak sprinting east, then turning south around the corner of St. Antoine toward Old St. Mary's Catholic Church.

"Get that fucker!"

The group of them began running east, crossing Monroe Street toward Saint Antoine. Except Salvatore, who merely sat in front of Sammy the Pincer and cried like a baby.

Meanwhile, Michael, having realized he had just killed someone, was almost in total panic. Almost. He raced to the I-375 bridge at Lafayette Street, crossed the freeway, then continued south on the surface drive. By the time he had reached Jefferson Avenue there was no one in sight behind him. Grown men chasing an eighteen-year-old sprinter was a fool's errand.

Michael moved so fast that none of the Sicilians saw his face. No one would be able to pin the shooting of Sammy on him. No one except Ken.

. . . .

Louis' graduation from Post Junior High was scheduled in January at the end of the school semester. It was planned as an early evening graduation in the school auditorium. Robert had spoken to Mack, who said he most definitely would be there. In fact, the entire family had planned to attend.

On the evening of the graduation Robert arrived early. He looked around to see if he might notice any familiar faces. He saw Principal Johnson and Mr. Brown, the counselor, but decided not to step out so they could see him. He had a large afro now and was noticeably taller, but they still might recognize him.

He thought, *"No need to upset Mr. Johnson."*

He did not see his family, so he stepped outside to check the parking lot and saw the 1964 Country Squire pull up. The entire family seemed to pour out, including Mack. As they entered the building, Robert merged into their procession of nine. Then Louis peeled away to join his fellow students.

The ceremony was well planned, and Louis was the main attraction. He won top honors for three straight years of 4.0 GPA. He was also the class valedictorian, mimicking the practice used in high schools. Principal Johnson, aware that Louis was one of the McCants that was involved in the rumble some years back, introduced him to the audience. Louis rose to a standing ovation. He gave a rousing speech and had all his classmates cheering for their future. At the conclusion of his speech, the students and parents gave him another standing ovation. One would imagine this was a college graduation, not just for ninth graders. Frank and Martha could not have been prouder.

After the ceremony Louis informed his parents that he was going to come home after hanging out with his friends. He was now fifteen years old and had surpassed all his dreams. Frank was especially proud of him. Before he left, his father asked him what high school he planned to attend, hoping he would say Cass Tech.

He proudly replied, "I'm going to join Richard at Cooley." Frank understood and put his aspirations aside.

He thought, *"Darn. Still no Cass kids."*

Robert told the family he had transportation and turned around a corner toward the parking lot, as they continued to discuss the graduation program. Then he saw Michael.

He thought, "*Wow. Guess I shouldn't be surprised that he'd show up.*" Then he noticed that Michael was following someone. The guy he was following seemed nervous, and did not appear to belong with any family leaving the ceremony. Robert followed both of them. The guy noticed Robert and left the lot, running to a parked car on the street. Robert called out to Michael, who stopped.

He said, "What's going on? Who was that guy?"

Michael replied, "Trouble. You'd better get home."

. . . .

The McCants got home from Louis' graduation ceremony and pulled into their driveway. But before they could get out of the car, they were greeted by their immediate neighbors.

"Oh honey, they broke into your house and trashed it. It was four guys. Others sat outside in their cars, watching the block. They didn't appear to take anything. Just destruction, my God! We called the police an hour ago, but they haven't gotten here yet!"

Frank leaped up the stairs followed by Mack, Robert, Richard, and Louis, who heard about the potential problem from Robert and decided to go home with him. They made Martha and the younger children stay outside until they could search the house. Finally, Richard came out to tell everyone they could come inside.

What Martha found when she crossed the threshold was heartbreaking. The home was trashed, but they also desecrated it. They smashed the toilet bowls and the bathtub, put holes in the walls, and left the water on, causing it to overflow and run onto the hardwood floors. All the plates and glassware in the China cabinet were broken. The living room furniture they purchased from the nice couple in the U of D district was destroyed. The dining room table was turned upside down, with most of the legs broken off. The little-kids' mattresses were wet with urine. The second-floor bedrooms were equally thrashed. The water on the bathroom floors were flowing into the floors below. They also defecated on Martha's and Frank's bed. When Martha discovered the bedroom disaster, she rushed into her closet and was relieved that it was undisturbed.

After a full inspection of the entire house, Frank, now somewhat calmer, said, "They must have been here a couple of hours. Possibly from the time we left the house. What were the neighbors doing? How do we recover from this?"

Mack was livid but also felt helpless like his father. Louis felt it was his fault. If he had not insisted that everyone go to the graduation this would not have happened.

Frank told him, "That's nonsense. They've been wanting to hit us for some time now." He could not help but think, "*Michael.*"

Martha cried for a moment then went into the basement, got a mop and pail, and placed them on the kitchen floor. Then she stripped all the beds and threw away the sheets. Louis took the mop and pail and began mopping the water off the kitchen floor. Richard got towels and laid them on the living room floor. He soaked up water, took the towels outside to squeeze the water out, then placed them onto the floor again, repeating the process over and over until most of the water was gone. Mack got fans and turned them toward the floor. Jack and Horace got brooms and dustpans and swept up debris. Mack, Robert, and Richard carried the living room furniture that was damaged into the back yard. When Martha began cleaning the mattresses Mack stopped her.

"No Mom. No one will be sleeping on these ever again."

All the brothers understood the message and began removing all the mattresses into the alley.

Frank did not join in on the cleanup, but merely sat on the porch pondering his next move. His youngest son Ervin, now seven, sat beside him. Both ignored the cold wind blowing northward.

Robert had a blank look on his face. A dangerous blank look.

He whispered, "I've got to get ahold of Michael."

Nine-year-old Jack merely stared at Robert.

· · · · · · · · · · · · ·

The next day Uncle Horace arrived with a new furnace and hot water tank. It would take only two days for a furniture delivery truck to unload all the new furniture and mattresses. When a surprised Frank asked the drivers about the deliveries, he was told they were from an anonymous donor.

He said, "Sorry sir, but the guy would not give his name. And by the way, sir, your appliances will be here tomorrow."

The following week Horace and Ervin came home with two six-week-old German Shepherd puppies. When their father asked them where they got the dogs Horace said, "I found a couple hundred-dollar bills under my new mattress with a note telling me where to buy them."

They named them Prince and Klaw.

It would take a couple of weeks to replace the damaged plumbing. It would take much longer for the family to recover mentally.

CHAPTER TEN

Draft Day

March 1971

Michael had been on a rampage since January 1970. For the past three months he had been torching west side drug dens, robbing the couriers, and intimidating the customers. He worked alone, fearful of his old associates. Every place he hit he left a note. 'BLAME THIS ON BUSTA!' or 'DON'T FUCK WITH MY FAMILY!' or 'I KNOW WHERE YOU LIVE TOO!' Just to make his point, he had visited churches where dealer's mothers attended and left notes on their cars to contact their sons and ask them about 'Michael'. Children were getting home from school with surprise notes in their book bags, asking their dads to contact 'Michael'. No one saw him, just the notes. He was truly a ghost.

A street bounty was now out on Michael. He expected as much and knew he could not stay in the area much longer. He had found new hiding quarters since his brother's graduation. He now occasionally slipped into a boat storage facility on the far-east side near Freud Street, just off the river. There were plenty of yachts inside for him to campout in. The long travel back west each day was for the best. It gave him time to plan his next move.

Robert was rarely home. When he did go home, he headed straight for his bedroom. His room had become his own again since Louis and Richard had built a room in the basement. The little-kids no longer camped out on the second floor. "I think we should sleep down here to protect mom when dad leaves for work," said eight-year-old Horace.

Frank's brother Horace called to update him on news about Michael.

He said, "The boy has gone mad! He's hitting those dopers hard, man! I'm telling you, he's a real McCants warrior! But he may have gone too far! He's torching dope dens and cars! And threatening family members! There is even word on the street that he killed that guy in Greektown last December! I don't believe it, but it is on the grapevine. You had better get him out of Dodge. You can bring him up here to Pontiac for a while. No one here will know him. Maybe even to Dad's folks out west in Brooklyn. Ha! I'm joking of course. Anyway, your brothers have got your back, whatever decision you make."

Frank hung up with a smile on his face. Then he considered the reality of his brother's call, looked at his reflection in the mirror, and turned away.

. . . .

At 3:00 a.m. in late January '70, just weeks after the family's home was invaded, the three youngest sons of Frank and Martha McCants closed their bedroom door, raised their bedroom window, then hopped down into the snow, closing the window behind them. The full moon was reflecting off the snow, lighting up the night air. They walked out to the alley and down onto Lyndon Street, then ran westward through the neighborhood, passing their elementary school, until they reached a home near Wyoming Avenue, north of Fenkell, one-and-a-half miles from their home. Jack, the eldest of the three, carrying a tube of gutter repair glue, spread the contents of the tube into the keyholes of four Cadillacs, plus the trunks. Horace, the middle boy, released the air from the sixteen tires of the vehicles. The youngest boy, Ervin, took the gutter glue from Jack, and spread it onto the air valves of the tires and the sixteen caps, then replaced the caps. Then the boys ran the entire distance home, entering through their bedroom window and back to bed. Martha just laid in hers, eyes wide open, listening to her husband's light snore and a bedroom window closing. It was 3:45 a.m.

Two days later, at 3:00 a.m., Louis and Richard, the middle sons of Frank and Martha, walked out of the second-floor balcony door, down the stairwell, and out into the alley. They traveled west along Lyndon toward Wyoming Avenue, then north to Fenkell, settling near a home just a block off the Lodge Freeway. Both boys carried four-way lug-wrenches. They noticed two men sitting in a nearby sedan, the engine running, both sleeping comfortably. Quietly, they loosened the lug nuts of the sixteen tires of four Cadillacs, then tightened them by hand. Then the two teenagers returned home, staying in the shadows until they reached the alley of Santa Rosa. Only Martha and Jack, her nine-year-old, heard the balcony door close. It was 3:45 a.m.

Two days later, at 3:00 a.m., Mack, the eldest son of Frank and Martha, walked out of the front door of his family's home. He drove his father's station wagon up Lyndon to Wyoming, then north of Fenkell and parked the car. He slowly moved through the houses on the block until he came upon a man standing guard at the back door of a house. He quietly crept up to the man, spun him around, and knocked him unconscious with one blow to the jaw. He then walked along the side of the house until he saw a man sitting on the porch. He climbed the side of the porch, coming up behind the man. He knocked the man out with one punch. He stripped the man of his coat and hat then put them on. He then walked down the walkway toward the street where he found a man leaning against a freshly wrecked burgundy Cadillac. The car was badly damaged on both sides. He approached the man with his head tilted down, and before the man became aware of his identity, he struck the man across the jaw, knocking him unconscious. Mack then walked back to the family car and drove home. But not before he took his car keys and scratched his family name on the new Cadillac parked in the driveway of the house. Martha heard him turn off the station wagon's engine and enter the house. So did Jack. It was 3:45 a.m.

None of the brothers were aware of the other's exploits except Jack and their boxing coach.

The following week Martha got a call from one of her gossip partners. When she hung up an hour later, she could only smile. Apparently, the word was going around the neighborhood that Busta was moving. The reason was continuous vandalism of his property.

All the schools were talking about the McCants' boys' assault on Busta, hitting him every night for a month. They were attacking his men, killing his dogs, bricking his windows, and writing graffiti on his house and cars. There was even talk of a shootout one night between the older boys and Busta's men.

Delores said to Martha, "You must be so proud of your boys for taking the fight to that monster. He is so afraid of your family now. Right on sista!"

Martha hung up the phone and smiled. Then she merely said, "Such silly gossip! Imagine, my little ones picking up bricks and attacking Busta's men. Why, they're still in grade school, and I put them to bed by 9:00!"

. . . .

Busta awoke to his phone ringing. He got up, grabbed it, and said, "What da fuck ya doin callinhare dis early?"

The response chilled him. He hung up, got dressed and was out of the door in minutes.

Busta knew his temper had gotten him in this predicament as he pulled up to the Mediterranean Boot Social Club. He entered and sat across from Shapatilo's office. He could hear shouting coming from within the office, but could not make out all of the voices, only his bosses. An hour later a strange White man came out of the office, frowned at Busta, then left.

Busta thought, "*Who da fuck is dat dude?*"

He got up to walk into Shapatilo's office but was met by a body bigger than his. It said, "No."

Busta sat back down. After another hour, Shapatilo came out and summoned Busta. He entered the office and sat in front of Shapatilo's desk.

Without looking up Shapatilo said, "Do you know what I've been doing for the past hour? I've been relaxin myself. I've been pushing out the meanness and meditating on good thoughts. I saw it on a late-night talk show. Sammy Davis Jr. was demonstrating it to the host."

He looked up at Busta and continued. "Do you know who that WASP was who left here an hour ago? He works for the city council. Word spread quickly about your work in that mixed block off Lyndon. That Spanish block, what's it called, Santa Tulip, Santa Pia, Santa Rosa? Yeah, that's it. Santa Rosa. I remember because my sweet mom, may she rest in peace, was named Rose.

"I distinctly remember telling you to stay away from that block. I distinctly remember telling you a city official once lived on that block. I don't want an explanation, just understand this. If those niggers get a fingernail broken, then I broke it. Me, the boss, not you. Notice the tone in my voice. Notice how calm it is. If those niggers get a bruised big toe, I, bruised it. You have got to PRAY that they don't have any enemies who would do them harm because if anything happens to those folks, I'm going to assume it was your black ass who harmed them. Now get the fuck out of my office. And take your bowling bag with you." Busta wanted to reply but understood it was best for him to just leave.

He thought, *"Just git up and go. Don't bother mentionin' my boys in da hospital from crashin day cars after day wheels falls off. Or gettin' day jaws broke! Don't pull yo shit and start blastin.' Just git up and go."*

He stood up and turned to the door to walk out, but did not get very far.

Shapatilo said, "I said, take your bowling bag, nigger!"

Busta was confused and thought, *"Ain't got no bowling bag. I doesn't bowl,"* but grabbed the bag. He walked to his car, holding the bag in his left hand, so he would not be able to pull his gun. He dumped the bag onto the back seat and pulled away.

When he got home, he started to walk indoors, then remembered the bag. He grabbed it only to notice a red stain on his leather seats.

"What da…! Got-dam bag stained my new seats!" He leaned into the backseat area and opened the bag. "What da fuck is in dis damn thang anywho?"

He jerked the bag open and looked at Drither, eyes still open.

· · · · · · · · · · · · ·

Busta was having a rough month. The business was flowing nicely, but he was being tormented by the McCants. "I know it's those mulatto motherfuckers. Messin with my crew and I can't do shit about it. And

I can't even tell the boss. He'll just say I should perhaps hire dem for protection!"

He had met a new girl and was looking forward to taking her out. She had chosen a blues club on the east side, off Joseph Campau, in Hamtramck. It was a Wednesday evening so he was expecting a small crowd.

At midnight, he picked her up at a new hotel, called the St. Regis, down the street from the General Motors Building, on West Grand Boulevard, near Woodward Avenue. He thought, *"Swanky place. She must be a professional."* They drove to the east side, parked the car, and entered the nightclub. It was a small but quaint basement studio. The room was full to capacity, around sixty strong, unusual for such an early hour during the middle of the week. Normally he preferred loud noisy crowds on weekends, but this would be a good change of pace after the rough month he had just endured.

The band was smooth and blaring, the singer right out of New Orleans. When they finished the first set, the singer thanked the band members, and gave a special tribute to the drummer, who was a local player named The Duke. When the lights came up a bit, the few women present all rose in unison and marched to the ladies' room, accompanied by Busta's date. With the lights on Busta could get a better look at the crowd. Then it hit him.

"All dhes motherfuckers inhare are men. And day as dark as me!"

He had never been in a place where all the people were dark complexioned. He was used to being in crowds of mixed complexions. But for the first time ever, he was surrounded by a sea of Black! Even the women, except Busta's date, were very dark.

Before Busta could ponder that thought further, Duke approached him and introduced himself.

He said, "I heard you da man! Glad to see you at my gig. Hope you're enjoying the evening. It only gets better."

Pointing around the room, Busta smiled and said, "I am indeed enjoyin myself. How can I not wit dis crowd?" He spun around in his chair and waved his arm around the room.

Duke said, "See that fella over there? He's my brother. Came to see me play. Those seven guys around him are my cousins."

Busta nodded greetings, tipping his hat. Duke continued, "See those guys over there? That's also one of my brothers and cousins."

Busta looked over at the eight men and nodded but was suddenly getting an uneasy feeling. Duke continued, "In fact, all these tables are reserved for my brothers and cousins." Busta was now getting a very eerie feeling about the place.

Duke smiled at Busta and said, "My brother over there is named Frank. Perhaps you've met him before. Frank McCants." Frank turned his chair around to face Busta for the first time. None of his sons were present. Duke had decided not to include them. He wanted a totally 'dark' theme that night.

Busta noticed that none of the men were paying attention to him, as if he was not there. All except Frank.

He thought, *"Now I understand why dis prick was so cool on dat porch dat day. Hell, he didn't need no guns."*

He glanced around the room. Some of the men were as big as he, not that it mattered. He obviously was being sent a message. It came in loud and clear.

He decided it was time to leave before the next set. He looked at his watch and at the ladies' room when Duke interrupted him and said, "Well, it's almost time for my next set. I hope you can stay. And don't worry about my wife's niece. She had a plane to catch, so she's already gone. Enjoy your evening. And by the way, my name is Horace. Horace McCants. I'm Frank's big brother." He smiled and walked back to the stage.

Busta drained his drink and walked out the door to his car and pulled away. He half expected it to blow up.

He thought, *"Dis has ta be da worse night of my life."*

. . . .

For the past year Robert had been completely entrenched in his studies. He had planned to graduate in December 1970 and immediately enroll in grad school. His plans were on schedule. Mack was doing well at U of D, just beginning his second year. Richard was now a junior at Cooley High. The racial stress at Cooley was all but gone, since most of the White students have graduated and few White freshmen were enrolling into the school. Louis was now a freshman at Cooley.

Robert felt somewhat strange to be a senior in college while Louis had just graduated from junior high, since they are only three years apart.

He thought, *"How did this happen? He's on schedule; yet, I'm light-years beyond him. I should have advised him years ago. He's smarter than me. Always has been, but he's got his sights on multiple things. Music being one of them. Guess you can't do both, practice music and study at the pace I'm studying."*

The three younger children were doing well, with Jack in the fourth grade, Horace in the third, and Ervin in the second. The boys continued to be extremely close and the new kids coming into the area learned very quickly who ruled the Clinton playground. The community was noticing another migration as Black families from the east side relocated to Fenkell and Livernois, just as the McCants had done five years ago in '65. The three younger boys had to establish their positions quickly with each new kid who arrived. Fortunately, the McCants boys were not bullies.

Martha's nerves had calmed down quicker than Franks. Coming home to find your house trashed was a disturbing thing. She understood that anything broken can be fixed. Besides, growing up in New York had prepared her for drama, even if she did attend prep schools. She still does not know who donated all the furniture and appliances. Her husband Frank, on the other hand, was not used to anyone bothering his family. So, walking into his home last January was quite disturbing. Her son Robert had been leaving envelopes of one hundred dollars every other week to help with the repairs. She had not informed Frank, knowing he would not accept it.

Over the past couple of years, Martha had become quite bored. There are only so many soaps one can watch, so she had decided to sell cosmetics to keep herself busy.

Frank had managed to relax somewhat after the meetings he was having with his family. He was very relieved that he never had to call on them, except on that night at the blues club. That was his brother Herb's idea. The last thing he would ever want was for one of his cousins or brothers to get hurt because of him. Or because of Michael.

Over the last few months, the couple rarely saw Robert. They believed he spent most of his time at his two jobs. They also believed there was a girl in his life after the way he acted three years ago. When he was at home, he did not bring up Michael. In fact, only young Horace and Ervin ever mentioned him. Martha could handle Robert being away at such a young age because he was so mature. Besides, she left home at sixteen, so she could relate. The fact that they had not seen Michael in five years did not seem to bother them, since his name continued to come up during troubled times.

Michael was still bouncing from carriage house to carriage house, boat to boat. He was having trouble sleeping since he occasionally had nightmares. He dreamed of Robert. And Sammy. Sammy the Pincer.

. . . .

On July 1, 1970, the US Selective Service System held the N70 draft lottery. The McCants twins, born December 5th, 1951, received draft number 27.

After an eventful January, the year 1970 came and went without any more drama. Michael and his brothers had made their point and the family was not being bothered anymore. The nightclub evening only brought closure to the situation.

Michael had been staying out of sight knowing the gangsters were still hunting him. He rarely crossed Woodward Avenue to venture onto the west side of the city.

On Saturday February 27, 1971, Robert entered his bedroom only to find a surprise guest inside.

"Michael?" Robert yelled in as muffled a voice as he could muster, considering his joy.

"What the hell! Where've you been? I haven't seen you since Louis's graduation a year ago!"

Michael replied, "Yeah, I've been busy since that night. Long year. Kind of cold outside, making travel more difficult. Had to deal with the punks who tore the house up, but I believe I've made my point."

Robert, somewhat puzzled, said, "So you know about that, huh? I didn't know word had gotten to you. We assume it was that dude Busta. Pops wanted to hunt him down, but mom stopped him. I even heard the boys talking about getting revenge. Funny to hear the little ones talking vengeance. Busta's boys destroyed everything. I had to find an escape because I was thinking like Pops. The last thing this family needs is one of us in prison. We had to get everything new. Even had to get new hardwood flooring on the main floor. New kitchen and bathroom floor as well. Fortunately, an anonymous donor sent new furnishings and appliances. Dad withdrew savings for the flooring, and we all contributed labor, of course."

Michael did not react to any of the news about the repairs. He asked, "How are mom and dad doing?"

"They're fine, I guess. Kind of hard on Pops, not being able to retaliate. He keeps forgetting he's old now. Hell, he'll be forty this year. So, you still call him 'Dad'?"

"Forget you!" snapped Michael. He continued, "Louis and Richard are at a house party up the street. They didn't even notice me as I walked through the crowd. I walked right passed them."

"Well, considering how you're dressed and the time you've been gone. They hardly ever see me either. I've been away in school most of the past five years. Since the family thinks I dropped out of school after you left, I don't get a lot of interrogations. Where are you staying?"

Michael replied, "Been hangin' out on the east side, not far from the river."

Robert said, "The little-kids vaguely remember you. Ervin was most hurt by you leaving."

"You still call them that? Little-kids? How are they doing? I go by their school occasionally to watch them on the playground. They aren't out much, however, during the winter. Is Horace still husky?"

Robert ignored Michael's last question and said, "Well, timing is everything. I've been called to report to Fort Wayne on Monday. Or I should say, we've been called upon to report. Big brother, we've been drafted. We had number twenty-seven, so it wasn't possible to not be called up. There is a letter in the China cabinet for you."

Michael replied, "No way! I never signed up for the draft!"

Robert said, "Yeah, I assumed you wouldn't, so I signed you up. You've got the entire world chasing you. You don't need the U.S. government after you as well. Anyway, I really blew it. My draft counselor, who I have to visit after each quarter, told me I could safely graduate in December '70, even though grad school does not start until this September. He was mistaken, or he lied. I should not have filed for graduation until this coming May. I let my ego get in the way. Sometimes I'm my worst enemy.

"Your draft card is over there on the chest-of-drawers. We have to report to Fort Wayne Monday morning at 8:00 a.m. sharp. I went to the fort last year for a physical examination. No doubt you never did."

Michael said, "Oh I get it. You signed me up, but you had planned on skipping out with a college deferment. Thanks baby brother. Don't know what I'd do without you. Don't know if I'm going though. Got some goons who've been chasin me for the last couple of years."

"Don't you think I know that! Mom says they still drive by. Word on the street is that you killed a guy."

Michael replied, "He tried to knock me into next week. My chest was bruised for weeks. I didn't intend to kill him, but my reaction was instantaneous. I can't allow nobody to push me down. He didn't just shove me. He meant to hurt me. He would have stomped me the moment I hit the ground. I've seen him do that before. It's his favorite move. Should have been able to avoid it, but he was faster than I expected. I suspect that my boy Ken set me up. He may have asked Sammy to kill me. It's too much of a coincidence that we should run into each other during a meeting Ken set up. Ken and I did a job in late November '69. Five hits in one night! But I saw his boys waiting up the block for us near the Twenty Grand. I saw them as I drove by. One of the reasons I cancelled the hit on the 'Twenty'. I believe Ken's the one who told Busta where we live."

Robert thought, *"Hit on the twenty? What's he talking about? What's a twenty?"*

Robert said, "Well, your best bet now might be the Army. Come with me Sunday night. Monday is just the report day, not induction day. We can leave late, during the night, and sleep in my car on

Dragoon until Monday morning. No one will be looking for you in that part of town. We have to be at Fort Wayne at 8:00 a.m. sharp."

. . . .

That Sunday, the day before he was to report for the draft, Michael was walking on Larned Street near Martin Luther King High and Elmwood Cemetery, just west of the carriage houses in Indian Village. He was coming from a friend's home, having spent the night there. As he turned the corner, he suddenly noticed a cop talking to a thug. Not just any cop, however. And not just any thug. Sumanski and Busta, discussing financial arrangements. He froze, but not before the two of them looked up and shouted simultaneously, "Mother Fuckin' Son of a Bitch!"

The chase was on! The two men were standing near the stands of the track field and had to run back to their cars. Sumanski beat Busta to his police cruiser and jumped in. Busta knocked Ray Ray over into the adjoining seat of the caddy, threw it into drive and took off after Michael, ignoring Sumanski's siren.

Michael raced north across the school's football field. He reached the other side of the field just as the two cars turned the corner from Mt. Elliott Street to Lafayette Street. As he was crossing the street, Sumanski accelerated, attempting to run him over. Michael knew that he could not make it across because Sumanski would just drive onto the sidewalk and run him over. So, he turned toward the oncoming car, and twenty feet in front of the cruiser he leaped into the air. He performed a forward somersault flip over the speeding car, then landed on his feet. He dropped to one knee then rose and sprinted once more toward Busta's oncoming Caddie. He did a swan dive directly toward Busta, who drove directly under Michael's arching body. He then began to pivot forward just before he touched down. He landed on the pavement, tumbled over once, then jumped to his feet, turned to his left and sprinted toward the Elmwood Cemetery's fence. He reached up to the seven-foot-high fence, grabbed a top spindle and cleared it in one bound. Then he continued his sprint, hurtling gravestones as needed.

Two police officers riding in a patrol car on Mt. Elliot heard Sumanski's sirens and saw Michael running in the cemetery. They stopped their car, jumped out and raced northward along the eastern fence of the cemetery, intending to cut Michael off. A rookie officer, proud of his running abilities, thought, *"I was a high-school champion sprinter. I will beat this sucker to the corner since he has to run at an angle."* As they converged Michael hit the eastern fence and cleared it before the officer finished his two-hundred-feet sprint, then bounded across Mt. Elliot and into the neighborhood.

The officer said, "What the hell! No way that guy is still running. He must really be hopped up on something. I have never seen anyone run like that!"

Michael understood Sumanski and Busta would kill him in front of others if they got the chance. His understanding of these facts only motivated him to continue to streak through the neighborhood. He raced up an alley off Mt. Elliot, passing pedestrians and children playing on the sidewalk. He ran through the neighborhood heading east, cutting through backyards, warehouses, and stock yards, staying between the two cross streets. He was occasionally confronted by yard dogs but was through the yards before the dogs could react. They do, however, give away his position. He continued to run east, crossing East Grand Boulevard, just north of Belle Isle, with a destination in mind. His carriage house on Iroquois. If he could reach the carriage house, then he should be safe. The police would not suspect that locale.

Police cars joined the search, continuing to race up and down Jefferson and Kercheval. He remained between the houses, running east, so the police could not find him.

He finally reached Iroquois, ran into the yard of the neighbor's house next to his final destination, climbed the shared fence, then ran to the garage side door and opened it, hoping the family was not home. A light snow had begun to fall, turning his black afro to white. Once inside he froze. Staring directly at him was a cute elderly couple, dressed in matching winter gear, gloves and all, holding snow shovels.

The lady pulled off her right glove, placed her hand over her mouth and said, "Oh dear. You must be my housekeeper!" She looked up at her husband and smiled.

Her husband said, "Those sirens must be for you, son. You'd better come with me."

The man closed the automatic garage doors, walked passed Michael and out of the garage, looked around the yard and down the driveway, then indicated for his wife and Michael to follow him. Michael was completely stunned but followed the man's directions. The woman met Michael at the door, grabbed his hand, and led him out of the garage, closing the door behind her. They entered the house and her husband closed the door behind them, taking one final look at the back yard.

The police patrolled up and down the streets and alleys of Indian Village and the surrounding communities, driving by the carriage house and up and down Iroquois several times. They searched all the empty houses and garages in the working-class area, but to no avail.

Finally, after two hours of patrolling the area, Sumanski called off the search.

"That mother fucker must be a freaken nigger Gypsy! There is no way he could escape us. Not in this area. Unless someone took him in. These White folks over here would be terrified of him. Could be these jungle bunnies in the adjoining blocks, but why would they risk it for a random west side nigger?"

Once it became dark the elderly man went out to his garage and pulled his car around to the side of the house. His wife came out of the side door and her husband opened her car door. She climbed into the front seat. Then he opened the back seat door, paused for a moment, then closed the door. After locking the side-entrance door the man climbed into the car, drove away from the house, turned left toward Jefferson Avenue then westward toward the downtown area.

He asked Michael, "Where to, big fella?"

Michael replied, "Dragoon Street, Sir, near Fort Street. I've been called to report for the draft and need to be at Fort Wayne tomorrow morning."

The man said, "Does the cop who is chasing you know who you are? Does he have your identification? If so, then you can't risk reporting to the draft board. The police have already placed an APB out on you. You may slip through, but you may not. The draft board may know about it when you arrive tomorrow. They will notify the police and hold you until they arrive. I would advise you to get out of town. From what you've told us, this cop wants you dead. Get out of town until this situation blows over. It may take quite a while, but you must stay away from your family. They have suffered enough if the trashing of their home was because of you. You are right in suspecting that Black fellow. And don't use my carriage house again. I don't want to get arrested for harboring a fugitive. I could lose my license. There are other ways I can help you, however, if need be."

He then pulled up his sleeve, so did his wife. They both had faded numeric tattoos on their forearms. Michael understood the implications of the markings.

When the trio arrived on Dragoon and Fort Street, the man pulled over but kept the car in drive. Michael got out of the car, thanked the couple, then proceeded down the street. As he departed the car the woman said, "Stay safe, my son. Stay safe."

. . . .

Michael and Robert met as planned.

Robert said, "I didn't know if you were going to show up. You look awful. Couldn't you get a change of clothes?"

Michael disclosed, "Yeah, I was heading in that direction when I ran into trouble. I need to update you on some things." Michael filled Robert in on all the events of the previous few years.

Then he said, "I am only telling you this because you need to know what to watch out for. The cop doesn't know Mack, just me. If he wanted Mack, our brother would already be dead. I know you're leaving but keep an eye out for the house until you do. If nothing occurs over the next few weeks, then you shouldn't have to worry. If they're coming it will be very soon. Busta knows about Santa Rosa, but I doubt if he shares that information with that cop. I can't stay here tonight with you, but I'll be back in the morning. You don't need to get arrested harboring a criminal. I have a friend that I can stay with nearby."

Robert added, "Based on what you just told me about earlier today, then Busta will have to explain to that cop why he was also chasing you. Therefore, the cop does know who you are. Let's meet at the entrance of the fort at 7:55 a.m. The gates should be open for an 8:00 enrollment. The line will be long by then, since all those White boys will get there early. They don't' practice CPT like we do. I'll hold a place for you if you arrive a little late."

Michael does not tell Robert that he is not going. Robert does not need to know that he was heading to the train station for passage to Gary, Indiana. Robert, however, already knows his brother will not be there in the morning. He just hoped he would be okay.

. . . .

The gate did open early but the entrance door did not open until 8:00 a.m. exactly. The line filed into the building until they reached maximum capacity. Those remaining in line were halted outside of the building. It will take three shifts of movement to register all the candidates. Robert made it in on the first shift.

He was home on Santa Rosa by 2:00 p.m. He did not discuss his conversation with Michael to anyone. That night he slept lightly, worrying about his twin.

. . . .

The two men on the porch gossiped about their boss as they sat smoking. No alcohol was allowed while they worked their shift. "So how much was the total tonight?" asked the tall young man. The other responded, "Just short of 10Gs. Nothing like what we get in Chi-town. Man, Gary is a slow-ass city. I guess the slowest fuckers from Mississippi moved here instead of the windy-one, huh?" and laughed. His laughter drowned out the light noise of a shadow as it descended from their roof. It was gone in seconds.

CHAPTER ELEVEN

Boot Camp

In the second week of March 1971 Robert was drafted into the U.S. Army and ordered to report for basic training. He informed his parents, who were surprisingly relieved.

Martha thought, "N*ow he belongs to the U.S. government for the next two years. Perhaps they can help him with his depression.*" There was a letter from the U.S. Government for Michael, but they merely placed it in the China cabinet with the previous letters and never mentioned it to Robert.

He showed up before the gates opened. In fact, he was the first in line. He did not want to stop his academic education, but since grad school did not start until the fall, he accepted this as a timely challenge. He reasoned that he was ahead in school by three years, so spending two years in the service might not hinder his schedule too badly.

Robert was sent to Fort Polk in Louisiana. He handled the basic training very well, getting commendable ratings from his trainers. Most of the inductees were surly, because they did not want to be there. The reputation of the army in 1971 was not stellar. Going to Vietnam was not on anyone's list of desired locales. For whatever reason, however, Robert attempted to maintain top ranking in any exercise thrown at the recruits. He could not help but excel.

One of Robert's fellow recruits was having a difficult time with Robert's success. Jamie approached a group of recruits and said, "That fella is making all of us look bad. He just has to finish first in everything. He needs to slow his ass down. I think tonight he should get a beatdown." Most of the recruits sitting near Jamie got up and walked away. Only Dick and Chucky remained.

All three of them were bigger than Robert, but not by much. After witnessing his workout, however, neither would want to fight Robert one on one. He was built like a middle-weight boxer, standing 5'8" and 155 pounds, with minimal body fat. That night the three of them walked over to Robert's bunk, threw a blanket on the sleeping lump, then pounced on it.

Jamie yelled, "What the …!" when he realized no one was under the cover.

He turned around to find Robert standing shirtless in the aisle. The shadows merely highlighted his pecks, abs, and shoulder muscles. Robert took one step forward and the three young men backed up.

Dick thought, *I didn't sign up to get my ass kicked,* and walked away. Chucky followed him.

Jamie, now very nervous with the entire barrack watching, said, "Dude, you're making all of us look bad. You've got to slow down. Why must you finish first all the time?"

Jamie's voice began to tremble, but he kept his position. Robert realized that Jamie did not want to fight, and said, "I'm sorry you feel that way. My intent is not to embarrass any of you. I don't know how not to put all my efforts toward a task. I've always been that way. I am not competing with any of you. They are not concerned with who finishes first. Just who doesn't finish. I have an advantage over most of you because of my size. Some of you guys are bigger and it's more difficult to move through the maze of obstacles. The instructors know this and really don't care. Just don't linger and act exhausted, and all of you will do fine. But don't ask me to change. Don't ask me to hold back. Cheer me on, and I will support you as well. Let's work as a team so that all of us make it through the first time. Guys, we're going to have to learn to work together sometime. Hell, we're getting ready to go to war."

He then looked over at Stan and winked. Stan understood he was being thanked and nodded. Jamie could do nothing but walk away.

Robert slept well that night. For the first time in weeks, he did not dream of Michael.

He completed basic training at South Fort in eight weeks, then was shifted to Advance Infantry training for an additional eight weeks. Fort Polk had a plot of land called Tiger Land at their North Fort. The site's purpose was to train the soldiers for Vietnam deployment. Tiger Land simulated a Vietnam village, with role players, booby traps and tunneling. Again, Robert excelled at this training, impressing his commanders. He never rattled whenever bullied by the instructors. In fact, he expected it, since that was what he would do if he were a trainer.

Upon completion of his training his commander made an exception of Robert and recommended him for officer training at Fort Benning. His exceptional academic record and his outstanding performance at the South and North Fort provided his commander with the rationale for sending a nineteen-year-old to officer training. The recommendation was highly unusual, but so was Robert's attitude. Before he was transferred to Fort Benning, however, he was given a psychiatric exam. He passed the exam without a hitch. The psychiatrist thought, *"There is something about this one. I can't put my finger on it. He has a peculiarity— an eccentricity that I cannot place. His level of focus is uncanny. Never met a Black like this one. Hell, never met a White person like him either."*

After a four-day week-end furlough during the Fourth of July, Robert entered Fort Benning infantry training then transferred to the Officer Candidate School. He used the time to relax, calling his mom only once. Twelve weeks later, he was commissioned an officer in the United States Army.

. . . .

"Kid is very serious." said the Commander. "Hard to believe he's only nineteen. Already has his college degree. Must have made an error in applying for his Masters. Otherwise, the draft board would not have been able to touch him. Probably should have slowed his study down a bit." "His shooting is stupendous." said the range instructor. "Usually don't find guys shooting this well unless they grow up sleeping with guns. Mostly country boys or kids whose parents take them hunting regularly. Strange thing though. He hits bullseyes regularly. But on silhouettes, he only shoots at the legs. Never a head shot or heart shot." The commander replied, "No desire to kill? That's a good thing. He'll change when the need arises. We all do. This kid is one hundred percent ghetto, perfect language or not. Don't let those academic mannerisms fool you. I suspect he's as raw underneath as they come. I'd want my son following him into battle."

. . . .

Martha was watching The Mike Douglas Show and talking on the phone with a friend when Frank arrived home from work and asked about Robert.

"Have you heard from him? Has he called? I don't know how successful he can be without an education."

Martha replied, "He has called, but very sparingly. Generally, while you're at work. They keep moving him from one training site to another. I don't know if he's having problems adjusting or what. All that moving around can't be good. First, he was in Louisiana for the longest time. I thought boot camp was short, six weeks then they ship you out. But he was in Louisiana far longer, almost sixteen weeks. Now he's in Georgia. Hell, I hope they keep him in basic training until the war ends. We have to hope that he gets some counseling as well. His sullenness over the past six years has been so concerning to me. And can he exist in the military without Michael?"

Frank said, "Well, he was an all-A student when he was in school. Hell, the boy taught himself how to read when he was three! He's probably been educating himself all these years. Knowing Robert's potential, if he'd stayed in school, he'd be a sophomore at Wayne by now. One thing for sure, now that..."

Martha thrust her index finger at Frank and walked away. He knew he had just gone too far. She said as she turned the corner, "Remember, you've got other sons, too."

· · · · · · · · · · ·

Mack had finished his second year at the University of Detroit and was ready to start focusing on his major, computer science, in the coming fall. He did not know if he wanted to be an engineer of the science or a developer. What he did know was that he wanted to make some money. Even though he was getting a full ride, having some pocket change would be nice. His scholarship paid for his books which he did not sell at the end of the year. His collection of college books, along with his high school books, was becoming impressive.

Mack had met several young ladies on campus but never became serious with any of them. In fact, after four years of dating he realized he had never taken any of his dates home. He sometimes wondered if he was ashamed of his mom. Because she looked White.

He thought, *"No, it can't be that. I take my male friends home. Besides, once someone meets Martha, they know she's cool!"* No, it was not his mother. It was his home.

When they moved into their home, he thought it was the best house in the world. That, of course, was in 1965, when he was only fourteen years old and coming from the projects. Now he was twenty and had been exposed to the diversity of homes in the northwest community. Mansions just northeast of the college. Tudors to the north. Nice brick colonial homes west of the school. Then there's the south of Fenkell Avenue. Wood frame housing, requiring painting every few years. Not all the homes, but enough of them.

He thought, *"Can I really be ashamed of my home? Am I offended when I hear kids calling our home 'plank houses'? Are my friends right about me getting uppity?"*

During the Spring of '71 Mack had become enamored with a girl who attended Wayne State. Her name was Linda and she lived west of the U of D campus, so he met her on his walk to school. They would greet one another as she walked south on Livernois Avenue, across from the campus. He first saw her as he was about to cross Livernois to the campus. This time, however, he continued to walk up the block to get a closer look at her. He was not disappointed.

One day he noticed they were carrying the same history textbook, so this was the opening he needed to start a conversation. She, however, could not linger long or she would miss her bus at Fenkell, so she handed him her phone number then continued down the street. After a few phone calls, they arranged to study together, even though U of D was on trimesters and Wayne was quarterly.

After they had been dating for six months Mack began to believe that Linda was the one. His parents married at eighteen, which he viewed as a mistake he would not repeat. Getting married after college, however, should work out well.

He had not shared that information with anyone, especially Linda. He had been to her home, a nice 2,000 sq foot brick home several blocks west of the campus. He, however, always found an excuse not to take her to his home.

He said, "Linda, you really don't want to walk all the way down there to my home and back, believe me." For now, he would just continue to focus on school and enjoy overnights at her place.

"As long as my parents don't find out," she replied with a smile.

. . . .

Richard was extremely proud of himself. In June he graduated from Cooley with honors. Not as good as Louis at Post, but good enough.

He thought, *"The graduation was great. Most of the family was there. Uncle Horace came, which was a pleasant surprise. Pops and Unc are getting closer, since the home was vandalized. They don't meet as often but Pops goes to visit him now, as a brother, a friend. And Unc comes around our home more often as well."*

Richard had applied to Wayne State and was accepted for the fall quarter. He only got a partial scholarship, but the tuition should be manageable, as long as he works part-time and commutes. He thought he might be able to use Mack's textbooks as well.

"Yeah, right. Mack ain't gonna let anyone touch his precious books!"

. . . .

Busta had been on the skids since late February. His reputation had really suffered after he failed to catch Michael near the high school. He told Trigger, who was not there during the chase but heard about it from Ray Ray, "I doesn't understands how he could leap over both Sumanski's and my car. I thought I had em!" His hatred for Michael grew every day. He now knows it was Michael who was sneaking into his home, spiking his drinks, then opening his curtains and tying him up.

He thought, *"Sick bastard tying up Ray Ray and Drither dat way. He must be sweet hisself. Drither didn't seem to mind dough. Guess I shouldn't speak ill of da dead, huh?"*

Trigger approached Ray Ray and said, "Has you noticed, Busta ain't been eaten good. He seem ta be out-of-it since January when he wents on dat date."

Ray Ray replied, "You mean since the boss kicked his ass for not catching Michael."

"Yeah, dat too," Trigger said.

Busta was aware of his lost appetite and the resulting weight loss. He, however, was not concerned because he had a desire to lose some weight so he could move better. He was now forty years old and realized just how uncomfortable he felt when he had to move quickly. His weight was down to 260 pounds.

"Got damn, can dat negro run! Like an Olympic athlete. He runs, jumps, dives, and cuts like a football player or acrobat. I's may never gits my fuckin mits on em. But if I ever do, all the runnin, jumpin, divin, and cutten ain't gonna help his little ass one fuckin bit."

· · · · · · · · · · ·

It was the summer holiday week, and Shapatilo was restless. He was really disappointed that he did not have Michael's head on a pike by now. He, however, had noticed that the hits on his properties had all but stopped. In fact, the entire area had quieted down considerably. Random hits here and there, but nothing that cannot be tolerated. Sometimes they even caught the culprits. He thought, *"That's when the fun begins."*

He reflected on the new calm since January and said to himself, "Maybe I'm being too hard on that fat nigger. The hits are indeed down since he put the fear of God in that quicksilver punk ass."

He got a call that evening and answered it. "Yeah, who da fuck is this?" he said.

The voice responded, "If you want to know who really hit your stash house, then check the back of their house's attic." Click.

· · · · · · · · · · · ·

Shapatilo and his entourage pulled up at Busta's house unexpectedly. He got out and climbed the stairs, with Busta meeting him at the door. He walked pass Busta, forcing the big man to step back.

He yelled, "If I find any evidence of you cheating me, nigger, you are dead! Stringbean, get your ass up here!"

Busta was exasperated. He said, "What da fuck is goin on?" Stringbean, a small thin man, walked into the house and moved passed Ray Ray and Trigger.

"I know boss. I know. You want me to check their attic, right?"

Shapatilo responded, "Why else would I bring your black scrawny ass with me? Climb up there and check for anything. Rat turds, roaches, spiders. Anything and everything. I want to know what's in that attic!"

Stringbean walked to the second floor of the house, then crawled up into the attic, using a nearby chair to stand on. No one usually climbed into the attic. No one had been up there for years. They just shoved cases or sacks into the opening. Any heavy weight not placed on a floor joist would punch a hole in the second-floor ceiling.

He checked the entire attic and reported back, "Nothing up here, boss. Just dust and spiders and shit. There's a board in the roof that's been cutout and placed back, however."

He came back down and asked for a ladder so Shapatilo could see for himself. Shapatilo climbed up the ladder with a flashlight and looked around for a brief moment, but he could not handle the dust.

He came down and said, "Okay, okay. I got a report about something, and I had to check it out. Everything looks fine. Get back to your rummy fuckin game," while walking out the house.

Hours later, Busta was still perplexed about the intrusion. Then he got a call from Stringbean. "You owe me, nigga. I just saved your fat ass at the risk of my own. I want twenty percent. I'll fill you in layta, my nigga."

. . . .

Three days later, Stringbean pulled up to Busta's house. He did not feel comfortable coming any sooner. Even though he worked for the boss, Shapatilo might be watching both of them. He arrived as arranged after midnight in Ray Ray's car. He told Busta to provide him with the ladder. He climbed back up into the attic and a minute later came down with a sack. $75,000 worth of the stash money, that had been hidden in a corner. Busta appreciated Stringbean saving his ass enough to put a small caliber bullet in his left temple.

He told Ray Ray, "Take Jake wit ya and go back ta ware ya picked him up at and gets rid of his ride. I'll handle da body. Den come backs hare and cleans up dis mess."

Busta was now perplexed. How did $75,000 get planted in his attic?

He thought, *"Of course! Michael planted dis dough up dare! He stole it, den when he drugged us dat night he planted da dough. Fucker took 50Gs for himself. The boss was pissed, but I don't knows why. I paid that ma-fucker his cash, so any missing dough is mine, anywho. Too bad Stringbean did not realize dat. Now he gone. Greedy bastard wit a tiny brain. Well, I jest added to da weight of his brain."*

. . . .

That night Shapatilo woke up with a startling revelation. He said aloud, ignoring his wife, who was soundly asleep, "If there was money in the attic, it technically belonged to Busta. He had already made up for the missing moola. Yet, it was the principle of the thing. He may have tried to stiff me, hoping I would not force him to replace the dough. But why would someone try to set him up? Who could have known there was money in the attic? If Michael stole it, then it was Michael who put it back. He must have gotten my number from Busta's place. But if Michael was truly trying to set up Busta, why would he call and not actually have the money there? What could have happened to it?" He paused for a short moment then shouted, "Stringbean!!!!"

. . . .

Robert finished officer training and was commissioned a Second Lieutenant. His commander received a lot of flak, especially since Robert was so young, but he did not concern himself with the rumblings of others. He had to put in two years, and it did not matter to him what rank he was assigned.

His commander merely said to his colleagues, "There's something special about this one. I heard from his commander at basic that he took charge of his barracks and helped all of them finish the training.

No repeats in the whole barrack. They worked as a team aiding those who fell behind. It was his effort that made that possible. This is a rare gift, and we must take full advantage of it. These are draftees for Christ's sake. They generally don't give a damn about each other or even impressing their instructors. Yet this crew changed overnight. One day they were sullen; the next they became comrades. And according to his instructors, Robert was mostly responsible for that. I just have the feeling we're going to hear extraordinary things from him."

A week later, Robert was on a flight to serve in Vietnam. The plane made a stopover in Germany. When it departed, he was not on board. Six weeks later, however, in mid-November, over eight months after bootcamp began, Robert was again aboard a flight for Vietnam.

CHAPTER TWELVE

Vietnam

Second Lieutenant McCants arrived in Vietnam on a hot November day. Fall would be a misnomer since the tropics only have two seasons: rainy and non-rainy. What he found that day in '71 was a highly dysfunctional array of troops. There was minimum discipline. Troops were dressed as they chose to dress. The Black soldiers were attempting to wear afros, not always conducive to the military helmets they were issued. Robert saw confederate flags, KKK insignia, Black power flags, Black Panther berets, and papers from Mohammad Speaks. The soldiers were segregating themselves in the camps and in the city of Saigon. Black night spots and White night spots. The brig was occupied by a disproportion number of Black soldiers. Marijuana was prevalent, but heroin was present as well. The music blared with soul music, country music, or heavy metal music, depending on the side of the camp you were living on.

First Lieutenant Campbell greeted Robert at the command post. "Second Lieutenant McCants, glad you could join us. I have read your file, which is impressive. You spent six weeks in Germany, doing special training. Care to share that experience?"

McCants replied, "I have had so much training over the past eight plus months that its now just a blur. The army has excellent training instructors. As good as any college professor I've ever studied under."

Lieutenant Campbell said, "Oh yes, I see you got your college degree at the age of nineteen! That's either a mark of brilliance or tenacity."

McCants, wondering if Campbell was setting him up, responded, "Yes, sir. I can be very tenacious. Sir, where am I to bunk? Where are the officer's barracks? I really would like to get out of this travel gear and shower."

Campbell had heard that McCants was short on small talk.

"Sure, lieutenant. I will have someone take you there immediately. We will have plenty of time to get to know one another." McCants did not like references to his age and wished it did not have to be a part of his file. He could not see where it made a difference.

"Hell," he thought, *"I'll be twenty in a few weeks."*

McCants turned to salute the lieutenant but was reprimanded before he could raise his arm. "Second Lieutenant McCants!" came a shout from his rear.

"Didn't they explain to you that you never salute any officer while stationed here? You would be alerting any snipers who the officers are. They would become prime targets." It was Colonel Austin McGregor, a West Point graduate he had heard about during the flight.

He turned toward the colonel and said, "I apologize, Sir. I understand. It will not happen again." He resisted the urge to salute the colonel, then excused himself and waited for his escort.

After he showered, McCants walked the grounds, then entered a tent with all Black soldiers. The voices in the tent dropped to a murmur.

One of the soldiers said, "Well, brother. I'd salute you but you might get shot. There are snipers hanging out in the next tent."

Everyone in the tent, including McCants, laughed. Another soldier offered McCants a joint, but he declined. "I'm surprised they allow that here," said McCants.

"How do you stay focused if you're high?"

The soldier said, "Brother, there is no way we can't be focused with Mary Jane around," and they laughed again.

McCants stayed within the tent for a short while, getting to know the soldiers better. He was eventually sarcastically told that what he was doing was frowned upon. Carousing with the lowest ranking soldiers. McCants understood, waved goodbye, and headed to the officer's canteen. Colonel McGregor met him at the entrance.

Before walking away, he said, "I'm glad you got that out of your system. Don't let me see that happen again. You are not a buck private. You are a second lieutenant in this man's army. Remember that."

McCants met the Vietnamese officers which he found very dedicated to the war effort. He tried to get to understand the war from their perspective. He understood these men were killing their brothers and cousins, similar to the American Civil War. When he brought up the subject, however, their response was simple.

A Vietnamese sergeant said, "For you Americans this is just the Korean War part two. End of story. You want to halt communism from spreading, and if you have to destroy my country to do that you will. I know you were invited in, and we probably would have already lost the war without your help. I just am not convinced of your motives beyond halting communism."

While McCants was visiting the Vietnamese officers the American command center was abuzz about his arrival. Later, during dinner,

Colonel McGregor, speaking to all officers present, said, "I read McCants' file before he arrived from Germany. It's not the norm to send newly trained officers to Germany. They usually send them directly here. Did any of you guys go to Germany?" There was no response, so the Colonel continued, "I was cautioned to read it before he arrived, which is somewhat unusual. I must say, he is a peculiar kind of guy." He, however, did not reveal what the file contained.

· · · · · · · · · ·

Doctor Karl Schutz read aloud McCants's file from Fort Benning:

"Lieutenant McCants from Detroit Michigan. Finished high school at the age of 16. College graduate at the age of 19. Won't be 20 until December. Finished first in his class in college. Finished first in each of the basic training exercises. Finished first in rifle training, even though he has no history of using firearms. Finished first in officer training. Standard testing indicated a very high IQ; he is near genius. Further testing requested. Concerns: his extraordinary ability to focus raises alarms.

"Well," Schutz continued, "that would explain why they sent him to us and not directly to Nam. Let's crack open that skull of his and take a look inside."

After six weeks of testing, Doctor Schutz could not come up with any tangible findings. He said to his staff, "Okay. Okay. Okay. We've had this gentleman here for almost two months. We have been unable to draw any conclusions to our research. He appears to be perfectly normal, just extremely quiet, introverted, focused. When approached he is very friendly, which is not normal for an introvert, very talkative, which is not normal for someone who's quiet, and very relaxed with others, which is not normal for his level of focus. When he's alone, just being observed, all these personality traits surface. However, when he's among his peers or working with us, he is quite normal. It's like he's a robot! He can turn off his energy when it's not in use!

"He reads a lot in his spare time, but the subject matter covers all areas. Crime novels, scientific periodicals, sports, comedy. Hell, he's all over the place. We cannot determine any one area that interested him the most. He's still in top conditioning even though he's been off the training cycle for weeks. Yet we've never observed him exercising. He's ambidextrous. But he will use his left hand for a week, then switch to the right hand which is rare. It's like he deliberately monitors the time spent on each side. Now tell me that's not weird! He sleeps just six hours a night, even when he's given enough time for eight hours. He falls asleep, barely moves during the night, then wakes and is up in seconds. Shit, he barely stretches when rising! Doctor Patel, what did you find out with your testing?" Doctor Patel had only been with the unit for six months. He was on loan from the British. Trained in India, he was considered a savant in mental health.

Patel, speaking with a Gujarati accent, said, "I have never observed anyone like him. I have tried to keep my views strictly based on western philosophy. However, He drove me mad with his incredibly consistent behavior! I deliberately tried to alter his reactions, but nothing worked. I found myself regressing back to my initial training in India, which I never do. But he made me do it! I am so frustrated! This sister-fucker is something different! I have seen shaman, after a lifetime of training, performing some of the mental tricks this boy does! And I don't think the boy knows he's doing anything special. I don't know. I just don't know. I am done with this sister-fucker! My God!"

Dr. Schutz smiled broadly, and sarcastically said, "Okay Patel. Okay. Wow! Tell us how you really feel. Ha Ha! Sister-fucker? Haven't heard that phrase before. That is not a way to talk about our Blacks!" Laughter filled the small room. "Why didn't you just call him the N-word! I have never heard you use that word. I would have called him a motherfucker!" The room erupts into more laughter. Dr. Schutz continued, "And you can't call him a 'boy' either!" Again, more laughter in the room. "Okay guys, settle down. Afterall, we are men of science. And Officer McCants, as young as he is, deserves a modicum of respect. Hell, a total level of our respect."

Dr. Patel stood up and said, "I must apologize. Sorry, I must apologize. You are correct. McCants is an officer in your military, and I must show him the respect he deserves. And I do respect him as a man. He is actually something extraordinary. He is just so intimidating on an intellectual scale. He must have frightened any teacher or school administrator who challenged him intellectually. I do have a recommendation. That he is not sent to Vietnam, but instead be given a position either here or in some American base. Some place that is not dangerous. I don't fear for him. I fear for his enemy."

. . . .

After only a week in the country, McCants was sent on his first mission. An experienced First Lieutenant Smith headed the platoon, with two experienced Vietnamese sergeants accompanying them. For the most part, it was uneventful. The two Vietnamese sergeants were an extremely intense pair, taking the mission very seriously. McCants was able to appreciate this. During an evening discussion he tried to explain his logic of not killing, if possible. It did not go over well with the two men, so he dropped the subject. Totally missing the point, he thought, *"Have never had difficulty making my point before. I wish I had studied Vietnamese while I was in college."*

At night, McCants would fall asleep and dream about his range instructor and his orders.

"Don't aim for the knees. Aim for the heart and head. A wounded soldier is an extremely dangerous soldier."

Each night, he had the same dream.

"Don't aim for the knees. Aim for the heart and head. A wounded soldier is an extremely dangerous soldier."

McCants was very happy to get back to his regular bunk. Now he was able to dream about home. He would dream about his parents and brothers. But strangely, he never dreamed about his twin.

. . . .

Over the next month, McCants was sent out on two more missions, with only a week's stay in between. Each time he reported directly to First Lieutenant Campbell. McCants was informed that Campbell had just arrived in Vietnam one month before he arrived, and these were his first missions. He was a third generation West Point graduate and believed he must make his family proud. McCants decided that he should watch Campbell's back, because he might take unnecessary risks. He was a well-trained officer and McCants could tell he was born for this role. He just needed to take his time. McCants questioned if he would.

They returned safely from their first mission. They were not so fortunate during the second.

Lieutenant Campbell ordered McCants, Corporal Baker, and Private Johnson to stay behind and protect their rear while he took the platoon down an eastern trail to scout the village ahead.

McCants said to Campbell, "Do you think we should be separated by such a distance? We won't be able to quickly support each other."

Campbell acknowledged McCants' concern but maintained his orders.

Thirty minutes later the rear guard's world exploded. Corporal Baker's gun was shattered, and his right hand mangled. His ammunition bag was also struck, stopping a round from striking him in the chest. Private Johnson, in a panic, went through all his ammunition within minutes. When he had used up his last clip, he tried to load one of Corporal Baker's damaged clips into his M-16. The clip caused his gun to jam, rendering him defenseless. He yelled out to Lieutenant McCants, only to find him lying face down in the mud, unconscious.

"McCants! McCants! My god, he's got a head wound!" shouted Johnson, now totally panicked. "He needs a medic right away!"

"Dant Da Da Don!!!!!!" shouted the four-year-old. I'm sup-er-man!!! I can fly just like Mighty Mouse!" "Boy, get off that bed before you fly through that window! Get over here, now!" "Watch me mommy. I can fly! I'm Sup-er-man!!!" "Son, please take that towel off of your neck. You're going to hang yourself. Mack, take your little brother into the bedroom with your other brothers."

"McCants! McCants! Can you hear me? We've got to go! The Gooks are here and they're going to rush…" *"Dant da da Don!!! I'm…. Felix the Cat!"* "Bam Bam Bam!…" came the reports from the North Vietnam soldier's rifles.

"McCants! They're coming!!! Give me your gun!" "Bam Bam Bam Bam Bam Bam!…" *"Dant da da…."* McCants, his eyes still closed, said, "Where are we? What's going on?"

Corporal Baker said, "Thank God you're all right! Sir, we're under fire! My hand is severely damaged. We need support. I've called ahead to Lieutenant Campbell, but it will take them some time to get here. Are you alright? Can you fire your weapon?"

McCants said, "Where is my weapon?"

Corporal Baker shouted, "It's on your lap, Sir! I tried to take it from you, but you had a death grip on it!"

McCants eyes began to focus, and he realized he had his index finger on the rifle's trigger. He looked over the groundcover just as seven North Vietnamese soldiers began charging toward them. He moved quickly, aimed, and fired. "Pow!"

The closest soldier fell in a heap, yelling incoherently. "Pow Pow!" came the report from McCants rifle. Two more Viet Cong soldiers fell, then squirmed in agony on the ground. "Pow!" Another Viet Cong soldier fell. "Pow Pow Pow!"

The last three charging VC soldiers fell, all screaming in pain. The air suddenly got very still as the smoke from McCants rifle dissipated. There was now total silence around them, only the distant cries of the young Viet Cong soldiers.

Lieutenant Campbell had ordered two squadrons to return to assist Lieutenant McCants. The rest of the platoon held their position. The two Vietnamese sergeants arrived, leading the two squads.

One sergeant said, "These guys are still alive. I will finish them."

McCants intervened. "Hold it, Sergeant. We're taking them back alive. Does everyone understand?"

The two sergeants looked at each other, then nodded to McCants. Corporal Baker looked at the wounded Viet Cong soldiers in amazement, then said, "Black Audie Murphy. Hot Damn!" Private Johnson, having wiped the tears off his face, thought, "*Who the heck is Audie Murphy?*"

. . . .

McCants was in the infirmary for two days. His head wound was not serious, just a grazing shot off his temple, along his hairline. The skin was not broken, just bruised, possibly caused by shrapnel. He also had a cut on his right shoulder that required stitches. The doctors, however, wanted to keep him under observation to be sure there was nothing more serious. Corporal Baker was not so fortunate. He had to be sent to Japan for more extensive medical treatment on his injured hand.

When McCants left the infirmary, he reported to Colonel McGregor. The colonel asked him to have a seat, then said, "Are you alright, young man? That was quite a blow to your head."

McCants said, "Yes Sir, I'm fine. Glad we were able to complete the mission successfully."

McGregor said, "Lieutenant Campbell did indeed succeed. As did you. I have two questions. Did you deliberately aim to wound the charging Cong or was it just happenstance? The second question is what the hell is 'Dant da da don!'", and he smiled. "Must have been a hell of a dream."

McCants rose, nodded at the Colonel, and exited the tent. He did not answer either question.

The two Vietnamese Sergeants were not happy the Viet Cong soldiers were kept alive. The hatred built up between them was born from the killings between the two armies over the last fifteen years. The Colonel was aware of their complaints. He contacted his Major and reported the results of the mission. He informed him of the seven captured soldiers, the method of capture, and the complaints of the sergeants. He also informed him of the report from Fort Benin about McCants penchant for aiming low.

The major responded, "Colonel, did he hit the target? Seven soldiers by one man? Were the men disarmed? Well good news, then. We can use the information we gather from them. Be thankful you have so talented a man on your force. Keep me apprised of the lieutenant's progress."

The colonel hung up the phone and said to himself, "I am grateful. I just hope his desire to aim low doesn't cost us."

Colonel McGregor had two concerns: that Campbell may desire heroic action and that McCants will not kill.

To resolve his concern, he placed the two new officers together on the next few missions. However, there was very little action in the day long expeditions. They walked out, questioned villagers, then returned to base. Rarely did they have to sleep on the ground. On the rare occasion they encountered enemy combatants, limited firing forced the Cong to retreat. Campbell noticed that McCants usually did not participate in the shooting, but merely observed the actions of the lower ranked soldiers.

When he asked McCants why he was not firing his weapon, his response was, "Because it has yet to be necessary. We have new soldiers here that are as raw as you and me. They will need as much experience as possible. Some of them can barely shoot their rifles, even after basic training."

A report submitted by Campbell to the Colonel described McCants as a top-notch soldier and officer, but he had one concern. The report read, "He continues to want to only wound the VC. This has been the pattern since he arrived. He rarely shoots his weapon. When he does, however, a VC is wounded and has to be evacuated. This ties up another VC soldier, which may be McCants' plan. He never shoots the assisting VC soldier and directs his men to fire elsewhere. The men are becoming aware of his strategy. Some are opposed, especially our Vietnamese partners."

A year later, after very light scouting expeditions with minimal action, Colonel McGregor was satisfied with the experience gained by his two lieutenants.

He approached McCants and said, "I have selected you to join Campbell on an important mission. Lieutenant Campbell will lead the platoon. He will inform you and the men the purpose of the mission as the need arises."

McGregor had grown very fond of McCants. He, however, was still concerned about his penchant for not killing. He had brought back several more wounded Cong. The Vietnamese sergeants, however, find this to be a detriment and continued to report it to their Vietnamese commanders.

. . . .

A major, stationed in Vietnam, made a long-distance call to a military psychiatrist in Germany. He said, "You've asked me to keep you informed about a certain lieutenant stationed here in Vietnam. I will be mailing you a report." The psychiatrist said, "Danke schön," and hung up the phone.

. . . .

Busta was somewhat irritated. He had been summoned to the Mediterranean Boot Social Club again and had no idea why. He thought, *"My product is sellin like hotcakes. I's makin a ton of dough fo dis ass-hole. What could he wants now?"*

When he arrived, he was directed to the same chair he sat on during his previous summons. Only this time he did not have to wait long before the giant escorted him into the office.

Shapatilo said, "Busta, I need a status on Michael. The big boss wants to know if there has been any progress."

Busta thought, *"What da fuck! I's been bringin in tons of dough and all he want ta talk bout is Michael?"*

He replied, "Boss, word is he left town. Nobodies seed him in months."

Busta started to mention his lookouts on Santa Rosa but decided not to. "With all da heat from da pol-lise, he may not be comin back no how."

Shapatilo, having received a second anonymous phone call a day after the first one in July, said, "Fuckin' great. Fucker kills Sammy, then disappears. It's been three years! Okay. You can go. And by the way, I'm sorry I intruded on your home back in July of last year. That Stringbean had me believing something that wasn't so.

"One more thing. You keep leaving your bowling bags."

Busta hesitated, then picked up the bag and walked out of the office and into the parking lot. He placed the bag into his trunk and drove away. Ten minutes later he was in front of a landfill. Busta opened the bag to see which of his boys was now dead. He looked in and said aloud, "Stringbean!"

. . . .

A shadowy figure peered through the broken window of a nearby house, watching two Cadillacs parked in front of a two-story frame house. He waited for hours, then a third Cadillac pulled up and a small spidery-looking Black man he did not recognize got out of the passenger seat and was escorted into the house. An hour later Busta's crew left the house without the guest, then Busta emerged from the house carrying a large rug. The guest never left.

The observer followed Busta's car to an empty lot, miles from the city limit. He dug a shallow hole, dumped the contents of the rug into the hole, then shoveled dirt back into the hole until it was somewhat level. He stomped on the dirt, trying to compact it, then drove away.

The observer understood the possibilities of this act and made a phone call. It was the second call made to this number in two days.

CHAPTER THIRTEEN

Helicopter Rescue

January 1973

Lieutenants Campbell and McCants continued to be teamed up throughout the remainder of their first year. The American sergeant, Brooks, and the two Vietnamese sergeants, Phan and Duong, accompanied them on most of the missions. Now, after thirteen months in Vietnam, the new year arrived for McCants as he and the men departed on a special, very secretive, mission. Colonel McGregor had already briefed First Lieutenant Campbell on the objections of the mission. He informed McCants that he would be informed of the details of the mission as the need arises. This mission, however, had the men spooked. They believed the war effort was a failure and knew that peace talks were underway between the U.S. government and the two Vietnamese governments.

Lieutenant Campbell's section consisted of Lieutenant McCants, two American sergeants, two Vietnamese sergeants, and approximately two dozen men. After disembarking from the helicopters, Campbell split the section into two squads, and personally led one of the squads. McCants, now twenty-one years old with a year of experience under his belt, led the other squad. Each squad had one of the Vietnamese sergeants for interpretation.

Campbell instructed McCants, "Lieutenant, take your squad north, scouting for troop movement. I will head northwest then veer back eastward toward you. We'll reconvene by nightfall. We are not here to engage the enemy, so do so only if necessary. We need to ascertain their whereabouts and report their location back to headquarters." McCants acknowledged the lieutenant's orders and headed north, directing his men into the forest.

McCants, as was his preference, brought up the rear of his squad, having instructed Sergeant Brooks to take the point position.

"Where are we headed?" asked Buck Private Smith to no one in particular.

Sergeant Brooks responded, "Who the hell knows. That pointy-headed Campbell just follows orders without any consideration to the consequences. Let's just get through this. I can't believe they flew us this far north. This war is almost over. Moving this far north makes no sense at all, since we know the Cong are moving south. We most certainly will encounter them if we keep marching north. No one wants to die for an 'almost' completed war."

Brooks and Smith entered a small village, followed by the rest of the squad. They found the village chief and Sergeant Phan questioned him. After the discussion, the Vietnamese sergeant was convinced this was a Viet Cong supply camp, even though there was little evidence to support his opinion. The supply of rice was plentiful, which was not normal if the Cong had been through here. After being briefed by Sergeant Phan, McCants conferred with Brooks, then contacted Campbell. He believed Phan was distrustful of any village this far north. McCants expressed his doubt of the village's involvement with the Cong and Campbell agreed and ordered the men to continue forward. What McCants and the others did not notice was the lack of young men in the village.

They were wrong about the village. Brooks, however, was right in his assessment about the Cong. A large contingent of Viet Cong soldiers, heading south toward the village, were moving directly toward their position.

"Let's hold up here for the night fellas," ordered Lieutenant Campbell, after they had reconvened. "I don't like this locale, and we're only a klick or so from an evacuation point, just south of our present locale, but the sun is going down rapidly, and I don't want to risk further northward movement in the dark."

As the two squads setup camp, the Vietnamese sergeants discussed with each other what was obvious to each of them about the village. Both sergeants were in agreement that something was amiss. They shared their concerns with both Lieutenants. Campbell informed them that he appreciated their input, but they were already committed to their mission. The village was now inconsequential. Sergeant Phan, upset that the Lieutenant would not take his warning seriously, angerly spoke in Vietnamese.

"Bạn nên lắng nghe tôi! You should listen to me! Did you not notice…". Sergeant Duong grabbed his arm. Phan, realizing he was raising his voice, apologized in English, and walked away. McCants, alarmed at Phan's outburst, began to sense that he may have made an error in his personal assessment of the village.

He said to Campbell, "Sir, I am now of the opinion that Sergeant Phan may have been correct. I don't know why, since there were no signs indicating Cong involvement in that village. But let's be honest. Phan and Duong know a lot more about this country than the two of us, and we didn't bring them along just for translation. We should regard them as experts and heed their warning. I've yet to experience them wrong before. Perhaps we should consider their suggestions before we settle here for the night."

Meanwhile the soldiers continued to unpack their gear. "Most definitely don't want to run into any VC tonight," said private Smith. "It's a full moon and everything is lit up like a bitch! Can even see you spooks in this night air," and laughed.

"Fuck you and yo mama," laughed Private Cook, the darkest man in the section.

"Those fuckers sho can't see me!"

It was the last thing he said before he was hit with a round through his throat, almost severing his head.

"Shit! We're under fire! Man down! Man down! Get the medic!" screamed the men.

Campbell, taking charge, ordered the men to hit the ground. Smith, however, froze for a brief moment, so Campbell rushed at him, knocking him to the ground. Campbell was hit a second later.

"The lieutenant's down!" yelled private Thomas. "Lieutenant's down! What's goin on?"

Brooks replied, "We're under fire, dumbass! Take cover immediately."

Thomas and Smith began directing fire northward toward the underbrush 200 yards away. The other men followed suit. Thomas was still exposed and was shot in the shoulder, knocking him to the ground. Smith rushed to him and began dragging him behind cover. Then Smith was hit in the leg but managed to get Thomas and himself behind cover.

McCants rushed to Campbell's side to check on his injuries. He had serious wounds to his chest and was having trouble breathing.

"Sir, I'm going to request an immediate evac. We are outnumbered with very poor ground coverage. Sir, I still don't know what our orders are."

A delirious Campbell, barely able to speak, whispered, "Nix that McCants. We have a mission that must be completed. We must detect a mobilization of the VC before they reach the river."

"Sorry, sir. But they've already crossed the river. This mission is over. We already have four wounded so I'm calling for an evac." He waited for a response from Campbell, but he was now unconscious.

Sergeant Brooks, seeing Campbell down, realized that McCants, a month past his twenty-first birthday, was now in charge. He began to command the troops while McCants radioed for an evacuation. After the initial barrage of fire stopped, Brooks settled next to McCants.

"I'm behind you all the way, whatever you decide. But if you want my advice, I think we need to get the hell out of here. I suspect we may be vastly outnumbered, and they have the high-ground and better cover. This poor coverage causes us to be spread too thin as well." McCants informed the Sergeant that he agreed with him and had already called for a retreat and evacuation.

McCants said, "I want you to take charge while I move to the point position. I cannot command from up there."

Brooks was somewhat confused why the Lieutenant would position himself so poorly but obeyed. He ordered the men to hold their fire until he could determine their situation. McCants moved to the head of the section, taking Private Cook's rifle and rounds with him. He laid Cooks clips along a log and checked Cook's M-16 to ensure it was still operational. He ensured a round was chambered in Cook's rifle, set to semi-automatic, and awaited orders from Brooks.

Occasional fire came from the north, but most of the next few hours were quiet. Only low chatter could be heard from the Viet Cong.

"Believe they are trying to determine our strength," Brooks said to Sergeant Phan. "We mustn't give away our actual size. Pass the word to the men to hold their fire. And no more talking. Phan, I need you to tell me if you can hear what they're discussing."

Brooks then crawled over to McCants' position to discuss options. He noticed that McCants was relaxed, even lightly napping. He also noticed McCants had Cook's M-16 laid out posed and ready. He spoke to the lieutenant.

"If Campbell was right, then an invading group of Cong are moving south. We are probably outnumbered and could be overrun with one blitz. Did you get an ETA from the base?"

McCants replied, "I'm sure you know the drill. No flying at night in this terrain since there is nowhere to land. They would be sitting ducks, and we would be as well trying to board the choppers. I suspect they are going to want us to retreat to that clearing approximately a klick south of us, just west of that village we were in. The one with all the rice!" he said sarcastically.

"They will let us know soon."

After a long pause, McCants whispered, "Dawn is an hour away. I can almost distinguish color already. Start sending the men back as quietly as possible. In small groups of three or four, a few minutes apart. Take one wounded with each group. We don't need to tie the men up any more than necessary. Make sure the Lieutenant goes first, followed by Cooper."

"Distinguish," thought Brooks. *"What school did this kid go to?"*

He replied, "Gotcha. I assume you're going to want to maintain your position here?"

"Yep," whispered McCants.

"And if you don't mind, get me Campbell's M-16 and rounds."

"Don't have enough already?" smiled Brooks as he went to get Campbell's gear, along with a supply bag of clips.

He whispered, "Young brother may be raw, but he definitely has moxie."

Minutes later the troops began moving south, very slowly, one small group at a time. After thirty minutes, McCants found himself alone. He could now move south as well, but then the Viet Cong would be free to advance themselves. So, he stayed.

"What the hell have I gotten myself into?"

For the first time in months, he thought about his twin.

"What would Michael do?"

He began to reflect on the cause of the conflict. "These fellows are just trying to unify their country. Most of them are only fighting because some old fool told them to. Just like all ground soldiers do all over the world. I don't agree with their position, but it is their civil war. Killing these young men just doesn't seem right. I bet most of them are younger than me."

His thoughts were rudely interrupted by a barrage of bullets whistling by his head. "Bam bam bam bam bam…", as hundreds of rounds pierce the air around him. A half-dozen northern soldiers began charging his position, followed by another half-dozen. Most were yelling loudly in the universal war cry, "Aaaaahhhhh!!!"

"Here we go…", said McCants and he began firing back.

"Pow Pow Pow!" went the report from the M-16, still set on semi-automatic. "Pow Pow Pow!"

The barrage of fire was stupendous. "Bam bam bam bam bam." Rounds rained in on McCants' position, striking all around him. "Pow! Pow Pow!" came his response. "Pow! Pow Pow! Pow! Pow Pow!"

All of the men were keenly aware of the firefight now occurring behind them. Private Smith, being supported by Brooks, said, "Sergeant, ain't McCants going to retreat? What's he waiting for? I can hear his M-16, and it's stationary. What the fuck is he doin?!"

Brooks replied, "Giving us time to get to the landing site, dumbass! Keep it moving, double time. And make sure Cook, Thomas and Campbell are secure. Somebody take Smith from me!"

All the men knew Cook was dead and they had a great concern for Campbell and Thomas. They also knew that McCants remained behind.

"Shit, hope the lieutenant can get out of there before the Cong realize we're gone," said Private Thompson.

Unfortunately, that time had arrived. McCants noticed a quiet within the Cong ranks. The Cong commanders, having sent a small contingent of troops charging toward the Americans, realized that only one soldier was returning fire. So, they ordered their remaining troops to charge the American position. A blood curdling scream arose from the Cong as the remaining troops came pouring out of the terrain. "Pow pow pow!", sang McCants' M-16. "Pow pow pow powpow pow powpow pow powpow! pow pow! Pow pow pow powpow pow powpow pow powpow! pow pow! Pow pow pow powpow pow powpow pow powpow! pow pow! Pow pow pow powpow pow powpow pow powpow! pow pow!" He changed weapons as he heard, "BamBamBam Bam BamBam bambam bam bam." Then, "Pow pow pow powpow pow powpow pow powpow! pow pow! Pow pow pow powpow pow powpow pow powpow! pow pow! Pow pow pow powpow pow powpow pow powpow! pow pow!" The two distinct sounds blended together in a symphony of deafening noise, constantly overlaying each other, and losing their distinctiveness. "Powbam powbam powbam, bampow bampow bampow!" VC soldiers fell continuously, collapsing over each other. None got within twenty feet of McCants as he continued to aim and fire. *Hit their knees and they can't run,* thought McCants.

"Hit their weapons and they can't shoot."

"Pow pow pow powpow pow powpow pow powpow! pow pow! Pow pow pow powpow pow powpow pow powpow! pow pow! Pow pow pow powpow pow powpow pow powpow! pow pow!" McCants continued to fire and reload until his rifle jammed. Then he switched to Campbell's rifle, switched to his left hand, and continued his amazing pace. "Pow pow pow powpow pow powpow pow powpow! pow pow! Pow pow pow powpow pow powpow pow powpow! pow pow! Pow pow pow powpow pow powpow pow powpow! pow pow!! Pow Bambambam bam bambam bambam bam bampowbampowbampow. PowPowPow! Pow Pow BamBamBam Bam BamBam bambam bam bam Pow pow pow powpow pow powpow pow powpow! pow pow! Pow pow pow powpow pow powpow pow powpow! pow pow! Pow pow pow powpow pow powpow pow powpow! pow pow!! Pow Bambambam bam bambam bambam bam bampowbampowbampow."

Bodies continued to fall one by one every time the sound of the M-16 was fired. His movement was robotic as he jammed one new clip into his rifle after another with minimal pause between firings. His focus was so intense he was no longer aware of his immediate surroundings. He only saw bodies running toward him and falling as more men came running toward him. He was totally unaware of the war cries as the sound got closer and closer to him. "Pow pow pow powpow pow powpow pow powpow! pow pow! Pow pow pow powpow pow powpow pow powpow! pow pow! Pow pow pow powpow pow powpow pow powpow! pow pow!! Pow Bambambam bam bambam bambam bam bampowbampowbampow. PowPowPow! Pow Pow BamBamBam Bam BamBam bambam bam bam."

Meanwhile, at the clearing, three helicopters arrived to pick up the troops. After the first two helicopters were loaded, the captain on the last helicopter said, "I count nine. Should be ten! Boy, where the fuck is yo lieutenant?"

Brooks, standing next to the helicopter, ignored the 'boy' remark, and replied, "I'm going back for him. You guys take off. You can pick us up at the initial drop-off site. Give us a couple of hours to get there." Sergeant Phan jumped from the helicopter to join Brooks and began running back up the trail.

The captain yelled, "Stay the fuck put soldiers! I'm giving the orders here! Get your asses on this chopper now! I'll give him five minutes! Then we are leaving!" Then he ordered the other helicopters to leave. Both sergeants stopped, but neither climbed aboard the helicopter.

"Pow pow powpow! Pow pow pow pow! Pow powpowpowpowpowpowpow! pow pow!"

Then total silence from the field. All that can be heard was the blades of the helicopter. They waited five additional minutes, but no one exited the forest.

"Sorry sergeants, but you're going nowhere!" the captain commanded.

"They must've gotten your man. Get aboard now! That's an order!"

Brooks and Phan reluctantly followed orders, knowing the captain was right.

The helicopter lifted up thirty feet then began to pivot just before Brooks yelled, "What the fuck!? Sumbitch! Put this bitch back down! There's our BOY! Well, I'll shit my pants! He's alive!"

Brooks began to sob, tears streaming down his face. "Mother fucking Son of a Bitch! He's alive! That Detroit mothafucka is alive!"

All of the men looked around and saw McCants walking casually through the brush one hundred yards away, carrying three M-16s and a supply bag. Cheers rained down so loud the pilot could barely hear his radio. McCants, covered in blood, had no smile, no frown, just a serious look on his face. A focused look.

When the helicopter landed, he approached it and said, "You guys better order a slew of medivacs. I just left about fifty-thousand or so wounded VC kids back there. They're piled on top of each other. They're going to need our help. And we'd better get them before their own boys do. We don't want to have to fight them twice, do we?"

The helicopter captain just looked incredulously at McCants as he boarded the helicopter, and away they flew back to base.

. . . .

The helicopters landed at the military base with medics running out to retrieve the wounded soldiers. Sergeant Brooks followed the medics into the hospital, preventing McCants from getting a written status report from him. He managed, however, to get the necessary paperwork he needed from the two Vietnamese sergeants. Both sergeants patted him on the back, smiled at him, and walked away as he nodded his appreciation. He wanted to check on Lieutenant Campbell but understood the urgency of reporting to Colonel McGregor first. He walked into the tent to an anxious colonel.

McGregor saw McCants get off the helicopter and thought, *"My God, what happened out there? The poor boy looks like he's been through hell and back. I've never seen anyone covered in blood after a firefight. It must be one of the injured men's blood. But it's all over his face as well!"*

When McCants entered McGregor's tent he yelled, "Soldier, why did you request an evacuation before you reached your destination?"

McCants understood military protocol, that McGregor already knew why they evacuated, but had to put on a show for the other officers present. So, he explained in detail, "Sir, none of us knew our final destination. Only that we were to push forward. Lieutenant Campbell was preparing to present the mission's objectives when we came under fire." This was not completely accurate. Campbell still had not briefed him when the firing started, but McCants had no intentions of presenting the lieutenant in a bad light.

McCants continued, "The Cong hit us south of the river. It was only after Lieutenant Campbell was wounded that we discovered the river was our destination. In fact, he instructed me not to call for an evac before we reached our goal. He was somewhat delirious by this time, or he would have understood our goal was already achieved. That we could report the precise location of the southward advancing

Cong platoons. I might add Sir, that Lieutenant Campbell was shot while saving Private Smith's life. He took a bullet meant for Smith, by shoving him to safety."

The Colonel internalized McCants' Campbell comment for later and said, "So your location was south of the river when you were attacked. Good to know. How many of your men were injured?"

McCants replied, "Private Cook was killed immediately, just before Lieutenant Campbell was shot. And Thomas and Smith received shoulder and leg wounds, respectively. We were forced to hunker down after that because the barrage of gun fire was extremely heavy. They were using what seemed like fifty caliber rounds making it nearly impossible to return fire. After a few minutes, they stopped firing, and the waiting game began. I believe, based on the following morning's events, that they were trying to ascertain our numbers and perform a blitz-like charge at daybreak, which is exactly what they did. If we had stayed in our location, we would have been overrun since we did not have adequate cover."

The colonel thought, *"Did he just say 'respectively'?"*

McGregor said, "The report I received from the captain was that they had to wait for you to board the copter. What caused your delay lieutenant?"

McCants replied, "I just wanted to make sure everyone was safely aboard before I exited my position. That's all, sir. Just wanted to be sure."

McGregor then asked, "Anything else you wish to report Lieutenant?"

McCants replied, "Yes, sir. I believe Lieutenant Campbell did an exemplary job and risked his life for his men. This should be noted in his record. I would commend Sergeant Brooks for his excellent command of the men after the lieutenant was wounded. He took over the command for me, as I radioed for the evac. Sergeant Phan was correct in his assessment of the village we reviewed. We should have listened to him. I also would like to request that we send in a rescue crew to retrieve as many of the VC wounded as possible. That is all, Sir."

Colonel McGregor said, "Well then, Lieutenant, get yourself cleaned up. In fact, check yourself into the infirmary. You seem to have another head wound, since there's some blood beginning to flow from your helmet."

As McCants walked away Colonel McGregor brought his right arm from behind his back and continued to read the report he had been previewing. It was McCants Germany psychological report from '71.

He thought, *"This comment about 'concern for the enemy' by this Indian quack may have been right on. Perhaps I should give this Dr. Karl Schutz a call."*

After the Colonel read the three reports from the sergeants, he was able to confirm why Lieutenant McCants was late boarding the helicopters. The comments made by the helicopter captain were true. "Son-bitch just came sashaying out of the freakin' trees like he was on a trek in the Outback."

It was not until McCants went into the infirmary that they discovered McCants did indeed have another head wound.

. . . .

McCants had to be sedated because of the head wound. He dreamed of the horrible battle he had just participated in. He dreamed about Superman and Mighty Mouse and dead soldiers and Viet Cong zombies and being teased as a baby killer. He dreamed of the time when he was four years old and he broke the window over his bed, cutting his elbow, while playing Superman, red cape and all. A wound that required six stitches to close the elbow cut and leave a permanent scar.

He dreamed of grape juice from grape vines growing in Vietnamese villages. Grape vines that could talk. Grape vines that could gossip, like his mother. He dreamed that the two Vietnamese sergeants in his squad were happy for him and despised him at the same time. And he dreamed that everyone was talking about him but getting his name wrong. *"It's McCants, not Murphy, dummies."* Then he went into a deeper RIM.

. . . .

McCants rose from the ground and thought, "I'm out of ammo!", and was jumped immediately. He caught the soldier as he dove through the air, twisted 180 degrees, flipped the soldier upside down and flung him to the ground. The impact broke the soldier's neck. Before McCants could turn back around, another soldier leaped at him, so he sidestepped and hooked his arm under the man's outstretched arm, twisted him completely around as he completed his turn, and threw the man back at two charging soldiers, knocking the three men to the ground. He reached down and grabbed his bayonet from his boot and drove it into the dying soldier's chest, then brought it up just as a fifth soldier thrust his knife toward him. He was forced to jump back one step as he thrust his bayonet deep into the soldier's torso, pulled it out, and jabbed a 6th soldier in the throat, then back into the fifth soldier's chest three times. Two more soldiers drove him backward, slashing at him with their bayoneted rifles. He grabbed the barrel of the closest soldier and pulled the man to him as he thrust his bayonet into his heart, then grabbed the eighth soldier by the neck and punched him in the temple, killing him instantly but breaking his hand. He then dropped the bayonet from his broken right hand and caught it in his left. He jammed it upward into the chin of the recovered second soldier as the third and fourth soldiers regained their footing. One of them charged him, reaching out for McCants throat. He brought his arm up sharply, knocking the feeble choke attempt away, then spun the man around and snapped his neck. The last soldier knocked McCants to the ground, grabbed a knife and attempted to stab him in the chest. McCants rolled to his left, grabbed the soldier's hand, flipped the blade toward the soldier, then thrusted it into the soldier's armpit, with the bayonet exiting out of the man's shoulder. He jerked the bayonet out and slit the man's throat. The soldier was still holding the bayonet as he drowned in his own blood.

He jumped up weaponless and spun to prepare for the next assault, but none came. Eight dead bodies lay at his feet, twenty feet from a pile of dead Cong soldiers. He looked closer at the carnage. They had wounds to their heads and hearts. Most of the soldiers had not started shaving yet. He switched on his amazing power of focus to prevent from crying. He would cry no more. He would not be permitted to mourn the dead babies at his feet. Dead babies just yards away from him. That was the responsibility of their mothers at that village with all the rice.

. . . .

When McCants awoke, he was in Japan. He had a cast on his right hand. He would never return to Vietnam.

. . . .

A major, stationed in Vietnam, made a second long-distance call to a military psychiatrist in Germany. He said, "As you requested, we're sending a certain lieutenant back to you. His updated report will accompany him." The psychiatrist nodded, smiled, and hung up the phone.

CHAPTER FOURTEEN

Back from Nam

When Robert left the hospital in Germany in March '73, at the age of twenty-one, he was immediately discharged from the army. No offer to re-enlist was made. He understood since the country was ending the war, the army needed to downsize and getting rid of officers was one of the decisions made by the upper echelon. This included ending the draft.

He had spent eight weeks of basic training, eight weeks of infantry training, four months of officer training state-side and Germany, thirteen months in Vietnam, followed by six weeks of hospitalization in Germany. He never questioned why he needed hospitalization for a broken hand.

Two years after leaving Detroit, Robert was back home and back on a college campus. Only he did not settle in Detroit, and he did not immediately tell his family he was back. They, he felt, did not need to know. He was back to his old secretive ways.

It took a few weeks for his transcripts to reach the University of Michigan administration office. He got an off-campus apartment in the western part of Ann Arbor, near the I-94 freeway. The shopping mall and theatre nearby were ideal for students, and he could melt right into college life. A lot of his classmates from Cass Tech were present on campus, but, since he did not socialize much at Cass, he did not attempt to renew acquaintances. At twenty-one, he was entering grad school, not finishing his senior year. He kept the last two years pushed back deep in his mind. He, instead, preferred to think about a time more than a decade or so ago.

. . . .

The boys jumped out of the old station wagon and tried to run to the backyard to play before their father could stop them. He was so angry that he did not speak the entire trip home. Before they could get around the building, however, Frank yelled, "Hold it right there. All of you. Get back here now! Now, somebody tell me what that was all about? All that fighting? Last week we visited Horace and you got into a fight with your cousins. This week we visited Herbert, and you fought the neighborhood kids. Even your cousins were embarrassed. Those were their friends you were fighting. Last month the same damn thing! What the hell is it with you guys? And don't tell me 'they' always start it."

Martha turned her head away and smiled but knew not to say a word. This was Frank's show, even though she secretly liked her 'Fighting Sullivans'. She had seen them in action and was amazed at their teamwork and skills. They fought as a group, overwhelming even older boys. So, she left all of them standing at the car and walked into their flat.

Eight-year-old Mack said, "But Dad, they started it. A comment about our 'pretty mother.' Or they get jealous because the girls are giggling about us or about Louis's wavy hair. Or because they

*said Michael beat-up on so and so which is ridiculous because..."
Frank said, "I thought I said I don't want to hear that same old
tune. I don't care who started it. You guys just want me to whoop
you!" He grabbed Robert, and said, "Robert, into the house now."
The boy said, "I ain't Robert, Pops, I'm Michael. Besides, I saw
what you did to those four guys in that barbershop on 12th Street
when they came around the corner to our house and messed with
Mom while you were at work. You went in there and cleaned
their clocks!" The boy then jerked free and ran into the front door
and out the back door. Bewildered, Frank looked around as all
the boys began to run into the flat. He said, "Where is Louis?"
Martha, standing in the doorway, laughed, and said, "It's your
fault. You had too many at once. Besides, they did see you bust
that place up last year. Those pimps never came back either, did
they?" Then she thought, "Guess those basement lessons we have
after school are paying off."*

. . . .

Robert had not seen Michael in two years, since the day of the draft
registration. He missed his other brothers, but he missed Michael
more. He had a bond with Michael and not having him near the last
two years was difficult. He also wanted to see the little-kids but did
not believe their seeing him would help with his privacy.

His apartment was in a quiet area away from student activity. He
could relax and sleep, something he really was looking forward to.
He wanted to clear his mind, to not focus on anything until classes
start in the fall. So, he slept and dreamed a lot. He dreamed a lot
about Michael.

He wondered why the army was not after Michael for dodging
the draft. So, he was forced to call his mother and ask her if Michael
had any mail from the army. She was happy to hear from him but
did not press him any further. She informed him there was plenty

of mail for Michael initially, but they stopped coming after January 1971. Robert assumed that Michael handled his own situation and therefore, dropped the matter.

.　.　.　.　.　.　.　.　.　.　.

In Mid-1970, the weekend after Robert McCants took his physical at Fort Wayne, an intruder entered the Fort's administrative building via an open second story window. He perused the facility until he found the results of the physical exams administered that week. He then replicated one of the documents, only changing the first name of the participant and the physical results from 1A to 4F. Then he returned the original document but placed the duplicate document in the 4F folder. He then exited the building the way he entered.

.　.　.　.　.　.　.　.　.　.　.

Busta was having another great year. Two years in a row. And the only thing he could contribute his success to was he had rid himself of Michael. His hatred for the boy was ceasing, now that Michael was run out-of-town. He was getting along with his boss, even though he knew Shapatilo had it out for him. He turned over collections on time and stayed away from Shapatilo's haven.

He thought, *"Dose fucken dagos hate my nigger ass and I feels da same way bout dem. If I ever feels da need I'm going ta prepare myself ta killing all of dem fuckers and jist suffa da consequences."* He still worked closely with Sergeant Sumanski, who he knew hated him as well.

"Sumanski hates Black but loves green! And as long as he do, I owns em, and he knows it. If he loses my money stream, he loses everythang! Fuckin Polock!"

Busta had been working out regularly since the race for Michael in the winter of '70-'71. Just jumping into the car was a hassle. He thought, *"By dat night I musta been up ta 285 pounds. Could barely git my fat ass behind da fuckin steering wheel. Fuckin Sumanski was even faster den me! Any running made my heart race sometin fierce! I turned forty dat yar, and thought I was goin ta have a heart attack."* So, he started playing tennis, stopped eating pork, and cut out the beer. Now he was down to a manageable 240 and could fit into his wardrobe. He thought, *"Unfortunately my wardrobe is ole, but I doesn't mind. I kin now buy new clothes foe a new body."* He did not want to buy the same old street clothes that all of the other Players were wearing. *"I likes da way dem NBA cats looks so I'll go dat route. I'll jest fashion myself offern da pictures I seez in da magazines dat feature NBA cats out partying. Especially dat New York Knick's guard 'what's-his-name'."*

He worked out at a popular gym on Woodward Avenue near Palmer Park, lifting weights. He also jogged the outer boundaries of Palmer Park, along Woodward, Seven Mile, and Hamilton Avenue, then back to Woodward. This route took him by Detroit's 12th Precinct. Sometimes, he ventured into the Palmer Woods community to see the pleasant homes of the Detroit rich or go into the private home area along the Detroit Golf Club. He enjoyed being in this area. Even though he was only three miles from his old home off Fenkell Avenue, it seemed a world away. A home he had to move from after the assault from the McCants.

When Busta got home his phone was ringing. He answered it and heard his boss's voice.

Shapatilo said, "I think I know where that nigger Michael is."

. . . .

Word there was a new hitter in town was starting to spread all around the Windy City. He came from Gary, Indiana. They discovered that the thief was scaling walls to get onto rooftops. He would cut into the roof with hand tools, then climb into the attics of houses, hide, and wait for the drop-offs. Once the money was counted and put away the thief would merely grab bags of cash off tables when no one was in the room, then climb back out of the attic onto the roof, then away. He never took all the money. Just enough so it might not be noticed immediately. No one ever saw him.

But he always left a note. "Tell them Michael was here." The technique had first been detected in Gary two years ago.

. . . .

"Boss," said Ray Ray, "That's old news. I've been hearing that rumor since '72. We ran Michael out of town that March night two years ago. He ain't never coming back. My boys even patrol around his mom's place once a month just to see if he reappears. Nothing. And I personally talk to the neighborhood cats. Nothing! The older son still walks home from U of D. The next boy is in the army. The next two are at Wayne. All of the other kids are still in public school. Nobody is talking about Michael. He's a done issue here in Detroit, I'm telling you. And someone is just messing with those dumbass niggers in Chicago. Maybe a copycat, or they're messing with they're boss' money."

Busta had heard it all and believed none of it. He believed there could not possibly be a copycat of Michael. All he knew was that hearing that name made his skin crawl. It also motivated him to become even more fit. He believed that his last act on earth was to kill Michael.

He said, "Ray Ray, git me in touch wit Chicago. Anyone who's connected. Wez gots ta talk."

He thought, "*What does da boss expect me ta do bout shit happenin'
in Chicago. Unless dis is a test. I'd betta at least come up wit a plan.*"

. . . .

Three months later, in the late summer of '73, Busta met with his boss.
He arrived before Shapatilo did, to ensure there would be no surprises.
He called the meeting so he should not have to be concerned, but he
had not trusted the man since the last bowling bag incident.

Shapatilo arrived at the club and they both walked into the
building. He unlocked the office and walked in, then Busta tried to
follow him, but his massive bodyguard bumped him and proceeded in
first. Busta did not truly appreciate just how big the man was until he
lost those forty-five pounds.

He thought, "*I don't knos how I thought I could handled dat mass
of being. Dat bump hurt! I don't care how ole he gittin. I'd betta start
carryin' my magnum.*"

Shapatilo said, "Okay Busta. It's your dime."

Busta looked at Shapatilo, then at the hulk, then back at Shapatilo.
Finally, Shapatilo said, "Okay Little Sammy. You can go now."

Busta thought, "*I's always wondered what dat big fucks name is. He's
Little Sammy. He must has been related ta dat dead guy. Da one Michael
killt. Maybe I should partner up wit Michael jest ta git rid of dis fucka.*"
The thought made him nauseous, so he suppressed it. Once the door
to the office was closed Busta said, "I has a plan ta stop da rip-offs in
Chicago. If it truly be Michael, den he won't be ables ta resist da bait."

Shapatilo was all ears.

. . . .

Robert was back in a groove. A day of classes, followed by a trip to the
library where he repeated all lectures from his notes. He was gaining

traction as a serious scholar. Every minute spent in class was reviewed. He would alternate between four hours of lecture and four hours of review. Once he got to his apartment, he rewrote his notes believing that writing something over again sealed it in his brain. He never felt he had a genius IQ, a remark he despised, but had heard all his life. He felt the label took away from the hard work he put in to succeed, as if his knowledge was naturally gifted to him.

It was now the holiday season and a shopping weekend. School would be out soon. As he walked home from the library, he ran into an old friend. It was Carol, someone he had not seen in over five years. Her afro was gone and was replaced with straightened long, flowing hair blowing in the cool wind and falling down her back. He believed she was still the most attractive woman in the world.

She said, "Robert? Oh my god, it's really you. Wow, you look great! What are you doing here? Sorry. Dumb question. So, you're studying here at Michigan. Great. Boy, I guess I just wasn't prepared to run into you again."

Robert said, "Hello, Miss Jennings. Or is it Bordeaux? It's nice to see you again. Hope everything is working out for you. Have a great day."

He smiled at her, then walked away as if she was not even there.

Carol said, "Robert. Perhaps we can catch up? Robert?" But he was gone—leaving the steam from her breath to blow away.

She said to herself, "Wow. I knew he was fine before, but now that he's grown, wow! I've never stammered before any guy. Oh, he just caught me off guard. No problem."

Robert walked to his car and drove to the mall. He did a little shopping, had dinner, then drove home. He thought, "*Glad I never spent my military earnings while away the last two years.*" Once he got home, he pulled out his books and spent the next four hours studying. He woke up with the light still on, walked into his bedroom, turned out the light and climbed into bed. He was asleep in minutes. At no time did Carol cross his mind. Instead, he dreamed of Michael.

. . . .

The black Trans Am pulled up near the meat packing district in Chicago. The driver parked in the shadows of a building, grabbed his bag, then closed the door, not bothering to lock it. He thought, *"I've got to stop using this car since it's been snowing regularly. Not the greatest traction on snowy roads."* He began running between buildings and crossing streets for approximately a mile, zigzagging from one block to another. His destination was a mile north and a half mile east, but he ran diagonally through the complex to avoid the main roads and passing cars. In the center of the complex was a four-story building. Most of the buildings were quiet. They were administrative buildings, and the staff was long gone. He climbed upon a three-story building then walked to the edge of the roof and looked down to a parking lot up the block. As he expected, there were several cars parked inside the lot. So now he waited.

Two hours later all the cars were gone. The lot was quiet, and the only sound was the distant traffic. He had an uneasy feeling. He thought, *"This seems a bit too easy. This is not the usual location for stashing large piles of cash, and there is minimal security. Just those two bozos walking the perimeter. Well, we shall see."*

He climbed down from the building, then crept over to the adjourning building near the asphalt parking lot. Then he reached into his bag for a set of shoes, which he switched into. These were custom sprinters track shoes, size ten. He did not want to get them wet in the one inch of snow. He placed his boots on the ground with the intention of retrieving them later. Then he pulled out a forty-foot rope and began ascending the wall of the building. He had surveyed this location three times during the last few months to ensure that it was a safe hit. Today was even quieter than the previous visits. This had his instincts on high alert.

When he got to the top of the building, he walked along the edge until he was above the shared catwalk. Then he lowered himself to the roof of the catwalk and walked across, avoiding the edge, since the catwalk's roof had a curvature for water runoff. When he got to the connecting building, he scaled the wall to the window above the catwalk and mounted the ledge. He took out a glass cutter and cut a small hole in the window then extended his hand into the opening to release the window latch. He then raised the window and was inside the warm interior. He was so focused on listening for sounds that he was unaware of the warmer temperature.

One floor up was the location of the cabinets with the coveted stash. He had walked through this building, delivering fake packages twice before during business hours, and knew the floor layout. He walked over to the stairs and climbed up one flight. He then walked up the hall to the room in question, reached for the doorknob, then froze. Something was off. Something was not right. He was not surprised to smell the presence of perfumes and colognes since the building had office workers. He did not, however, expect to experience this particular smell. This particular cologne. It reminded him of a ride in a '70 Caddie some years ago. A burgundy '70 Caddie. His brain began to scream, *"Busta's here! This is a trap!"*

He turned and sprinted back down the corridor as the large door opened. Bullets began to fly just as he turned the corner. He ran to the stairs, but instead of running down the stairs, he ran up one flight, then circled back up the corridor, running one floor above his pursuers. He always had three exit plans and an emergency G.O.O.D. plan, and this was the G.O.O.D. plan. "Get that mother fucker!" was the common comment he heard as he sprinted to the end of the corridor, around the corner, then up the next corridor.

Some of the men ran down the stairs. A few, however, having heard the door above them close, ran up the stairs to the next floor then into that corridor. By the time they had gotten to the corner of that floor, Michael was jumping down the northern stairs. He stopped at the second floor, fearing men would be on the ground outside. He climbed out of a second story window and walked the outer ledge, grasping the side of the building. He was right. Several men were now patrolling the grounds.

When he got to the end of the building, he waited for the men to leave, then jumped down to the ground. One man heard him and returned. Michael hugged the building until the man turned the corner, then grabbed the barrel of the man's gun, struck him in the jaw, rendering him unconscious, then tossed the gun away. The man fell to the ground. Two other men came running at the sound of the struggle. Michael grabbed the first one that turned the corner, twisted him around, then pushed him into his partner, knocking both of them down. He then jumped up high, and landed on the second guy's exposed knee, hyperextending his knee cap. He then spun around as he dropped to the ground, slamming an elbow onto the first guy's neck, knocking him unconscious. He then rolled over to his side and punched the screaming man in the temple, knocking him unconscious. Michael thought, *"Three down, 30,000 to go!"* and took off, maintaining the G.O.O.D. plan.

Busta was alarmed. "What da fuck happened? Why ain't dat fucker dead yet? How did he even git off da fucking floo, ya motha fuckas. Ya had em dead-on. How da fuck did he git away? I ain't chasin dat quick motha fucka. Ya dumb motha fuckas sons-za-bitches had betta not let em gits away!"

Lights came on all over the complex. Michael anticipated lights so he pulled a slingshot from his bag, with a handful of ball bearings. He knocked out light after light until the area near him was dark again. Then he moved on until he reached an open court. The lights were covered in this area so he could not disable them.

Shots were still being fired in his direction so he could not stay long in one location. He tried to cross the large lot but saw men running toward him in all directions. So, he had to alter his exit strategy. He ran straight toward a twelve-foot corner wall, hit the wall running, then with three quick steps against the two adjoining walls was able to grab the top. He hoisted himself onto the wall. The men tried to follow him, but none of them could scale the high walls. They ran along the wall, running in the direction Michael was moving. He arrived at the end of the wall, leaped onto a car hood outside the tall wrought iron fence just as the men arrived at the locked gate, trapping them inside. He jumped off the hood of the car as the men fired at him, then hurtled the car parked across the street. Bullets continued to fly.

He turned left and ran one hundred feet, saw more men running toward him from the other direction, so he scaled another fence along the sidewalk, putting himself back into the complex. He ran along the inside of the fence, with new pursuers now running along the outside. They occasionally fired at him, but he never gave them a still target so they were unable to hit him, especially running on slippery roads and sidewalks. When he got to the end of the lot he scaled the fence again, before the men reached the corner, and turned right. The men continued to fire at him as they reached the corner. Michael crossed yet another street, hit one car bumper, jumped up to a tree branch, then hoisted himself into the tree.

One of the men said, "That mother just jumped into that tree! Snow and all! Where the fuck did they find this guy?"

Michael jumped onto a higher branch then ran along the branch until it bent downward. Just as it was about to drop him, he somersaulted onto the top of the fence, then somersaulted onto the ground outside the fence, then took off again, running directly away from the men. The trapped men continued to fire upon him until they ran out of bullets, which was soon. Michael did not stop running until he reached his car. The 'Get Out Of Dodge' plan was now over. As he pulled away, he lamented the loss pair of boots.

The men slowly walked back to the building to report to Busta. One of the men said, "That fool runs like a gazelle!"

His partner said, "No, he don't. If gazelles ran like that, lions would have starved to death years ago."

. . . .

Busta called Shapatilo as scheduled. When he hung up the phone, he knew his career was over. He climbed into his '74 burgundy Cadillac, which he had parked out-of-sight in one of the garages on the lot. He was sweating uncontrollably and felt very uncomfortable. He reached into the glove box and pulled out a handkerchief and patted his brow. Then, as he sprayed on a little cologne he kept in the glove box, he thought, *Michael may have just signed my death warrant. Lord, I've all da times hates Chicago!*

CHAPTER FIFTEEN

Elder McCants

Three years later

Robert pulled up to the condo complex at dawn on a Saturday afternoon in July '76. He had recently completed his studies at the university and was about to embark on a new career. However, he was troubled about his past and needed to close one chapter before he moved on to the next. That chapter opened when he was just four years old with a visit from his grandparents.

. . . .

The car pulled up to the Eight Mile ground-level projects, home of the McCants. The middle-aged couple inside the car sat for a moment talking, before stepping away from the car and walking to the door of a unit. They knocked on the door, and a middle-aged woman answered. She said, "Hey sista and brotha, what can I do you for? Yaw Jehovah's Witness, ain't yaw?" The man looked at his wife, realizing his mistake, apologized to the woman for disturbing her day, then moved to the adjacent door, four feet away. He knocked on that door, and in a moment a pretty, young White woman answered. Only he knew she was not White. She just looked White. She was holding a child, about one year old. She shifted the boy in her arms and said, "May I help you?" However, she immediately knew who they were. They were her husband's parents. Her thoughts were, "God, he looks just like his son."

The gentleman introduced himself and his wife and accepted the invitation to enter. They now entered the forbidden home of their son, Frank McCants.

. . . .

Robert walked up to the door of the tan colored condo and politely knocked. A middle-aged Asian man answered.

The man said, "Nǐ hǎo, wǒ kěyǐ bāngzhù nǐ ma?" The man's daughter walked up behind him and said, "Please excuse my father. May we help you?"

Robert apologized for disturbing the family, then walked to the next condo. When he knocked, a senior version of his father answered the door.

The man took a long look at him and said, "Hello. You must be Robert. I have been expecting you for three years. Ever since you enrolled at Michigan. Please come in."

. . . .

The two women looked at each other but did not embrace. The younger woman was not nervous, but apprehensive. Her apartment was a total mess, with diapers hanging from the bathroom clothesline, toys spewed over the floor, and the sound of a toddler crying in the bedroom. The kitchen sink was full of dirty dishes with clean dishes and silverware standing in a dishrack. A small boy was sitting in a corner reading a book. A toddler came from the bedroom, runny nose and all, climbed up on the couch, and began playing with a toy gun. The eldest boy followed his younger brother and sat next to him on the couch, looking tentatively at his grandparents, whom he had never met before. He said, "Ma, someone left the bedroom window open."

The mother took the cowboy off the couch and asked the couple to have a seat. They politely declined. She assumed why. "Guess they don't want to get their clothes dirty," she thought. The gentleman pulled over a couple of kitchen chairs and asked his wife to sit. He joined her. The mother said, "As you've already figured out, I'm Martha, Frank's wife. He isn't here at the moment. He had to run an errand. This is Louis, the baby." She sat Louis on the couch next to Richard. "That's Robert in the corner with the book. He's four. Mack, the big fella sitting here, is five. And that's Richard with the toy gun. He just turned three." She looked around to see who she forgot but was suddenly caught off guard when the children's grandmother said, "My, they are so beautiful! My grandsons. I didn't know what to expect." Martha thought, "What the fuck does that mean?" but suppressed her feelings. Dr. McCants said, "I am sorry we did not call ahead but we did not have your phone number. I have waited six years for this moment, and Willamae insisted on coming since we were in town. As you know, we live in Ypsilanti and are rarely in town. Our youngest are now in high school, and they keep us fairly busy with sports and all." Martha thought, "Liar. You are always in Flint or Pontiac visiting your other sons. Hell, I know you are on your way to visit Horace's home!!" She smiled, however, and said, "We appreciate the thought."

.   .   .   .

Robert crossed the threshold into a new world. A world filled with African art and artifacts. A collage of drums and masks and statuettes. These were mixed with nineteenth century pictures of northern Blacks in fine suits and dresses. A picture of a man standing next to Frederick Douglas. He walked to the living room and at the elder's invitation began to settle onto the sofa.

Then he stood back up and said, "Hello Grandfather. It's a pleasure meeting you again. It's been twenty years. I was only four the last time we met."

The man looked somewhat startled for a brief moment, then remembered. "The boy in the corner reading a book. That was you, Robert, wasn't it?"

After an awkward pause, Dr. McCants said, "Robert, I have been keeping up with you since you arrived in town. This is a small community, Ann Arbor and Ypsilanti. The academic community between the two universities has a culture all its own. Anytime a McCants arrives on either campus I am informed. This includes your Brooklyn cousins as well. They are not McCants, but they are my nieces and nephews. Plenty of your cousins have come through here. Several are studying at U of M right now, so you've probably encountered them without knowing it.

"You must be in your final year of study. You have picked a fine field to get your doctorate in. As you may know, history was my field of study. It will be a pleasure to share my experiences with you. Especially with all the news coming out of the Motherland."

His grandfather noticed his last comment was somewhat perplexing to Robert. He thought, "*Obviously, he does not keep up with current events.*"

As Robert listened, he thought that this was not the introduction that he was expecting. This is not how he remembered it twenty years ago.

. . . .

Robert found the chatter in the living room disturbing, so he took his book and went into his bedroom. Martha noticed him leaving but was too preoccupied with her guest and the other children. She put Louis, who had climbed back into her arms, back on the couch near Richard and said, "May I prepare you some tea or coffee? It will only take a moment." Willamae declined, thanking her for the offer. Mr. McCants ignored the offer and said, "The boys look healthy. As you know, we had seven. Boys that is. You are more than halfway there." Martha chuckled then said, "Perhaps, but this is it for me. It's more than I ever imagined and more than I can handle. I grew up in a home with plenty of children but plenty of help as well." Willamae seized on this opportunity to ask, "So dear, tell us about yourself. Where are your folks from? I can sense a bit of West Virginia." Martha took offense to the remark. She thought, "This racist uppity bitch. My god, if only she wasn't my mother-in-law. I've met plenty of upper-class Negroes just like her. If anyone has roots from Virginia, it's her." She defiantly replied, "No ma'am. I was born and raised in New York City. My mother may have some Virginia roots, but not West Virginia. I was enrolled in Michigan State when I met your son."

. . . .

Robert replied, "No sir, I have already achieved my doctorate in history. I have also earned full tenure at the university. I don't quite understand how that happened, since I have yet to prove my worth."

Dr. McCants just stared at his grandson but did not react to the remark. He thought, "*The boy will find out in time.*"

"Sir, I'm going to get right to the point. Let's not pretend there isn't major friction between you and my father. I am told I can be direct, so I might as well be so now. I am finished with my studies. I am only here to close out an open chapter in my life. It opened twenty years ago when you visited my family for the first and only time. I don't count the time at the Mound Road projects, since you merely drove by but didn't get out of the car. You pulled up, looked around, then left your grandsons bewildered that you wouldn't visit." Mr. McCants started to interrupt, then realized he had better let the young man finish.

Robert continued, "This is my story. I finished high school two weeks after my sixteenth birthday. I finished college three years later, a mistake I will never forgive myself for. I was so focused on my race to the finish line that I didn't realize it might destroy me. I found myself a year later, halfway around the world, shooting at people who look more like me than you do."

Robert paused, knowing he had gone too far. "I don't mean that literally. But they were poor and oppressed and I was helping maintain that oppression. I shot men and boys over there."

Robert was getting more and more animated as he spoke. "The army said I killed a lot of enemy soldiers, but I don't believe them. I don't believe I killed anyone, but they have tried to convince me otherwise. They sent me to Germany to convalesce, but I know I was there for observation. It wasn't the first time. Since my return, I have regained my focus and completed my studies. Now I am ready to use that education. But it's a strange feeling knowing I have no more studies to perform. They don't have a level beyond the PhD!"

Dr. McCants realized his grandson was losing it, so he intervened. "Son, try and relax. I am aware of your level of sensitivity. I know more about you than you realize. You and your brother Michael. Just hold still for a moment and catch your breath."

The room remained quiet for a while then Robert said, "How do you know Michael?"

. . . .

Frank arrived home just as his parents were leaving. He hugged his mother, and they talked as his father walked to the car. The grandfather did not expect to find a grandson sitting behind the steering wheel.

"Hello young man. I thought you were busy in your room reading a book?"

The boy said, "Naw, that was my baby brother. My twin Robert. I'm Michael. We are always confusing people. I was born twenty minutes before Robert, which is why I'm the oldest. It really irritates him to know that I'm the oldest. Sometimes we fight over that mere fact. I usually win, however, you could never get him to acknowledge that."

Dr. McCants was shocked at the child's vocabulary and directness. The entire time, the young child looked directly into his eyes, as if they were peers.

He thought, "He's only four, but he talks as if he were much older. And he's aggressive, unlike his twin."

He said, "How did you get out here? I didn't see you leave the apartment."

Michael said, "I've been climbing out of that window since I was two. How else am I going to see the world? My dad gets upset, but what's a fellow to do? I'm ready for school but they won't enroll me. By the way, you are my father's father? You look a lot like him, only older."

Mr. McCants was enchanted by this little boy. He said, "Yes, Frank is my second son. I have seven sons. Some of my boys are also married and have children just like you."

Michael said, "Not just like me. They are dark, like my Pops. But I guess they do look like me. I've met Uncle Horace's boys plenty of times. Uncle Herb's sons are still just babies. Horace's sons and my brothers play, but of course, I also fight! I like to fight, which gets me in trouble. Robert only wants to read. Or talk to Mom, which he does a lot. I can read his mind, so I don't need to read books or talk to Mom much. Anyway, are you coming back soon? You should bring your pretty wife back as well. I can tell she doesn't like my mother, but I don't care. My mother doesn't like her either. She's torn between you, however, since you look so much like Pops."

Dr. McCants could not believe his ears. He thought, "What a precocious little boy. His IQ must be off the charts. I must get to know him better." Just then Frank came out of the house, knowing one of his boys was missing. He saw his father talking to someone inside the car and knew where to find the missing child. As he approached them, he heard his father say, "We must visit more often, my boy," and knew he had a problem he could not fix cordially.

He said, "Father, I see you've found Michael. Son, please climb down and go back into the house."

Michael looked at his father, then climbed down, walked over to the open window, jumped up, and grabbed the windowsill, then pulled himself up to a seated position. He looked directly at his grandfather and said, "It was my pleasure Grandfather," then backflipped into the room.

. . . .

Dr. McCants said, "You remember the first time we met at your government home on Eight Mile? You didn't come out when I met your twin, Michael. He was sitting in my car. I still don't know how he climbed up through that window. Anyway, we had a long conversation, almost man-to-man! You and your brother are obviously gifted. You display your gift via academia. He demonstrated his socially. I regret not following up on my promise to him. To visit more often.

"If we are being direct, then let's be direct. You are still suffering from your war experience. Yes, I have read your military discharge summary and your progress reports here at U of M. I know you were in Nam. If you are going to work in the field of teaching, you must resolve that issue. As far as our issues, I believe we have got to resolve them as well. You and I have lost a lot of time together. Let's not allow the past to continue to separate us.

"I am the eldest son of my parents. My family is huge. I have hundreds of cousins. My father had eleven brothers and four sisters. I have two brothers and a sister but am not allowed to visit any of them. My grandfather did not approve of my marriage to Willamae, your grandmother. She and I met on this very campus. My father was disappointed that Michigan did not accept my application. Then he found out that I didn't even apply. I met your grandmother while driving around this school in my father's Studebaker. I found out she was planning to attend Eastern, so I never submitted my application to Michigan, only here at Eastern.

"Willamae comes from a long line of Abolitionists. They are a proud people that loved their African heritage. Her people had run away from Virginia before the Civil War and her great grandfather joined a group of abolitionists in Detroit back in the 1850s. I thought that was a worthy heritage, but my father and grandfather were still upset that I was seeing her. I suspect my great-grandfather set a standard that they religiously followed. They had already arranged a marriage for me, which did not sit well with me. So, I ignored their request and married your grandmother. They immediately disowned me, and for years I was not even allowed to visit. I had to change my surname to your grandmothers, which initially was very painful. I became Joseph McCants.

"I had seven sons, but even they were ostracized. I suspect my great-grandmother or grandmother had something to do with the all-male outcome. Even my boys can only have sons. When the war ended in '45 the tension between my family and me began to relax. Even so I still can only call my parents, not my siblings or cousins, if I need family help. They have, however, allowed my eldest son Horace to be the primary contact with the family." Then he thought, *"I suspect he's done so on occasion with that Busta fellow."*

Robert heard his grandfather, but felt his experience only made his treatment of his son Frank even worse. He said, "I am just now hearing this. My father never talks about it, perhaps because he doesn't know the entire truth. But don't think I don't know about your family. I know plenty about them but am just now making the connection. They were famous in Detroit long before you were born. There is plenty of information in the archives at the city's Burton Library. You're a historian so you must know this.

"The details of your disenfranchisement, of course, are not recorded in history. But you just repeated it with my father. You even kept his brothers from him for the first five years of his marriage! And for that I cannot forgive you. My father struggled needlessly. He would never accept your help if it did not come with love. And that you and Grandmother could not give. I won't place all the blame on you. Some of it truly lies with Grandmother and her family. Her abolitionist roots. Yes, I've studied them as well."

· · · · · · · · · · · ·

Frank did not mince words. "Father, I am glad you finally came to visit. I now know I must get a phone, so I can communicate better with my family. I heard your comment about visiting my boy. That's not going to happen. You show my wife no respect, which shocks me since you were treated the same way by your family. I would have thought that would have taught you not to repeat that same bigotry, but obviously it didn't. I am glad you had time to stop by here on your way to Pontiac. Yes, I know where you're heading. Horace told me he was expecting you."

Mrs. McCants was approaching Frank from the rear, so he lowered his voice. "Father, please do not come back until you can embrace Martha the way you embrace Horace's wife." He turned to his mother and said, "I love both of you and miss you terribly. Please visit more often," then walked away, leaving his parents standing at their car.

. . . .

"Grandfather, I am glad you invited me into your home. It was a pleasure seeing you again. However, I need to know you can love my mother as you do me. As you do your other daughters-in-law. She is a beautiful woman, and my father loves her so much. My mother is as Black as your other son's wives. If you look deep enough into her family tree you will find Africa, just as you have in yours. The fact that her skin tone is near white does not change that. Sure, she created a pool of light brown babies. But don't you have enough Black grandsons, like my brother Ervin?

"My brother Mack is exceptional. Having him as a big brother was like having two fathers in the house, which was needed at times. He is now a computer programmer analyst and a proud dad. Richard has finished college and Louis will be finished next year. All three of my younger brothers are in high school. My father and mother did this without any help. They raised their boys in a rough inner-city and we ruled the day! We stayed out of jail. Michael took a 'walk on the wild side', but he will eventually come around. Like one of our teachers once said, he may have reached adulthood way too soon. We did not meet our mother's people either, so not having the two of you around was hard, but we had our parents to lean on. And your sons, my uncles, were very loving."

Robert looked over his grandfather's shoulder, then said, "Please offer Grandmother my greetings and apologize for my intrusion. I should have called ahead. Goodbye." Robert stood up and walked out of the door without looking back. He got into his car and drove away, his mind now focused elsewhere.

Dr. McCants sat on the couch for a while pondering the meeting. He was deeply regretful that he allowed time to pass without ending this estrangement. It took his grandchild to make him aware of his failure.

Then his wife came from the kitchen, having heard the entire conversation, and said, "Why did you allow that boy to talk to you that way? He needs to find himself a *Bible* and fix his ways. He needs to find Jesus."

He looked at her, frowned, shook his head, and walked out of the condo.

CHAPTER SIXTEEN

Chicago

Late Summer '76

Michael pulled his car into a long winding driveway at 12:45 a.m. and turned out his lights. From this vantage point the residents of the home would not be able to see his vehicle. He waited an additional fifteen minutes, then exited the car and walked in the shadows of the home in Chicago's famous North Shore Drive. The home was situated among similar million-dollar homes with plenty of diamonds and pearls. Hidden safes with cash and bearer bonds. He entered the home through a patio door.

The golden retriever was nervous at his presence, but he calmed the dog with a treat then cuffed his ears. After an hour of rummaging through the house, he opened the refrigerator and pulled out some sandwich meat and milk and made himself a snack, making just enough noise to arouse the occupant. He sat in the living room, at the base of the winding stairwell. As he expected, a senior woman, about sixty years old, eventually appeared, somewhat apprehensive. She looked around the room, hesitant to come down, and was about to walk back to her room when Michael dropped a spoon onto the floor. He then switched his position from the stairs to the back of the room. Now she was hooked.

"Who's in my living room?" She wondered.

Strangely enough she was not afraid. Not with a loaded Smith and Wesson in her left hand. She kept the gun out of sight and started down the stairs. The room was dark except for the moonlight, and she preferred it that way. If she was going to confront an intruder, it was best that she did not disturb her vision with bright lights.

Michael could clearly see the woman as she walked by the window. He thought, *"The sun has not been her friend. Even with cosmetic surgery."* Finally, she reached the end of the couch, sensing a presence in a corner chair.

She said, "Young man, I am armed, and I don't have a problem using this. If you want money, there is some in the armoire to your right." She walked to the center of the room to get away from the furniture, then stopped. She did not want to be knocked over or bump into anything.

She said, "Okay, you obviously didn't come here just for valuables. What can I do for you?" At no time did her heart rate or blood pressure rise. She was as calm as she was while sleeping.

Michael slowly rose from the chair, aware of the lady's left hand. He slowly stepped forward into the moonlight and said, "Hello Grandmother. Nice to finally meet you."

. . . .

Robert was finally finished with his education and could begin working. He was awarded a PhD in History from the University of

Michigan and was granted a position to teach. At twenty-four, he would be one of the youngest professors at the university. He thought, *"Considering the two years in the service this was not bad. I think it's time, however, I stopped planning my future and started living my life."* He had an apartment near the western campus of the school and occasionally drove back to Detroit to visit his family. Very occasionally.

Mack was now married with a child, which Robert still had not met. Richard was working for Detroit Edison after getting his degree from Wayne State. Louis would be starting grad school in the fall and had just started working for Michigan Bell. The younger crew were in Cooley High.

Martha's work in cosmetics was successful, providing her with the spending money she needed. She did not have to ask Frank for any money, and she even contributed to the bills. He had bought her a used car, so she was now mobile. She had even considered enrolling in the local community college, Wayne County Community. Her sons told her to just come on over to Wayne.

At forty-five, both Martha and Frank had maintained their health. The drama of the late 60s was over.

. . . .

"Martha, its time you moved out on your own. You are now sixteen. My mom put me out when I was sixteen. I have not seen her since. And I was pregnant. Living on the streets of Harlem, pregnant, ain't easy."

Martha knew why her mother wanted her gone. It was the money her dad's mom had given her. And that White man she had just met.

Martha said, "Ma, you can't pass for White. You just can't! He's going to find out eventually. Besides, you know how grandma feels about us trying to pass."

Her mother responded, "She's your grandma, not mine. I am no longer tied to that old bitch. I would encourage you to do the same. Here is an envelope she gave to me for you. And here is a grand and a bus ticket to Detroit. We may never see each other again."

Martha opened the envelope. Inside was a picture of her grandmother and Martha as a baby. There was a note attached. It read, "You can write to your sisters. I would encourage you to do so. But you get one phone call request from me and one only. Use it wisely." A phone number was included with the note.

A month later she met Frank.

. . . .

Michael said, "You were put out of your mother's house when you were sixteen and you put my mother out at sixteen. So, my mother never met your mother. What was she, a quadroon from West Virginia? I can hear West Virginia in your voice. And your father was some white dude, right? Anyway, my mother's White-looking paternal grandmother helped to raise her but rarely touched her. I suspect, like you, she only looked White. I gather that from the one photo I've seen. You knew her, didn't you? She was pretty mean looking. No wonder my mother was never very maternal to her sons."

Betty was now sitting at the dining room table. She had placed the gun in a drawer and retrieved a cigarette and was enjoying the drag from it. She was so relaxed that her body language went from upper class Chicago to street Harlem.

She said, "You know when I first got here, I was pronouncing the city's name Chi-car-go. My husband had to correct me more than once. I suspect he was confused how a rich New York high society woman could have so many common habits and ways. I had to learn quickly what to do and what not to do. By the time I met his parents I was the perfect parrot.

"When I first arrived, these rich Whites were standoffish towards me. But they still treated me better than those uppity Negros in those Harlem brownstones. No matter how I behaved or dressed, they knew my story. Nope, I couldn't fool them. They knew I was Black, just not one of them! I couldn't even go to their churches, even though I could pass the 'brown-paper-bag' test!

"My husband wanted children, but I couldn't take the chance that one of them might come out looking like you. Besides, he didn't know I had a teenaged daughter. And, who wants to have kids after they've already raised one?" Michael smiled earnestly. There was no reason to take offense and he doubted she meant to be offensive. She was just low-class pretending otherwise.

"You are a really handsome young man. How many of you are there? How many kids did my Martha have?"

Michael said, "You really don't know? You didn't attempt to keep an eye on your little girl? The only child you would ever have?"

Betty grew a little angry and said, "Why would I? She was the apple of her father's eye! He treated me like shit, but he loved his Martha! In fact, he treated all the mothers that way. But he loved his brew of babies."

Michael looked surprised. Betty enjoyed the shocked look on his face.

She said, "You really don't know, do you? Martha doesn't talk about her father?"

Michael decided to change the subject. He did not want to hear about his mother's past through this miserable woman.

He said, "To answer your question, Mom had seven pregnancies and eight children, all boys. I'm a twin. My name is Michael and my twin's name is Robert. He's a professor at the U of M's history department. I'm just a thief."

Betty did not flinch. She said, "How many look like you? I mean, did any of them come out looking like me?"

Michael smiled and said, "Sorry grandma, but no. They are all about my complexion, except the baby. Ervin is Pops complexion. Pops looks like a handsome Sidney Poitier, right off the banana boat. He's educated through high school. His father is a professor at Eastern Michigan. And like you, he does not approve of us either. So, I have uppity-nigger grandparents on both sides! Ha!"

Betty took offense at being called the N-word. The 'uppity' part she embraced. Try as she might, she could not resist asking, "Did you bring any pictures?"

· · · · · · · · · · · · · ·

Mack dated Linda until they both graduated in 1973, then they got married. It was a large ceremony with family and friends from the neighborhood and the school. His mother's special guests were the nice Irish old ladies, the O'Learys, who lived across the street. She often would say, "I just love their accent!"

Eventually, he got a job with a major bank in downtown Detroit as a computer programmer analyst and she worked as a personnel rep at Blue Cross, Blue Shield. She got pregnant a year later and they had a son.

She asked, "Mack, can you get the baby? I'm in the shower." He had already fetched the boy, since he loved holding him. The baby soon settled down. He called his son little Frank, and she reminded him that, "The boy will never learn his name if you keep calling him that." So, he called the boy 'Mumbutu' or 'Shaka Zulu' or 'my African warrior'. She would just shake her head.

Linda said, "How's your brother doing?" Mack said, "Which one, baby? I have a team of brothers."

She said, "Robert, of course. The one everyone is so concerned about. The one we never see. He still has not visited since the baby was born."

Mack said, "Give him time. I know it's been three years, but he's still adjusting to being back from the army. He was stationed in Germany, but he probably had to encounter plenty of soldiers coming back from Nam. It had to have had a negative effect on him. I don't know what job he has in Ann Arbor, but if it keeps him happy…"

Linda knew her next question was a dangerous one. "Your younger brothers talk about Michael, but that seems to be a taboo topic." Mack cut her off and said, "Yes, you're right. It's a taboo topic."

. . . .

Michael had noticed the deteriorating condition of the house over the weeks he surveyed it. The interior was in the same poor condition. It required maintenance, both inside and out. That implied that the man of the house was no longer around.

She noticed him looking around the room and said, "Yeah, kind of rough, I know. Look Mike. My husband died before his parents kicked-the-bucket. So, his inheritance, which he'd been counting on, never happened. We were living off his earnings. Obviously, we went a little too far 'keeping up with the Joneses'. I'm now living off his pension and social security. Any and all repairs are cost prohibited. The last time I got an estimate the prick said I needed forty-grand. Then there's the taxes. So, I'll be selling the house soon and hope I can walk away with enough to support myself. Sure can't go back into the line of work I had thirty years ago! Ha!"

He smiled and said, "Too bad you can't invite your nigger grandsons to visit. They could fix this place up in a week." She merely frowned at the thought, then decided, *"Perhaps that wouldn't be a bad idea."*

. . . .

Frank looked over at his wife. She had a strange look on her face. She seemed troubled. He said, "What's wrong, Baby? You look like you've realized after all these years that you don't love me anymore."

Her glazed eyes came back into focus, and she said, "Shiiiiitttttt! No way my nigga! No way. You're stuck with me until the end of time. I was just trying to reach out to the boys. My grandma used to do that. I never learned how, but I keep on trying."

Frank said, "Well, you can relax. All of them are fine. I know they are."

She smiled to disguise her feelings. She could not help but believe that it had been too quiet, too peaceful. She thought, *"Something must be brewing. As long as Busta is alive, we are not safe. I should have told Frank to just kill that sucker after Louis graduated. Then we would be safe. But then Frank would never be the same. He doesn't have it in him to destroy a life without cause. Shit, give me the knife. Give me the gun. That mother fucker would be dead in minutes."*

. . . .

Michael said, "Grandma, why would you want to stay in this old mansion? Why not move to a smaller but manageable home? Why not sell this monstrosity and move to Florida? Live in your beach house. They've got plenty of White folks in Florida."

She smiled at him, knowing he was trying to get her goat, or maybe he was truly trying to help. She said, "I would love to move to Florida. Yes, we have a beach house there, but I'm behind in the taxes in both homes. But you're right. If I sell this house, I could move down there and save face! Or I could move into one of those retirement complexes. But I can't sell this house without having the maintenance completed. I would never want his family and friends to find out just how bad off this house is. Those folks live near the Florida home too. I would never live it down. No sir-ree. I have to fix this sucker first. And stop calling me Grandma!"

He said, "As long as you never call me Mike again." They both laugh.

Then she got serious. She said, "Michael. How did you get in here? This house may be falling apart, but it's still secure. How did I not know you were here? Why didn't my boy bark at you? What are you, Michael?"

Michael knew she peeked his ace, so he came forth and said, "Grandmother, I'm the best B and E man you have ever seen. I've been good at it my whole life. My twin is a better student than I was and now he's a professor. I used to use his knowledge to take tests in school. Blew my teacher's minds that I aced all my test, even though I was rarely in class! Don't get me wrong. When I apply myself, I succeed as well. But that wasn't for me. I like to steal. But I only steal from bad guys. Never the common man. I have never broken into anyone's home and stole from them. Not ever. Just dope dealers, pimps, and the like. I'm so good at it that I had to leave Detroit. There's a contract out on me there and now Chicago is getting too hot for me as well. But don't worry, not that you are. Nobody can catch me. I run like the wind. Hurricane winds!"

. . . .

Richard and Louis were still only dating. Louis had gone through all the eligible girls in the neighborhood, so now he only dated girls from the campus or his new job. The woman of his dreams looks nothing like his mother. He reflected on that and realized that none of the girls his brothers date resembled their mother. It had never occurred to him, especially since all his life he watched men drool over her. He, however, could not help but notice that all his father's brothers married women with plenty of melanin. All his cousins are darker than he and his brothers. Noticeably darker. Ervin looks just like them, not that he and the rest of his brothers don't. Just not as much color. He heard his uncle talking about dark women once. Something about chocolate. Licking chocolate. He did not truly understand what he meant until he dated a very dark girl. "*Oh My God*!" he thought. He has been hooked on dark girls ever since.

Richard was unaware of Louis's preference for dark skin. It just seemed natural to him to date brown girls. No real rationale. It seemed to him that the majority of lighter girls in the community went to Immaculata on West Outer Drive, so there was a larger pool of brown cuties to pick from at Cooley. Richard considered his father's choice. He doubted if her skin color was a factor in his father's attraction to her. She was just damn beautiful. He never thought about his mother's light skin unless someone else was making a big deal about it. Then one day he had a revelation.

"Grandpa punished Pops because he married a light skinned girl! Oh my God! It never crossed my mind. That racist bastard! No wonder he never comes into our house or treats mom cordially. That elitist" …then he stopped his thoughts. He could be way off base. It would be better to just drop the issue for now.

.   .   .   .

Betty said, "So does your mother still live in Detroit or did she move back to New York?"

Michael knew his grandmother was picking his brain. He responded, "If my mother wanted you to know of her whereabouts, she would have told you. I'm kind of old to fall for that, Grandma. You don't need to know her married name or how she's doing. I'll just say she's doing fine."

His grandmother responded, "That's fair. I deserve that."

The room got quiet for a while then Michael said, "I've been here for an hour before you detected someone had intruded. I reviewed your finances. You haven't been paying attention to them, have you?"

Unexpectedly, she began to cry. The tough Harlem chick was long gone and had been for quite a while. She was now just a kept woman, even if she did not want to admit it.

She said, "Roger, that was his name, Roger Hornsby, did everything for the household. He never shared anything with me. I didn't even know how to write out a check until recently. I never knew where the money was or where it went. Now I find out that we're bankrupt. That's why the son-of-a-bitch shot himself! My in-laws are of no help. They never liked me or my West Virginia ways. I tried hard to project New York, but I guess some of my old habits began to surface. Mom moved us to New York to get away from the Sticks of West Virginia, where they knew she was Black. My father was a White official in the town, and I began to look like his White daughters. She tried to pass in New York, but it was so obvious to most, that she failed. I met your grandpa at fifteen and got pregnant immediately. So, my mom put me out. Had Martha in '31. I didn't even finish ninth grade. Now I'm back where I started and am at my wits end!"

Michael boldly said, "Do you think your husband's family ever figured out you were a Black woman passing for White? Do you ever think that is why they treat you so?"

She ignored his question and continued, "Anyway, how did you find me? I've never written Martha, so does she know where I am?"

Michael replied, "Granny, I have known your address since I was four years old, so of course she knows. Mom wrote a letter to her 'sister mom' back in '52. She asked her to please reach out to the family to find you. The most recent letter had your address on it. I've had it memorized since then. By the time she got the information, however, I guess she had recovered from her trauma of abandonment. I've always wondered what a 'sister mom' was and after meeting you I don't want to know."

Betty ignored the obvious insult and said, "Boy, how did you find her letter? She was always taught to keep her private stuff out of reach of the world. No one is supposed to know her very personal stuff. I just know she didn't leave no letters laying around. How did you get to see a letter written years earlier?"

Michael paused, then said, "Mother, on rare occasions, would go into her room, close the door, and pull out a secret box she had hidden in the back of her closet. I know because I always wanted to see why she sometimes closed her door. So, one day I hid in her closet. She came into the room, closed the door, and opened the closet door. I thought I was busted, but she didn't see me! I held my breath until she reached in and grabbed a box buried at the bottom of the closet. After what seemed like forever, she put the box back. Later, when she was outside hanging clothes on the line, I went into her closet and got the box. There were her letters to New York, which were returned, and the ones sent to her. I assume the returned letters were addressed to you. There was also a slip of paper with a number on it. That evening I snuck and dialed that number, and it rang seven times, then someone picked it up.

"The person on the other end said, 'Michael, what ya doin messin wit yo mama's stuff, boy. Ya put dat stuff back and neber touch it a'gain!' and hung up. I peed my pants and have never gone into her closet again."

His grandmother laughed and said, "Damn boy, that was a good imitation of that old witch! Do you want to know who that person was?'

"All information pertaining to my family will come from my mother. I am not here to be educated."

There was a short moment of awkward silence, then Michael said, "Also old lady. I'm not here to rob you. I just wanted to see the monster who hurt my mom. But my anger is gone, since I see how life has treated you. My mother is very happy. She has a very loving husband who would walk heaven and earth for her. My dad is a warrior, and he turned his sons into warriors. I'm going to leave you now. I hope you find a way to get out of the predicament you're in. Good-bye."

Michael stood, walked out of the living room, down the hall, through the foyer, and out the door, not bothering to lock it. At no time did he look back.

. . . .

The following month the Widow Hornsby received a letter from the Palm Beach County tax auditing department. She opened the letter, knowing it was going to say that they were going to place her home up for auction for non-payment of taxes. She already had several threatening letters just like this one. Instead, this letter read, "Dear Mrs. Hornsby. We have received the payment for your taxes, in full, including the current taxes due. Thank you for your attention to this matter." All she could do was cry.

The next month the Widow Hornsby received a letter from the Cook County Tax Department. She held her breath hoping for a miracle. It worked, since the letter stated, "Dear Mrs. Hornsby. We have received, paid in full, your tax payments for the years 1972-1975. Your property tax account is now current." She began to cry once more.

The following week a work crew knocked on her door. When she answered the door the foreman of the crew said, "Ma'am. We have been paid to make any necessary repairs to your home, interior and exterior. We have also been offered a bonus if we finish in two weeks. So, if you're in agreement, then let's get this show on the road." The widow Hornsby stood there staring at this big White man. He just smiled as she began to cry.

The day after the repairs a realtor visited Mrs. Hornsby, inquiring if she wanted to sell any of her properties. The realtor made her an offer she could not refuse.

CHAPTER SEVENTEEN

Colonel McGregor

In 1978 Colonel Austin McGregor met Mack at a restaurant in Detroit's downtown business district. He was in town from Chicago, where he was a sales rep for a software company. Mack was on the National Bank of Detroit review team. Their colleagues had gathered for drinks after a long sales pitch made by McGregor's firm to Mack's employer.

McGregor walked directly across Woodward Avenue from the bank in downtown Detroit and entered Nichols restaurant. He immediately saw Mack sitting alone at a table and approached him.

He said, "Hello Mack. I'm Austin McGregor. We just completed the presentation with you and your team. Are you going to join the group or are you waiting for someone?" He paused as if he wanted to sit for a moment.

Mack smiled and said, "Yes, I'm waiting for my wife. She works nearby and will be getting off at 6:00. We have a babysitter tonight, so we need to take advantage of this opportunity. And yes, please sit."

McGregor sat across from Mack and casually said, "That was a good interrogation you gave our sales reps. You understand the software world pretty well. Your company obviously holds you in high regard. And you're so young. I normally don't see guys in their twenties given this level of responsibility."

Mack smiled and responded, "Thank you. I've been here for five years now. This is my first job out of college. My major was Computer Science, so this assignment was a perfect fit for me."

McGregor asked, "So what school did you attend? Where did you get your degree?"

"I attended the University of Detroit. It's a small campus in the northwest part of the city."

McGregor briefly paused, then continued, "So you've got a common Irish name, as do I. Can I assume… nope, never assume, right?"

Mack got a little serious and said, "The name comes from my paternal grandmother. My grandfather's elitist family did not approve of their marriage and refused to allow him to continue to use their name. Grandmother had a slave heritage, so the name comes from an enslaver from the nineteenth century. Like so many of us Black folks."

McGregor said, "Of course. I didn't mean to imply anything more, since so many African Americans have Irish names.

"I was stationed in Vietnam in '71 and worked with a second lieutenant named McCants. That's why I asked. He was also from Detroit and spoke highly of the city. That is, when he spoke, which was rarely. McCants was a very quiet fellow. I thought maybe you might be related to him because you look an awful lot like him. That's probably why you may have noticed me staring at you during the meeting. Even your voices have a similar pitch. His name was Robert."

Mack replied, "Well, yes, I do have a brother named Robert and he was in the army, but no way was he an officer. He didn't finish school, and he was stationed in Germany. Hell, if they'd sent him to Nam my mom would have freaked."

McGregor replied, "Well, then we're talking about two different fellas. Perhaps a cousin. Anyway, he was a hell of a soldier. I would follow him into battle any time. Listen, don't mean to bend your ear all evening. We'll see each other tomorrow, I'm sure. Have a good evening."

McGregor rose and walked away. He now knew Mack was indeed Robert's brother. McGregor thought, *"Mack doesn't know a lot about his brother's recent past, if he thinks he was stationed in Germany. And the dropout comment? He's lying or completely confused about his brother. Robert had a degree."*

· · · · · · · · · · · · · ·

McGregor's need to find Robert's family was important to him. He felt eternally grateful for the sacrifice Lieutenant McCants made to save his platoon. He hated that it resulted in McCants being sent back to Germany for more psychological evaluations.

Weeks earlier McGregor was contacted by a man named Smith who served under him in '73. Smith asked if they could meet for coffee, so McGregor, sensing that Smith was struggling, accepted the invitation. They met in a coffee shop on Dearborn Avenue. He was right. Smith was fighting an addiction he got overseas.

> *"Sir… it's so nice to see you sir. I'm glad things are going well for you. As you can see, I'm struggling a bit, but … That's not why I asked you to meet me. Sir, I saw the Lieutenant yesterday. Lieutenant Robert McCants.*
>
> *"Colonel, I will never forget McCants. Never. Hell man, he saved my life. He saved all our lives. We would have been overrun by the Gooks if he had not sacrificed himself for us. The fact that*

he survived was a miracle. But look what it cost him. I heard he was sent back to Germany in a straight-jacket." McGregor was daydreaming now and just ignored the last remark. His mind drifted away for a moment until he heard 'robbing dope house'. He stopped Smith and said, "You saw him robbing a dope house?"

Smith said, "I was standing right on the corner when he ran by me, bag in hand. Boy, can he fly. I yelled out, 'Lieutenant!' but he just kept going. Then I yelled, "Robert' and he slowed down for a moment, glanced back at me, then took off. I know it was him. Later, when the commotion died down, the lieutenant returned! He just walked up the street like nobody's business, walked straight up to me and said, 'Why did you call me Robert?' I was dumbstruck and could not talk. His walk was different, and his facial expression was more expressive. Not serious like the Lieutenant used to be. Then these guys came out of the dope house checking the street, so he pulled his collar up, glanced again at me, then walked away. That's why I called you, Colonel. There's a contract out on him. They are calling him Michael. Apparently, he's wanted by dudes in Detroit as well."

. . . .

After the final work session the next day, McGregor and his crew wrapped up their presentation equipment and prepared for the drive to the airport. McGregor wanted to say goodbye to McCants, but he knew he had to be careful with another request to speak about the lieutenant.

McGregor approached Mack as he was about to leave the conference room and said, "McCants. It was a pleasure to work with you. I am sorry, but I believe I need to continue our discussion from last evening. There are too many coincidences to leave the topic unfinished. My Robert is about a year younger than you. He is your height and almost your weight and has your wavy textured hair. Mack, there is no way my Robert is not related to you. I am very concerned with Lieutenant McCants. He left the army under stressful circumstances, and I need to know he's alright. If he's truly gotten himself in trouble in Chicago, then I owe it to him to help. He's now calling himself 'Michael'."

Mack grabbed McGregor's arm so hard it hurt.

He said, "What did you say? Michael? He called himself Michael?" McGregor had to pull his arm free.

He said, "So you do know him. Listen. We've got to talk. I will cancel my flight and return on a later one. But we must talk tonight. I only came on this trip because I saw your name on the agenda. I can fill you in on things I believe you don't know about your brother. Good things, but some troubling things as well. Will you meet with me?"

. . . .

Mack exited the phone booth after calling home and informing Linda that he would be late that evening. Then he sat across from McGregor, in the Caucus Club restaurant in the Penobscot building, the tallest building in the city until the Renaissance Center was completed.

McGregor said, "Okay Mack, I'm going to get straight to the point. You seem to prefer that method.

"My Robert McCants was twenty-one years old when he left the service in March '73. He went to Cass Technical High School, a fact that was highlighted in his report. He started college at sixteen and finished at nineteen, in only three years. He got his degree from Wayne State University. He is an extremely focused man, so much so that he makes some people nervous. I know all of this because I made it a point to research him after he was sent to Japan by our commanders.

"He had a lot of brothers, I don't remember the number, but he had no sisters, which was easy to remember. He finished at the top of all his training classes, which does not surprise me. How am I doing?"

Mack said, "Go on. Continue."

McGregor looked intently at Mack and said, "No, it's your turn. Where am I mistaken. Because if I am, then I'll stop wasting your time."

Mack sat for a while then said, "My brother Robert dropped out of school in the fall of '65 and essentially disappeared. He would show up here and there. He was extremely depressed, a condition which was not surprising to my parents. I won't get into the particulars there. He started working at Wayne State when he was sixteen, which matches your Robert. So, what he was doing from thirteen to sixteen could have been attending Cass. That would make more sense, than my thinking he was just hanging out. They did move him up an entire year during his eighth year, so he could have been in high school when I started in January '66. I know he went into the service in March '71, after being drafted. He had draft number twenty-seven so there was no getting around the military. They kept moving him around from one post to another, then back again, so we assumed he was not doing well."

McGregor interrupted Mack, "No sir, that meant he was doing extremely well. Robert excelled in everything, so they sent him to Officers School. Then to Germany… I don't know what that was about…Then to Nam as a Second Lieutenant. He was a hero in Nam. He saved his entire section."

Mack said, "Robert lives in Ann Arbor, so no one could possibly see him in Chicago. Whenever I call him, he answers his phone! I check up on him weekly. My wife insisted on it! My mom has even visited him there rather recently. So, no way he could be living in Chicago. I just assumed he was working in the Ann Arbor area. Now you're telling me he already has a degree from Wayne! Then perhaps he is attending school at Michigan? I spoke to him a couple of days ago. He's coming to visit the family next week."

McGregor said, "Okay. I'll grant you that. Perhaps he couldn't be in Chicago. This makes me feel more relaxed. But there's more…"

McGregor went on to discuss the mission in Vietnam when McCants' section was trapped. After an hour, Mack had a full understanding of the heroics McGregor's Robert performed. Then McGregor said something rather disturbing.

"The lieutenant insisted that I order our helicopters to fly back to help the wounded Cong soldiers. That was not our M.O. and highly unlikely, considering the number of enemy combatants, and the location. The next day a flight was made over the site, but there were no injured or dead soldiers there. The Cong do not leave their injured or dead behind.

"Later our two Vietnamese Sergeants presented a report to me. They had internal connections to the village grapevine about the Cong. They heard that a very significant amount of Cong soldiers was killed in action on the very day and location where McCants' section was trapped. A lot of the dead were from a village nearby and the mourning in the village was traumatic. The sergeants were on that mission with the lieutenant, so they recognized the site description.

"Mack, our men were ordered to cease fire to prevent the Cong from determining the section's size. Besides, the Cong were under cover, so our boys had nothing to shoot at. Robert was the only one in a position to shoot and he waited until all his men were evacuated before he started firing. They must have charged his position, exposing themselves to him. Robert was a dead shot! The report stated that McCants employed three M-16s. It was a remarkable firefight! Sergeant Brooks said they could hear his reports and distinguish them from the Cong's AKs. The volley of shots rang out for minutes, possibly over a thousand rounds! The sound must have been horrendous!"

Mack noticed McGregor getting a little too excited so he interrupted him and said, "You would have me believe one man killed an entire enemy force alone? This is nonsense. Only John Wayne can do that."

McGregor said, "Yeah, and Audie Murphy, which is what they were calling Robert. The Black Audie Murphy!"

The two men got quiet for a while. Then McGregor said, "The trouble started for Robert when word began circulating that all the Viet Cong soldiers were dead. He began hearing the rumors and approached me about them, insisting he had not killed anyone. He insisted he only shot them in the legs. I had seen men suffering from the stress of battle before, and Robert was rapidly advancing toward a breakdown, so I contacted the health authorities, and they ordered Robert shipped out immediately. He had a second head wound and a busted hand. We had already planned to send him to Japan anyway to get some R and R. Only he did not return from Japan.

"He was my lieutenant, and I was responsible for him. After previous missions, when he'd returned with wounded prisoners, I saw that the reports on him were real. That he only wanted to wound, not kill. I should have kept him behind so I could determine his mental fitness. Someone with Robert's views and beliefs about killing should be further examined after their first encounter. I knew his final mission could result in a major firefight, but I sent him out anyway. And I errored in not including him in the final briefing with his first lieutenant. So, you see, I owe him and need to follow through with this new report of his potential plight.

"The official writeup was that his head injury was serious enough for him to require hospitalization. But that was just a cover for the real reason he was leaving. No one wanted to ruin his record with an implication of mental disorder. As he walked to the plane he became a blank slate, only staring straight ahead. I'd seen it before. Nothing existed for him as he walked toward the plane. He had gone inside of himself, and no one could tell when he'd surface again.

"War destroys minds. Especially gifted minds like Robert's. What we saw and did over there should have destroyed all of us. The ones who came back normal after committing atrocities are the real people you should fear. According to the Vietnamese sergeants, Robert killed over seventy-five men in minutes. Not with a bomb, either. He single-handedly killed young men, who were trying to kill him and his men, for a ten to fifteen-minute period. He walked away from it in a trance. His heart told him to wound the enemy. But his brain knew that was not rational. He saw one of his men killed right in front of him. That had to have an effect on him. He saw a private almost get his head shot off, and his commanding officer receive multiple chest wounds, along with two other men suffering gunshot wounds. And he knew that his entire section could easily be overrun if he did not stop the Cong. If they were not held back, the section would not have been able to evacuate. Even the copters would have been exposed.

"While he was back in Germany, he was sedated because he kept having nightmares and was calling for his brother Michael. Mack, do you have a brother named Michael? It took weeks of sedation to calm him down. He was hospitalized in Germany for six weeks, then sent home with highly commendable recommendations. They covered up his time in the psych ward, listing it as recovery from head injuries. Only the top brass was given the official report. And no report implied that he killed any enemy combatants, only wounded them. So, the only medal he got was for holding the enemy back so the men could be evacuated. That is on his record. Besides, there was no proof that he killed anyone. He was never presented with any medals, but they are on file. Injured during battle, valor, bravery… all that super stuff.

"I am a West Point man, so I am the U.S. Army. The U.S. Army recognized when he was in officer training that there may be issues with Robert, which is why he was initially sent to Germany in the first place. In the end, however, their initial psych assessment of him was right. He should never have been sent to Nam. He was a weapon of mass destruction, and we almost destroyed his mind."

Mack could only stare straight ahead. McGregor checked his watch, stood and said, "Mack, I suspect there is a part of the story that you're holding back from me. Elements that occurred long before Robert went into the army. Anyway, it was a pleasure meeting you. Now please go find your brother." They said their goodbyes and McGregor caught a cab to the airport.

Mack just sat in the restaurant after McGregor left. He could not help but wonder, "*What has Robert really been doing all these years? He must have been at Cass when I thought he was roaming the streets. And that business about working at Wayne? Yeah, right. He was pursuing a degree! These last five years in Ann Arbor are going to prove to be a big surprise.*

"*I'm not going to bother him with this visit from McGregor until I see him next week. I know he's not in Chicago and that's all that matters. But this Chicago, Michael business? Michael hasn't been seen in years. Well, I'll just wait to talk to Robert next week.*"

. . . .

Robert McCants arrived on the Michigan campus early Monday morning, before other instructors and students. The campus was quiet, and it gave him the time and space to prepare for his last lectures. He only had commitments for Monday then he would relax the rest of the week and head back to Detroit this coming weekend to visit his family. They were expecting him. He had already contacted Mack to let him know of his plans.

He also wanted to find a way to contact Michael. He could not help thinking about his twin. He half expected him to walk up to him as he used to do in Detroit. Just out of the blue.

Yes, he needed to see his brother after so many years of separation.

. . . .

Michael was wary of the hyperactivity required to hit the bad guys and run. He was getting too old for that lifestyle. The look in his grandmother's eyes when he told her his occupation was telling. His brothers were all settled down. Jack was graduating from Cooley High this year. He had missed all of the graduations since Louis' in January '70. It was time for him to go home and settle down. The years are starting to fly by. Running the streets was getting old. He also could not get that guy who mistook him for Robert off his mind. What if that happened again. What if someone mistook Robert for him. Poor Robert would be defenseless. But he knew he could not settle down, nor would Robert be safe, as long as Busta lived.

There was a ransom out for him. It was old, but that still would not stop men from considering challenging him. He still carried a side-arm, but ever since he shot Sammy the Pincer, all those years ago, he had dreaded shooting anyone else. He always shot over guy's head, so he did not know why he shot Sammy. Except he instinctively knew Sammy was going to kill him.

Fortunately for Michael, his reputation proceeded him. Most men feared him, after hearing just how quickly he killed a made-man like Sammy. One day, however, someone will try him. *"Yep,"* he thought, *"its time to go home. Leave Gary and Chicago. Seven years is long enough. I need to find and eliminate all my issues. That is the only way I'm going to find peace."*

He considered just how he would do that. He thought, *"Every time I drive to Gary, I can't help but notice the Indiana Highway Patrol cars hawking me. Have even had to outrun them a couple of times."* Outrunning them, was getting harder and harder. He was constantly changing cars because of the police. So, I-94 east was out of the question. *'I could try Milwaukee and the ferry boat across Lake Michigan to Muskegon. But once I'm on that boat I'm trapped, with no escape. The odds are probably ten to one in my favor of not being noticed, but I need better odds than that."*

He decided to drive all the way to Green Bay, then across to the upper peninsula of Michigan to the Mackinac bridge, then south on I-75. He thought, *"Man, what a long trip. It would take over sixteen non-stop hours, instead of four hours. But at least if I use that route no one would be tracking me."*

. . . .

Robert drove a leisurely 65 mph eastbound on I-94, dropping his speed to 55 mph once he entered Detroit. He was eager to see his parents and brothers. His dreams about his brother were still bothering him, but he pushed the thoughts away. He was just happy to be going back home. As he approached the northbound Lodge entrance, he noticed a large luxury car was preventing him from moving over to the left lane, so he started to slow down to allow it to pass him. The car behind him, however, did not slow down and the luxury car did. He was boxed in and missed his exit. So, he tried to get over to the exit at Woodward Avenue but was unable to. Another large car had him boxed in as well. He thought, *"This is no coincidence. They have me trapped in this lane."* He accelerated to get in front of the car to his right, to no avail. After he passed the I-75 exit, the car to his left began moving into his lane, forcing him to the right, which was now free.

He thought, "*They are trying to force me off the freeway. Probably here at Mt. Elliot.*" Just as he got to the Mt. Elliot Street exit, the large car on his left crashed into his front bumper and he was knocked into the exit lane. The lead car continued down the freeway. Now, he knew he was in trouble. He drove off the freeway but then did the unexpected. He slammed on his brakes, causing the trailing car to collide into his rear bumper. Then he jumped from the car and ran up the ramp and across the surface drive, blocking the car from exiting the freeway. The two men in the car jumped out of their vehicle and gave chase up the ramp.

They were turning the corner of the first building on Mt. Elliot when one of the men suddenly became airborne. Robert clothe-lined the man with so much force, he flipped over and landed backward on his face. Robert crouched down and knocked him out with a jaw-breaking blow. The other man suddenly stopped and came running back at Robert, but he punched the man in the chest, knocking him off his feet and onto his backside. Robert then spun himself around the man and punched him in the back of the head. It was only then that he noticed the two men were White.

He thought, "*What the hell is going on? I thought these would be Busta's men, but they clearly are not.*" He looked up and saw two more men climbing from the freeway, so he grabbed the unconscious men's guns and ran toward East Grand Boulevard, hiding behind parked cars. While the two men checked on their friends, Robert jumped into a nearby phone booth and called Mack. He told Mack he was being pursued by mobsters and would run into the deserted Packard plant.

There were some entrepreneurs trying to make a go of the empty plant, but for the most part it was deserted. One of the workers, however, noticed him running by and began yelling at him, which alerted the pursuers. Soon the place was covered with men and cars. Robert was truly trapped.

. . . .

Shapatilo received a call from Grosse Pointe. "Shapatilo, what year is it?" He sighed and responded, "Boss, It's 1978. What's up, Boss?" The boss said, "And what year did my cousin Sammy get killed in Greektown?" Shapatilo said, "I don't remember, Boss. 1970?" The boss said, "No. It was 1969! I remember because he was going to celebrate his 50th the next week. He was born in 1919, so…That would mean that his 50th birthday would be in 1969! Capeesh! Now, how many freakin' years ago was 1969? Come on, tell me, how many years ago was 1969?! Tell me ya schmuck!" Shapatilo said, "Nine years ago boss. Almost nine years ago." The boss then said, "So that means that MICHAEL is nine years older ain't he! Sammy ain't going on fifty-nine, is he? But MICHAEL has aged another nine years. And do you know why? Because you ain't killed that nigger yet! I'm getting old. My mother is getting ancient. Her nephew has been dead for nine freaken years. We want that fucker dead before the year is out, do you understand me? Cover the city until you find his black ass. I want him dead!" Click.

CHAPTER EIGHTEEN

Standoff at the Packard

Mack called the house to talk to his father about the Packard situation. Jack, sensing an urgency to the ring tone, answered the phone. After Mack explained Robert's predicament, Jack said, "I've got this. I'll call everyone after I talk to Pops." Instead of informing his father, however, he called his older brother Louis to pick him up, then called Richard to meet them at the Packard. Ervin and Horace were waiting with Jack when Louis arrived on Santa Rosa to pick him up.

He did not inform their father because he did not want his father involved in another situation with gangsters. He knew his father had no limits when it came to them. He believed he needed to shield his father from this one. Besides, his father would undoubtedly get the rest of the family involved. To Jack, the night at the Hamtramck nightclub was a mistake.

He thought, "*Dad still thinks it's the 40s. Him running around with his brothers Herbert and Horace, kicking ass and taking names. Well, those days are gone. All the 'brothers' are old men now. Hell, my youngest uncle is twenty years older than me! Pops is forty-six years old, and Uncle Horace is forty-nine! We don't need to get any of our uncles or cousins killed over our mess. They've got families and careers. None of them are gangsters, even though they try to act like they can be."*

Mack was surprised and very annoyed when Jack arrived at the plant with both Horace and Ervin, and not their father.

He said, "What are you doing here? And why did you bring these kids? What did Pops say?"

Jack, now eighteen years old, said, "I didn't tell Dad. He doesn't need to be caught up in this mess, damnit! And the three of us are not little-kids anymore. I heard about what you did at Busta's place when you were only eighteen. Knocked out all three lookouts. Well, how old am I right now? And the three of us are now bigger than all of you! Hell, you've got a wife and kid at home. Shit, I heard she's pregnant again, Mr. Computer Programmer!"

Mack was now furious. He glared at Jack for not following his instructions. He got back in his car and drove to a payphone, where he called his father again. Ervin and Horace, understanding Mack's concern, pulled Jack aside.

Ervin said, "We should be calling Michael. He'd get this shit straightened out really quickly. You know what he did to that fellow in Greektown."

Horace frowned and said, "Well, do you have his number? I sure don't."

Jack just looked up at the sky, threw his arms up in exasperation, and walked away.

·　·　·　·　·　·　·　·　·　·　·　·

Frank was in his bedroom with the door closed. Martha knew not to enter when he was on the phone in the bedroom with the door closed. She, however, always knew trouble was brewing when he made calls from their room. The calls always involved his brothers. So, she eavesdropped via the bathroom heat vent and heard the entire conversation. She was completely unprepared for the news.

Frank said, "Horace, I just got a call from my oldest boy. Robert has gotten himself in trouble. I'm sure it has to do with Michael. It's with those Sicilians down near Greektown, or Grosse Pointe or wherever they hang out. They got my son trapped at the old Packard plant on the Boulevard. I'm sure Busta has a hand in this too, but I'll find out when I get there. Mack and the boys are there right now, but it's only the six of them. I need you, brother. I need the entire clan. And I don't intend on calling Dad. Get back to me as soon as you can."

Horace replied, "Understood. I will call you back in ten minutes," and hung up the phone.

Frank exited the room, found Martha looking worried at the dining room table, but ignored her and ran into the basement. She walked into the bedroom and closed the door. He knew not to enter the room when she closed the door.

· · · · · · · · · · ·

Martha was beside herself with worry. She heard Frank talking about Robert's situation and understood the dire nature he was facing. She went into her closet, pulled out an old leather case, and opened it with a key taped to the side of the case. Inside were mementoes of her youth. Pictures of her father and mother. Pictures of her siblings. And a picture of a woman holding a newborn. The young looking forty-eight-year-old woman did not look very happy to be there, but still sat for the picture. It was her grandmother holding her as an infant.

She continued to rifle through the papers until she found the little black book. It was a phone book, with numerous phone numbers of her extended family members. It had been quite a while since she needed it. She had numbers memorized of the siblings she called regularly. Martha, however, was only interested in one number and had never called it. She was told many years ago that she had only one opportunity to use that number, and she had been saving for the right moment. This had to be that moment. She confirmed the door was still closed and dialed the number. The line was answered on the seventh ring.

The voice on the line said, "I knews ya be callin soon. Wha ya wont baby-girl?"

Martha answered in a child-like voice, "Grandma? I need your help."

· · · · · · · · · · · · ·

Robert had been trapped on the top floor of the old Packard warehouse on East Grand Boulevard and Mt. Elliot Street for two hours. He knew his brothers were on the perimeter, but they could not get to him, due to the large number of Shapatilo's men. He could not get a message to them. If he could, he would tell them to leave. He had tried to escape through various sides of the complex, but each side was being patrolled by suits. They had such control of the area that the large crowd was only able to stand a block away. He was more likely to escape this trap alone once it got dark, but he did not want any of his brothers in the background. Every time he raised his head a shot buzzed by him. He chose not to shoot any of the suits, just keep them at bay. A hat here and there, but no bodily injuries.

Mack had been attempting to talk to Shapatilo for quite a while. So, when the gangster walked by him, he said, "Look man, I keep telling you; That's my brother Robert. You said you were looking for Michael. He ain't here! Robert is a student at Michigan, do you hear me! And he was a marksman in Nam. If he wanted to, he could kill all these guys, but he doesn't like violence. But if he decides to defend himself your guys are in big trouble. Your guys are all dead."

Shapatilo ignored him and was just short of sending his boys to grab all the McCants. Mack understood this and he had no intention of trying to fight this mob. Twenty-five against six are terrible odds. Especially when they are armed. The police were there merely for crowd control. They allowed Shapatilo and his men to run the show.

Suddenly an off-white '72 Ford Country Squire station wagon pulled up and Martha jumped out. A police sergeant tried to stop her from entering, but she ran passed him. He did not want to tackle a White woman, who may be related to Shapatilo, so he let her enter. She walked passed Mack, to his utter surprise, and approached Shapatilo, leaning in close to him to give him a slip of paper. He was surprised that this short White woman was allowed in by the police but accepted the paper. After he read it his face ashened, and he walked to his car and made a phone call. When he returned, he summoned all his men and ordered them to leave. The police, baffled by his actions, left soon afterwards and the crowd began to disperse.

After his men were gone, Shapatilo walked over to Martha and spoke quietly to her. He was still wondering who she was and assumed she was somehow connected. Only later would he find out she was Michael's mother.

He said, "I am very sorry we have inconvenienced you ma'am. We won't be bothering you or your family again." He then walked to his car and drove away. Martha looked at her sons for a brief moment, then roughly said, "Get your brother out of there and get your black ass' home!" She took one last look toward the top floor of the structure, then hurriedly walked to her car and drove home.

A confused Mack looked at Richard and Louis and said, "What in the hell just happened? Mom shows up and the mobster drops the siege?"

Louis asked, "What could she have promised him? What did she do?!"

Mack said, "She didn't do anything. She just gave him a piece of paper. That's all! The punk ass went to his car, then came back and called it off! Then the MF apologized to her! What is going on?"

Jack said, "Wait until Pops finds out about this! He's going to freak! Thank goodness. The last thing we need is fifty-odd McCants out here."

Louis said, "Mom talking to a gangster! What could she possibly have said to him?"

Mack said, "I told you she didn't say shit! She just gave him a small piece of paper."

Richard said, "Man, Pops is going to really go ballistic when he hears this. Getting Mom involved in our shit! Again!"

Mack ran into the plant and called out to his brother. Robert was shocked to see all the suits leaving.

He said, "What's going on? Why are they leaving? And did I see Pops pull up in the wagon? What the hell is going on? Pops didn't get his family involved, did he?"

Mack just looked at him and said, "Calm down. Let's wait until we get home. Give me your car keys. Ervin can drive it home. We can discuss everything later. I suspect none of us are going to believe it. And when we get in the car, you're going to tell me what's really going on in Ann Arbor."

Twenty minutes later the family was back on Santa Rosa.

· · · · · · · · · · · · ·

Frank was beside himself. He had made several calls to his brothers and was getting his gun from the basement locker when he heard his car pull away. He ran upstairs just in time to see Martha turn the corner.

"Where in the hell is she going? She knows not to leave here without telling me. She knows I need that car. Shoot! This is not the time for her to try and get involved with these damn boys!"

Forty minutes after Martha left the house, Frank's brother Horace pulled up into the driveway with two of his sons, followed minutes later by Martha in Frank's squire. She blared her horn at Horace, and he knew to get back in his car and get out of her driveway. She pulled up into the driveway, as Frank walked down the porch steps. The neighbor who shared the driveway knew not to complain. Martha left the vehicle at the driveway entrance, knowing someone would move it later. She looked rattled, but okay. At forty-six she was still youthful in her movements, but Frank saw age in her face for the first time.

He thought, *"Where in the hell did she go? Hell! That boy is going to be the death of her."*

She walked toward him, placed her palm on his chest, looked him deep in the eyes for a brief moment, then walked up the steps and into the house, just as Horace was parking his car on the street. Frank ignored his brother's presence and followed Martha inside. Mack and Robert parked on the street and headed for the front door. Horace instinctively knew to stay outside. Mack and Robert should have followed their uncle's instinct.

Frank was livid. His dark face was shining from the sweat pouring from his brow.

"Where the heck have you been? I KNOW you didn't go to that plant without me! I KNOW you didn't leave me here alone and go to those boys!" Mack started to speak but Frank gave him that 'Frank-glare', so Mack grabbed Robert and went back outside.

Frank continued, "Please tell me you didn't get yourself involved! Please tell me you didn't take my role away from me. Those boys are MY responsibility, not yours. We both raised them, not just you. Tell me you didn't go to those gangsters and beg them for mercy! I've got my entire family ready to go to war with them and now…. What do I say to Horace out there! What do I say to my warrior clan! My six brothers. Their seven sons. Now what, baby, now what?

"I thought we went through this before? I thought we discussed this when Busta came here? You said you understood but do you really? This is very dangerous stuff that must be handled in a certain way, or someone could get hurt. With you in the middle of it!"

The other brothers pulled up over the next few minutes. Richard and Louis were together. Jack and Horace were in Louis' car. Ervin pulled up in Robert's car, which had been towed off the freeway ramp onto the surface drive. They parked along the street, intermixed with the neighbor's cars. The boys heard their father and stayed out on the sidewalk. All except Horace, almost seventeen years old, who ran right in and walked up to his startled father so quickly he bumped Frank backwards.

He said, "Stop yelling at mom! Don't yell at my mom! She saved Robert! And don't blame this on Michael! He wasn't even there! This is that man Busta's fault. You should have handled him long ago. You had your chance so you should have taken that man out! He wants your son dead and you're standing here, with your so-called militia, doing nothing. Pops, this ain't no rumble! Your rumble days are over long ago. This is war! Give me a gun and I'll go kill Busta's ass!"

He ran into the kitchen and grab a butcher knife and came back out, "I'll get that Busta!"

His mother grabbed her huge son, awkwardly hugged him, and said, "Okay son. Okay. Your dad and I've got this. He wasn't yelling at me. He was just upset. Just like you. Calm down."

Frank said, "Okay Horace. You're right. It's Busta's fault. Now put the knife down. You'll need more than that. He's a lot of beef!" He looked at his son and started laughing.

Martha glared at him, but he continued to laugh, as his eyes teared up. He was proud of his son's rage, but also realized that one of his boys was finally bigger than him.

Mack, hearing his father laughing, finally entered the house, followed by Robert. Mack indicated to the others to stay out, so they joined their uncle Horace and cousins.

Martha walked up to Frank, placed her small hand on his left cheek, and said, "Tell them it's handled," and walked into her bedroom, closing the door behind her. Her son Horace was no longer hysterical and began to cry. Frank stood there staring at Horace, no longer laughing. Then he looked at Mack, avoiding Robert as best he could.

He said, "Mack, what just happened? Tell me son, what did your mother do?"

Mack said, "Daddy, I really don't know. One moment this White dude and his men were ready to assault the factory, then mama pulled up in her white stallion! She didn't even say anything to the guy! She just handed him a piece of paper. He read it, walked to his car, made a phone call, then returned, calling off his men. I have absolutely no understanding of what happened. Mom is just a miracle worker, that's all I can say. She seems to always pull a rabbit out of her hat when we get in trouble, and she did it again."

Robert spoke up, "Pops, you may not realize it, but mom has a family too. Maybe she's Italian and we just don't know it."

Frank said, "Shut up boy! Don't you think I know my wife? She's Black, just like me. Her mother and father were Black and so she's Black. End of story. Now, what are you going to do about this mess. It ain't over. I'm done with this 'Michael' drama. What are YOU going to do about MICHAEL! You're going to let Michael get you and your brothers killed!"

.   .   .   .

Robert would spend the night on Santa Rosa, even with all the tension in the house. It was now awkward sleeping in his old twin-sized bed, after using a regular bed in Ann Arbor, but he did not mind. This was not unlike the beds in the military, so it did not take long for him to adjust and he almost fell asleep. Except there was tapping on the back door. He got up to answer it and was not surprised to see Michael looking in on him through the windowpane. He opened the door and let him in. They spoke in hushed tones. Tones that only Jack would hear.

Michael said, "Seems as though you've had a rough day. I'm really sorry you're getting caught-up in my mess. I was worried this might happen and I am working on ending this shit once and for all. Give me some time. I've got plans in the works. Just give me some time." Robert knew he did not need to reply. Michael reached out and merely touched Robert on the shoulder, even though they had not seen each other for many years. He then walked back out of the door, dropped from the top railing to the ground, and was gone in seconds.

.   .   .   .

Martha, in a pleading voice, said, "Granny, I need your help. My son Robert is in trouble with the local Mafia. They think he killed a made-man."

Her grandmother said, "I's toad ya nots to call me dat. I's ain't nobodees granny. I's no yo issue and will takes care bouts it. Day doesn't think Robert killt da man. Day think Michael did em in. Youse needs ta take care bout Michael. I's got Robert. Memba, dis yo onliest call," and hung up.

. . . .

A mob boss in New York, having a conference with his son Rudolfo, answered his phone. He said, "Ciao. What's cookin?" The response was, "Looken fo Lastanza, dats whats cooken. Ringo gives me dis numba long time back if I needs somin handled. Is ya dat man?"

Lastanza had never met the person on the other line, but he instinctively knew who she was. He thought, "Oh!... My!... God!... Jesus! I thought Ringo's old bitch was dead! Last time I saw her was at his funeral back in '62." He stammered, "Ma'am, how can I be of service to you? It will be my pleasure to provide you with any assistance possible." Rudolfo had never seen his father react that way because of a mere phone call.

The voice replied, "I's gots a probem in Da-troi. needs ya to fixes it fo me. And I's aint dead yet." Five minutes later, Lastanza was on the phone to Grosse Pointe, Michigan.

. . . .

A mob boss in Grosse Pointe received a call from Shapatilo. The boss shouts into the phone, "I don't give a fuck what situation you're in now, just get your fuckin ass out of wherever you are and back to your den. You gots me!!! I don't want to get anymore freakin' phone calls from New York on account of you! And I'd advise you to apologize to that lady," He then slammed down the receiver.

. . . .

A middle-aged woman heard her grandmother on the phone. It was very unlike her to answer the phone, but when she did, it was always for her. The woman waited a few minutes then entered the lounge. Her grandmother was just hanging up. She said, "Grandmother, was that call for me or you?" Her Grandmother replied, "Now ya nos I's don't take ta taken no calls unless day fo me. And no, ya caint kno who called neitha. I's sho she be tellen ya herself soon nough." The middle-aged woman paused, then boldly asked her grandmother another question. "Grandmother, have you been experiencing any trepidation lately." Her response was, "As large as dis family is, I's all da time feelin tripdation. Only at 95, I's too ole to do much bouts it. And if ya must kno, yo big sistas used up her onliest call tonite. Had allsredi fixed one hern problems. Nigga from Harlem headen her way. Fixt him up good, woodn ya knos it. Ha! Dat was fun! An by da wai. One yern sista's boys gots da 'glow', gotsdamit! Whoda no. Not my 'glow' but my fuckn pappi's 'glow'! Neber seen nuttin lik it! Somehow it just slip thru. Wish I'd seen it earlier, when I was a youngin, I betcha."

. . . .

The following Monday morning, Martha awoke and got the boys off to school. She then took a long hot bath and returned to her room to dress. She found a note on her pillow.

The note read, "Check your secret stash." She dressed quickly, frightened that someone was in the house while she was in the tub, then checked her closet. Everything was intact.

She said aloud, "No one knows about this box." She lifted the box and examined its contents.

She thought, *"Everything seems to be as I left it."* She tried to put it back, only to find that it did not quite fit as before. So, she pulled some items out of the closet and found a medium sized box beneath shoeboxes. She opened the box and found ten bundles of $10,000 each, and a note, with several accounting pages attached. She read the note, then placed the box back in the corner with the note and pages.

She further pondered, "*Who knows about my 'secret stash'?*"

. . . .

A ghost moved along the shadows of the pristine lawns on the shores of Lake Saint Clair in Grosse Pointe. The phantom entered a dining room window, left open to take advantage of the lake breeze. The light security of the home had drifted off hours ago. The figure walked up the flight of winding stairs to the master bedroom, where he found an elderly man sleeping soundly. He returned downstairs and entered the kitchen, moved a chair into the corner, then sat and waited. At 3:00 a.m. the old man walked downstairs into the kitchen. He opened the refrigerator, removed a plate of cold cuts, then started to close the door. The light from the refrigerator, however, illuminated the figure in the corner, causing the elder to drop the plate.

He stammered, "What the...," then heard, "Relax. If I wanted you dead...you know the rest of it. That's a nice white silk bedspread you have. Please have a seat. And it wouldn't pay for you to do anything rash."

Castanza grabbed a chair, pulled it from the table, and sat down. "Okay," he said, "what do you want? Are my boys outside okay? And if they are, they fuckin' won't be in the mornin'."

The guest said, "Sir, I'll get to the point. You have a stooge within your midst. Feeding information to Busta. He believed you were going to send Sammy to kill him. That's why Sammy was taken out. The kid who fingered Michael was lying. He worked for Busta. How do you think the shooter got away? There was a car waiting for him a block away. Shit, they circled the block to see Sammy's body. They drove right by your boys."

Castanza was stunned. He thought, "*We didn't have a hit out on Busta. Sammy wasn't going to hit Busta. Who started that rumor? I must have a rat in my house. And how does this guy know so much, unless he was there. Unless someone has a big mouth.*"

The shadow continued. "Ask yourself who had a reason to kill Sammy? What grudge could Sammy and an eighteen-year-old teenager have. Michael was just a kid ripping off dope houses. Let me say this. What do you do to dopers who sell in your community? Yeah, right. Well, that's what Michael was doing. You are Sicilian and won't put up with that shit. Michael is Black and won't put up with that shit either. Capeesh? You don't have junkies standing on your corners. Breaking into your homes. You are responsible for the degradation of Michael's community, so don't be surprised that he was fighting back. But his target was Busta. He wouldn't even know who Sammy was."

The mysterious shadow disappeared without the old man realizing it. He was so engrossed in the thought of Busta killing Sammy that he did not notice he was now alone. He did, however, notice the small but thick binder laying right in front of him on the kitchen counter.

. . . .

Castanza was getting ready for bed when his phone rang. He answered it, then listened to a profane Italian screamer from 600 miles away. He eventually hung up the phone then made a call to a number in Detroit, a number given to him in Italian. The phone was answered on the first ring. He said, "Hello, ma'am. I understand you are experiencing a problem which I am here to resolve. I'm going to give you a phone number. I want you to give this number to a Mr. Shapatilo. You will find him with your son, Robert. Do not say anything to him, just give him the slip of paper with this number. He will recognize it. And I am extremely sorry your day was ruined. It will never happen again. Have a good evening." He then hung up the phone.

CHAPTER NINETEEN

Busta's Revenge

Last week of May 1978

Shapatilo was fuming. It was 6:00 a.m. and he could not sleep, so he called Little Sammy to meet him at the club. His boss, Castanza, in a fury, had ordered him to find and kill Michael. Yet, when he had Michael corralled, Castanza had called off the assault.

He grabbed his clothes, left the bedroom so he would not disturb his wife, then said to himself, "I'm so confused! What the fuck just happened?

"The old prick has been ordering me to kill Michael for nearly a decade, then when I had him cornered, he calls off the hit! I had my whole crew out there! The whole fuckin' crew for Christ sake! We'd been patrolling those highways for weeks! Maybe the boss knows something I don't know. Maybe Michael didn't kill Sammy. Actually, I don't give a fuck who killed Sammy. He wasn't related to me. Truth be told, I hated the big fucker. He thought he was untouchable, invincible.

Ha! Three bullets to the heart settled that notion. Who knows who put the hit out on Sammy? Next, he'll be calling me telling me Busta killed Sammy. Ha! Or that Busta had Michael kill the fucker. What a freakin joke. Hell, it don't matter because Busta is making me a ton of dough. So, unless I get information that says otherwise, Busta can have my mother-in-law killed. If the boss don't want Michael dead, then the case is closed."

He drove to the club and entered the building. Little Sammy was already inside. Before he could sit at his desk, however, the phone rang.

He answered the phone, "What the fuck do you want and why are you calling me this early?"

He heard Castanza's voice and said, "Sorry, Boss. Didn't know it was you. My phone's been ringing constantly since I got back last night."

They talked for a while then Shapatilo hung up. For a moment he just stared at the walls.

Then he yelled, "Little Sammy, get the hell in here!"

When Little Sammy arrived Shapatilo said, "We got a rat in the office."

. . . .

The McCants family was ready to move to the next phase of their evolution. Mack's son was now three years old and acting like a McCants boy. Linda, his wife, was expecting another child. Robert was preparing to lecture summer classes at Michigan. Richard and Louis had graduated from Wayne State University. Richard was working at the local electric company, Detroit Edison, and Louis was working for Michigan Bell.

Jack was graduating from Cooley High School the next month. He wanted to join his father at the plant, but Frank would not allow it. He insisted that Jack attend Wayne, which he would start in September.

Horace and Ervin were still at Cooley High, with Horace ready to enter his senior year. Both boys liked to double-date, something Jack found amusing.

By now, Martha had really blossomed as a cosmetic sales lady. Frank had gotten her a nice Chevy sedan, which, unlike the house, she kept spotless. He was still relegated to the station wagon. As she fussed over her car, Frank thought, *"I need to be sure she never leaves me stranded again. She's been asking for a car so..."*

The two youngest sons wondered at times how Michael was doing. They noticed, however, the calm in the family after the Packard incident.

Ervin said, "You know, the house is really quiet with the older guys gone. Mom is always on the road, selling her cosmetics, especially in the Sherwood Forest and U. of D. districts. I think she wishes we could live there someday."

Horace replied, "Yeah well, by the time they can afford it, they won't need it. The three of us will be gone and they will have an empty house for the first time since their first year of marriage. If you're going to plan their future, get them in a quieter neighborhood with a nice size home, not one of those monstrosities in Palmer Woods."

Jack overheard the conversation and added, "Nobody mentioned Palmer Woods. I think Ervin was referring to the more normal sized castles, like in the U of D district," and the three of them laughed.

Ervin said, "I do miss Michael. You guys saw him as a troublemaker. But I saw the excitement in his eyes when he was around. Not like that quiet ass Robert, with his head in a book all the time. I don't recall Robert ever playing with me, but I have vague memories of Michael playing with me when I was three."

Horace said, "Well, they are probably imaginary memories. He left home just before you turned three. But I know what you mean because I was four when he left, and I do remember him playing with the three of us. Don't you Jack?"

Jack just looked at the other two and said, "You guys are so petty. You probably don't even know that Robert went to Vietnam and was wounded in the shoulder. I overheard Mack telling Louis and Richard. He didn't go into any details, just that he was not in Germany, like we thought. He also got his PhD and is teaching at Michigan. Now that's a big turnaround from being a dropout loser.

"Not to change the subject, but I'm about to graduate and could make some good money at Dad's plant, but he won't let me work there. He won't let any of us work there. I think it has something to do with his dad. Pops never went to college, so he's hell bent on making sure that all of us go. He must have really disappointed that old fool father of his."

Ervin replied, "Yeah, but you shouldn't refer to him in that manner. There's more to the situation than we know. One day Pops will have to tell us. He can only keep it from us for so long. And we already know about Robert's shocking story."

. . . .

Little Sammy said, "So boss, let me get this straight. Now you want to kill Busta."

Shapatilo said, "Ain't that what I been sayin! We got to kill that fucker, and soon!"

Little Sammy said, "So boss, Busta bin keepin book on us, on the operation, cops and all, right?"

Shapatilo backhanded the sitting giant on his forehead. "Ow, boss. I wish you wouldn't do dat. It hurts!"

Shapatilo said, "Then keep up! Busta's been keeping a record on our activities. Don't know how the boss knows, but he gave me details that only Busta and I knew about. Hell, I didn't even know that Busta was paying that fucker Sumanski. He's got his own private cop in his pocket and wasn't sharing him with me! Mother fuckin' niggers. Just can't trust em."

Little Sammy said, "So boss, now I can kill dat nigger Busta?" pulling his head back.

"I've never liked dat one. He thinks he better than Little Sammy. I can tell, but he ain't better than Little Sammy now, is he? I may be sixty, but I can still handle dat nigger. Somebody shoulda told me he killed my baby brother. If I'd known he kill my baby brother, I'd squashed dat nigger long ago."

Shapatilo added, "Yeah, well we'll just wait until he closes his books for the month. When things die down from the Packard. He'll be relaxed thinking I'm happy about his earnings. And stop with the 'dat' shit, will ya! You even starting to talk like that big fucker."

. . . .

Early June 1978

Busta was feeling uneasy ever since the Packard incident.

"Damn, the boss had Michael trapped and didn't finish da job. He had 'em in his hands and dat White-lookin' nigga-bitch mother of his got 'em out of there. Who da fuck is she? Ray Ray told me she were somehow connected, but I didn't think she was Sicilian. And she married dat Black nigger and gave his ass all dem boys. Wow, she musta really fucked her family up. But not so much dat she ain't still got hooks."

He had sent the boys out to get more information about the Packard incident. He wanted to learn as much about Michael's mother as he could. He even considered sending Ray Ray and Trigger to New

York. As he dwelled on a potential trip for the boys, he heard a car coming up the road and saw the big Lincoln pull into his driveway.

He thought, *"Brothers drive Caddy's while da boss's boys drive Lincolns. Two plus two equals four, so dat would be da boss's boys."*

The four Sicilians walked up the driveway to Busta's home. He invited them in through the side door which led up to the kitchen and down into the basement. Little Sammy and the Gimp walked down into the basement, while the other two men stayed outside in the driveway.

. . . .

"Busta! Git yo ass inhare now! Didn't I tells ya we gots work ta do! Put dat book down and git to the shed! I's goan beat da black off yer, den ya goin to dat field likes I's told ya. No mo schoolin. Youse eight now and it ain't gonna do ya no good down har!"

. . . .

"Busta. We have to go. I can't stay here any longer. Ma is crazy and will work you until you are dead. Pa won't be getting out of prison for ten more years. By then Ma will have ruined you. You'll be eighteen years old with no education, and you're too smart for that. I was lucky. Mrs. Johnson educated me. I've been working in the big house ever since she moved here. Why she moved from Connecticut, I'll never understand. She must have really loved Mr. Johnson. But now she's dead, and I don't plan on staying around here for Mr. Johnson to use me as a fill-in for his wife. And I'm not going to start sharecropping with the two of you. I'm leaving Mississippi tonight, with or without you. There is a train leaving for Chicago and you can join me or not. If you are, be at the depot by 8:00 p.m."

. . . .

"Busta, I'm getting married next week and moving to Detroit. Since you've dropped out of school to work in that meat packing plant, you're old enough to stay here alone. And you were getting such good grades too. If you want, you can move with me and my husband to Detroit. Except you've got to give up that gang life of yours. Always fighting in the street. Let me know pretty soon."

. . . .

Shapatilo sat at his large oak desk waiting for his phone to ring. He knew he would soon be getting a phone call from his boss again.

He thought, *"Every hour on the hour. He calls every hour on the freakin' hour. What kind of schedule does that old fucker keep that he can call me every hour on the hour. I told him today was the day!"*

He heard his crew returning and knew it was Little Sammy because the floorboards were screaming.

He did not look up when the office door opened.

He said, "So you're done? Did he squeal like a pig?"

Busta said, "Yep boss. I's done. And he did squeal a little." He placed a bowling bag on the desk and sat in the chair facing the desk.

Shapatilo looked up, completely startled. He said, "Busta, I wasn't expecting you. Yeah, have a seat. What's this?" and began slowly reaching for his desk-drawer.

Busta anticipated Shapatilo would reach for his gun. He quickly stood up, leaned over the desk, and punched him hard in the nose, knocking his chair back into the wall.

As Shapatilo winced in pain, Busta sat back in his chair and said, "Open da bag."

Shapatilo did not need to. He knew what he would find. Busta said very slowly, "Open da fuckin' bag, motha fucka." Shapatilo, still dazed from the punch, struggled to lean forward, but he didn't need to open it because it was not closed. The head of Little Sammy was too big for the bag to close. He glimpsed over the top of the bag and gasped in horror. Little Sammy's eyes were staring blankly at him. He may have treated Little Sammy poorly, but he loved him like a brother. Enraged, he went for his gun again and was met by four rounds from a magnum. As he fell backward, his foot kicked up the desk, knocking over the bag. Little Sammy's huge dome rolled out of the bag and fell to the floor. Busta got to his feet, stepped over the head, grabbed a small cash bag from Shapatilo's desk, then walked out of the office. He got in his car and drove west. Further west of the city than he had ever been before.

A reward was put out for Busta.

. . . .

Mack said, "Triple doubles. Louis, go straight to jail." He lifted up the miniature race car and placed it on the board spot labeled 'Jail'.

The McCants were having their weekly monopoly game tournament. The three younger brothers were visiting Mack's house. Friday night, just before they began hanging out at a neighborhood house party. The following week they would be at Louis's home, then Richard's home. Horace thought, *"The fourth week we can just party, since Robert and Michael live so far away."* The boys really enjoyed the games since they missed out on them in the sixties when they were too small to play. Monopoly was the family game that the older boys could share with their parents. Somehow, however, the seventies came and no more family games.

Horace thought, *"Mom got a job, and everything changed. No more gossip or soaps for her."*

Linda just watched the games, sitting in a chair holding her three-year-old who wanted to play as well.

Mack said, "Make sure you keep Kenyatta over there. I remember one year when little Jack walked up to the board and flipped it over. Pops was so mad because he was winning."

The boys laughed. Linda could only imagine just how happy this family must have been, chaos and all. She really liked having the boys over once a month. She planned for this Friday all week, getting the dinner menu just right. Her friends even knew not to call her on her special Fridays.

. . . .

Michael decided to hang out on the east side while in town. He had already drove by Santa Rosa to see the boys, catching a glimpse from the corner roof of a building on Lyndon. He thought, *"The boys have grown a lot. Hell, they're men. Horace is bigger than Pops! And Jack, I'd swear Mr. Sherlock looked right at me, for no reason. I'm up on a roof, for Christ sake. Why'd he look up toward this roof?! Anyway, I'll go by Mack's later. It's about time we made peace. Right now, I need to attend to some business."*

Michael jumped into his midnight blue '69 Chevy Malibu, that he had parked at the grocery store off Livernois Avenue, and headed north to the Lodge Freeway. He was headed for the east side.

He drove to Mack Avenue and parked in front of Green's Barbeque Restaurant. He thought, *"Haven't been in here for quite a while."* He ordered a meal then sat and waited. As expected, his friend Ken walked in.

Ken said, "What the…! Michael! Got dam motha fucker, how you been? Dam brother, now you a man! The last time I saw you was in Greektown. We was posed to hook up, but when I got there, you was gone. And a dead dago lay on the ground! That wasn't you, was it?" and laughed.

Michael said, "If I was gone, then how did you last see me in Greektown? Anyway, what's been going on, my brother? How's life been treating you? I've been hanging out west in the windy city. Rippin' and runnin'. Runnin' and rippin'. I'd hope I'd run into yo ass today. I know it's been nine years, but I'd hope your habit of eating ribs on Thursday night hadn't changed. Well, it's Thursday ribs night, right? Have a seat, I just ordered some ribs and chicken."

The two men talk for a couple of hours. Then Michael shared, "So you've expanded your crew. Cool. I've got a job but no crew. Not here in Detroit anyway. Let me clue you in and you tell me if you've got any interest."

· · · · · · · · · · · ·

At midnight Ken and his crew pulled up to a building in the Davison and Dexter area. They parked on the side street, entered the alley off Dexter Avenue, and walked to the back entrance of a medical building. When they got to the back door, Ken showed them the alarm system and told the crew to wait for him. He knew how to get around the alarm, but only one man could go inside until the alarm was turned off. His boys looked puzzled at each other but waited outside. Ken climbed up the outer wall into a window, then came back to the door minutes later.

He said, "I've killed the alarm. Let's go." They climbed up the stairs into the office. The office door was already jimmied when they arrived.

Ken said, "What the…?" but entered. They found the cabinet in the back of the supply room and rifled through it.

Ken said, "What the fuck? Ain't no money in here! Are we being played or what? I was told there would be a hundred grand in here. Let's get out of here."

He thought, *"Michael's playing me. He didn't just arrive at Green's. He's setting me up, but I don't know how or why. He must know about the Twenty Grand crew that was waiting on him, or about Sammy, or both. That's why he canceled the hit on the Twenty. I knew I slipped up when I mentioned seeing him in Greektown. Prick som-bitch always was smart. Too smart for his own good. This is gonna cost him. I'm gonna find him and take him out myself. I know where his parents live."*

. . . .

Frank and Martha rolled over, somewhat exhausted, their contrasting flesh even noticeable in the low light of their room. He said, "Baby, I'm getting too old to handle you. Man, can I go back twenty years? Huh?"

She smiled and said, "So you want to go back to having to deal with a seven-year-old Mack, plus Louis and Richard. Dealing with Robert and Michael? I'll let you do the math."

He smiled and said, "Baby we've done it. Just don't get pregnant after tonight." She broke out into a loud uncontrollable laughter and almost fell off the bed. The gifted bed from a stranger. "Okay, calm down. I know my stuff is still potent."

She giggled and replied, "That's not why I'm laughing. I was just wondering where the freakin' gun is so I can shoot myself!" They both started laughing uncontrollably.

He said, "Shoot me first. Please!! I don't think I can deal with Michael anymore." They continued to laugh until they had tears in their eyes.

Then she said, "Baby, we really did it. All these years. All these family conflicts. And I don't think you have to worry about any more McCants boys since I've been fixed! Imagine nine boys!

"Sweetheart, I really love you. More than I love my sons. I know I'm not supposed to feel that way or say it, but I love you endlessly. You've shared your life history with me. Now it's time you know mine."

They talked until the sun came up. Then they tried to make a baby again.

. . . .

Mid-August 1978

Busta was playing it low by staying in motels along Michigan Avenue, the original route from Detroit to Chicago before the interstates were built. He moved around a lot to different small communities west of Detroit. Communities that had Black populations, only staying two or three nights per location, always parking in the back, and only going out after dark. He wanted to head south or even to Chicago but believed the highway patrols of Michigan, Indiana and Ohio would be on the lookout for him. He had been in hiding for the last two months, ever since he killed Shapatilo.

He got up one morning and drove to a party store, parked, and just sat in the car. He was reflecting on his life. He understood that he was at the end of the road. He could possibly return to Mississippi, but at forty-seven he felt it was too late to start over. Besides, they would eventually find him there. His stash was gone, so all the money he had was in his pockets. A few grand. "Fuck, I wish I'd not turned da monthly dough in yet! But dey was probably waitin until I did befo dey hits me."

As he sat there an unfamiliar car pulled up next to him and a familiar face got out. He thought, *Hell! It's fuckin' Michael! Dis is unbelievable! Da gods do love me! Da motherfucker doesn't even sees me. What da fuck is he doing in dis Podunk town!*

He pulled out the magnum thinking, "I can jest blast himhare and be done wit it. Hell, I mights even git away since I's not known in dese hare parts."

Busta decided to wait until the man came out of the store, but then thought it would be better to follow him. Find out where he was hiding out, then kill him without witnesses. The man came out of the store, looked directly at Busta, gave him the 'Black-Power' salute, then climbed into his car. He opened a cold can of Vernors Ginger Ale, then took a long, drawn-out gulp. He continued to sit there, draining the can in seconds. He then got out of the car, walked up to a trash can, and dropped the can inside. He climbed back into his car, started the engine, threw it into drive, and nonchalantly pulled away.

Busta was transfixed by the man the entire time. "Dat was Michael! But it weren't Michael. What da fuck is goin on? He didn't even react ta me atall. He looks directly ats me acting likes a college nerd, drinkin' fuckin' pop! Shit, he was wearing a freakin' U of M sweater! I must be losin' my mind. I musta fallen asleep and dreamt dat shit up. It never really happened." A few minutes later he realized his mistake.

"Oh shit! Dat was his twin brother Robert! Shit! I jest blows it! I coulda found Michael through dat motha fucka. Which way did he go? Shit! Dat was my moment and I blows it!"

Five minutes later, Robert pulled off I-94 and into his apartment complex, more focused than usual. He thought, *"That was Busta in that car. So that is where he's been hiding out since he killed those gangsters. East side of Ypsi. The police and the mafia must have a heavy net over the city if he's hiding out this far west.*

"He recognized me but was confused. For a moment he thought I was Michael. One day I'm going to get killed by some punk ass trying to take

out Michael. It almost happened just now. And that shit at the Packard? Pops was right. I've got to get Michael under control, or we might all go down. I would kill myself if one of my brothers got hurt because of Michael, and I did nothing to stop it. I can't wait for Michael to employ his so-called plan.

"I saw Busta's right-arm position. He was holding a gun. That's why I looked directly at him, then waved. I needed to disarm him, make him aware I was not who he thought I was. That's why I stayed and drank that harsh ass Vernors Ginger Ale so fast! My throat was on fire! Macho my ass. That's a real man's drink!

"He didn't follow me, so I don't have to defend myself tonight and kill him."

· · · · · · · · · · · · · · ·

Kevin, Ken's right-hand man, got a call and answered it on the first ring.

"Who dat?" said Kevin, trying to mock a character he saw in a movie.

The room was silent as the caller informed Kevin of circumstances that occurred last month. Kevin hung up the phone and looked at his boys Rick, Pedro, and Dicky, then said, "Let's ride."

The three quickly jumped into Rick's car and drove toward Ken's home. When they arrived, Dicky climbed the porch steps and knocked on Ken's door. Ken opened the door and stepped out onto the porch, barefoot and butt-naked under a bathrobe.

He said, "What the fuck you guys doing here at my house like this? All strapped up and shit. What's up?"

Kevin was holding a crowbar at the back of Ken's car. He planted it under the trunk lock, then forced the lid open.

Ken yelled, "Hey man, is you crazy! You fuckin' up my ride!" Kevin reached behind the spare tire and pulled out a bag and poured the contents on the ground. Ten bundles of hundreds laid visible for all to see. Ken looked surprised and dumbfounded. Then it hit him.

"Michael, you played me well. Looks like you win mother fucker."

These were among his last thoughts before he was thrown into the trunk of Kevin's car, minus the robe. No shots were fired, but he was dead before the car hit the road.

. . . .

The four men got out of the Lincoln and approached Busta's home, but only two of the men entered the house. The 6'6" 300-pound behemoth struggled to follow Busta down the basement stairs. Seeing the old steps flexing under the massive weight load influenced the Gimp to stay on the landing.

When Santino 'Little Sammy' Castanza arrived onto the basement floor he said, "Busta, Little Sammy here to see about dat little black book of yours. Where you keep dat little black book?"

Busta thought, "Shit. Dat book was stolen during da last car theft. So if he's askin fo it, den dey must already gots it." Busta stepped forward to reach for the desk drawer. Little Sammy reached out and swatted his wrist away.

He said, "I'll get it," and pulled the drawer open, but it only partially opened. He reached into the drawer but was unable to fit his huge hand into the small opening, so he called the Gimp down. The Gimp struggled to walk down the stairs as well, due to a shorter left leg.

When he finally reached the floor Little Sammy said, "Little Sammy can't get his hand in dat drawer. It won't open all the way. Reach in there and get dat black book out for me."

The Gimp hobbled over to the desk and reached into the small opening. He reached far back and suddenly began screaming and pulled out his hand to find a huge rat trap clamped onto his fingers. Busta pulled his magnum and shot the Gimp in the head, then aimed at Little Sammy, but was knocked onto the desk by the big man. Busta found himself flying through the air, as Little Sammy grabbed his jacket and hurled him across the room. He then charged Busta but clanged his head on the low-hanging heat vents, causing the 6'6" massive man to pause, then lean forward. This put him out of balance and allowed Busta to roll by him.

Busta crawled behind the overturned desk. Little Sammy tried but could not reach over the desk. His two friends entered the house and raced down the stairs, their .38s pistols drawn, only to be met by Busta's magnum. He emptied the gun into them, then rolled away from the desk as Little Sammy regained his balance.

The giant again rushed Busta, but the now limber Busta easily evaded him. He sidestepped the lunging giant, then rushed up the stairs, leaping over the two dead bodies. Little Sammy tripped over the desk as he grabbed at him and crashed to the floor. He grabbed his .45 automatic and fired it through the floorboards, but Busta anticipated this and stood outside next to the house until Little Sammy's gun was empty.

Busta now took his time walking back into the house. He could hear Little Sammy struggling to get off the floor and he thought about the trouble he used to have getting off the sofa, or the car seat, or out of the bathtub.

He eventually returned to the basement with a reloaded magnum, an old axe, and a new bowling bag.

. . . .

Sumanski pulled up to Mediterranean Boot Social Club but saw Busta's car, so he pulled around the corner and waited. He did not want Busta to know his boss called him. He is not sure what Shapatilo wanted, but it cannot be good for Busta. Sumanski thought, "I can't wait to be free of that motherfucker. My dependence on him has gotten out of control." A minute after Sumanski arrived, Busta left the office, jumped into his '78 burgundy Caddie and drove away. Sumanski pulled up, parked, and entered the building. A moment later he ran back to his car and called in an APB on Mr. Wilson 'Busta' Johnson.

CHAPTER TWENTY

The Bridge

On a late evening during the fourth week of August of '78, a police command car pulled up on the street directly in front of the McCants residence. A tall, athletically built, police commander, about ten years younger than Frank, got out of the car. Within minutes, a second and third car arrived. Hearing the unusual traffic, Frank and Martha exited the house as the commander approached the porch. He climbed the stairs and asked them if he could speak to them inside.

Once inside the unusually quiet house, the commander asked Frank and Martha to please have a seat. Their son Jack entered the adjoining living-dining room and sat at the dining room table, near his parents.

The commander began with, "Mr. and Mrs. McCants. My name is Commander Cavaletti of the Detroit Police Department. I have bad news for you this evening. One of your sons has been killed. It was Michael. Unfortunately, he fell off the MacArthur Bridge to Belle

Isle, after an altercation with a Mr. Wilson 'Busta' Johnson. Both men are dead, having been shot by the police during an altercation on the bridge. Divers have retrieved Mr. Johnson's body, but as of this moment, we have yet to find Michael. I am very sorry for your loss."

. . . .

Six hours earlier

The two youngest McCants boys rode on the East Jefferson Avenue bus to Van Dyke Avenue, then departed the bus. They were going to visit two sisters who lived nearby on Fisher Street. However, they had noticed some other young girls across the street from the bus and wanted to get a better look at them, even though they had two more stops to go.

Once across Jefferson, Ervin said, "I knew this would be a waste. Those are westside Immaculata types. All light-skinned and all. They probably don't even go to Cass. Now we have five additional blocks to walk. I hope these friends of yours have some color."

Horace smiled. He loved Immaculata types, with their creamy skin tones and silky hair. The boys walked three blocks east on Jefferson to Iroquois, then turned up the block. Horace gazed at the huge homes on the block and said, "Wow! I didn't know these girls were rich. Look at these mansions! Like Palmer Woods! This is going to be great."

Ervin thought, *"He has never been invited to any homes in Palmer Woods. Why does he think this will be any different? Only cream-colored girls live in homes like this anyway."*

The boys had never been to this part of town. Pristine mansion after mansion, set deep on each lot, creating large immaculate front yards with two and three car garages, and even apartments or carriage homes above them on back lots. Few cars were parked on the street. Most were tucked away next to the homes or stored in the garages.

Halfway up the block, they encountered an elderly lady working on a flower bed near the curb of the street, and Horace immediately regretted picking this block. Old White ladies scared him. She was busy tending her flowers and had not noticed the boys. Just as the two brothers reached her driveway, she started to rise, but stumbled. Horace hesitated to move, nervous about approaching an elderly White lady. Ervin, however, thinking of the O'Learys across the street from them on Santa Rosa, moved in quickly to prevent her from falling.

She thanked him for his assistance but was unable to focus on his face, so she said, "Oh my, I can't see you very well. I must have dropped my glasses."

Ervin said, "No Ma'am, they are hanging around your neck."

She smiled and said, "Of course they are. That's why I wear this dumb chain around my neck. There, now I can see."

She looked deep into Ervin's face and said, "My, such a nice-looking young man. And polite too. Thank you for saving me from falling. Now that would have been a disaster! I don't bounce well like I use to," and smiled.

As Ervin continued to assist the lady, her husband came to the living room window and looked out. He saw a man holding his wife's wrist and rushed out of the door, golfclub in hand.

She saw him approaching and said, "Now now, dear. Relax. This handsome young man just saved me from a terrible tumble. Put that dumb club away. Heck, you'll be out of breath before you even get here." Her husband slowed down and said, "Well, my mistake. It just looked like...."

The lady waddled up the walkway toward the sidewalk where Horace was standing, looking extremely nervous. He thought, "*That dummy almost got us in trouble. If the police show up, how are we going to explain what we're doing here? This is obviously a White neighborhood. I don't think those girls live in these mansions.*"

When the woman reached the sidewalk, she glanced up at Horace, gasped, and said, "Honey, it's the 'housekeeper'!"

. . . .

The news of the murder at the Mediterranean Boot Social Club had been circulating for almost three months. The street people knew, however, there was more to the story. Everyone knew about the four bodies found at Busta's house. It was obvious to the neighbors that Busta did not invite four White men into his home. Not without his crew there. There was definitely a connection between the two incidents. The police continued to be on the lookout for Busta, the main suspect. A reward from the owners of the club had quickly circulated and several additional unsanctioned cars joined in on the pursuit. Ray Ray and his crew wanted to help Busta, but he had not been in contact with any of them since that fateful day. The driver of a midnight blue '69 Chevelle Malibu, however, had a special interest in finding Busta. He was not interested in the reward. He wanted Busta for personal reasons.

Michael had been hiding in a garage in Southwest Detroit, awaiting word on Busta's status. After feeding information to Castanza, he half expected Busta to be dead. Unfortunately, his plan failed, Shapatilo was dead, and Busta was on the run. Now that a reward for Busta was public knowledge, Michael planned to join in on the hunt. He used a police scanner, which he had purchased in Chicago, to listen to police updates. According to the information he received from the scanner, the last sightings of Busta was in the Southwest part of town. Michael believed that Busta would try to hold up until nightfall, then slide out of town southward to Ohio, avoiding the major highways. He assumed that Busta might want to get back to the South, which is why Michael was holding out near the southern route of Fort Street.

Michael had to be careful because the police were looking for him as well. He suspected his old warrant from the winter of '71 was still outstanding. If he got careless then he could fall into the same trap that awaited Buster. However, he just felt compelled to complete their unfinished business. They both wanted the same thing; the death of the other.

. . . .

Horace and Ervin sat in sturdy bright lawn chairs as the lady poured them a second glass of lemonade. Then she went back into the house.

Her husband, seating across from the boys, said, "So you are not our 'housekeeper.' That's the nickname she gave the young man. His name was Michael. Both of you resemble him, but you, Horace is it, look just like him. I thought for a moment that you were him. You know the name Horace comes from the Latin name Horatius. It means time or timekeeper. Are you a timekeeper Horace? Is that why you keep looking at your watch?"

The boys had heard the story about Michael before, just ten minutes ago. Horace wanted them to get on their way before the gentleman began the story again.

Horace thought, *"Nice couple but they are really old. Older than the O'Learys. He keeps repeating himself."*

Ervin said, "Sir, we do have a brother named Michael, but I can't imagine him coming this far east, near the river. It was in '71? He would have been nineteen. Horace is seventeen years old, and I'll be sixteen years old in a few weeks."

The elderly man said, "I know you're not him. You said you had a brother named Michael before, so you don't need to repeat yourself. I'm just saying you resemble him. Glad to know your Michael is probably our Michael. How is he doing?"

Horace spoke up. "Michael left town in '71 and no one in the family has seen him since. He was always coming and going. We only saw him periodically since we were small. Our brother Jack claimed he would see him while we played on the playground during recess, but I didn't believe him. I never saw him. Michael has a twin brother named Robert. He is a college professor at the University of Michigan."

The man said, "Your parents must be very proud of him. And the rest of you boys as well. I can tell they did a good job raising you. We didn't get to know Michael that well. He had some problems, and I'm sure one day he will work them out. He was so young when he was here before. Draft age as I remember it."

Ervin thought, *"Michael was of Draft age in '71. That's the year Robert left for the service. I wonder if Michael also got drafted and is still in the service?"*

Horace looked at his watch again just as the woman came back outside.

He said, "Sir, it was a pleasure meeting you and your lovely wife, but Ervin and I have an appointment with some friends around the block. We must be going now."

The lady said, "Dear, these young men obviously came here to visit young girls. We have taken enough of their time. Here boys. I've packed a small bag of sandwiches and other goodies for you and your friends. Now run along and enjoy the rest of your day."

As the boys rose, the man smiled and extended his hand, and both teens shook it. Then Ervin, ever the ladies' man, extended his hand to the lady. She reached out to him, he grasped her hand, raised it up as he bent over slightly, and planted a light kiss on her wrinkled knuckles. She smiled; her husband chuckled, and Horace choked.

As the boys walked down the driveway, Horace said, "Now what are you going to say to the cops when they get a report of an attempted rape!"

Ervin just smiled and said, "My first and last kiss with a White girl."

The boys walked to the corner and turned right. Then they saw the unexpected. The neighborhood dramatically changed. All the houses two blocks over were shotgun houses.

When they arrived, they walked onto the porch of the girls' home and knocked. The girls came bustling out and one of them said, "You guys are late. What have you been doing, checking out other chicks? Well, we've already planned our day. We're going to walk over to Belle Isle. These will be the last warm days for a walk that far. You can join us if you choose to." The boys chose to join them on Belle Isle. First, however, they asked to use the facilities, after drinking so much lemon aide. As they looked at each other Ervin smiled.

Ervin thought, *"Love me some east-side girls."*

Horace thought, *"Oh well. At least they are Cass Tech girls."*

· · · · · · · · · · · · · ·

Michael checked his fuel tank to ensure he had enough gas. He never liked to have a full tank while playing 'pursuit', but certainly did not want to run out of fuel. He also felt the need to check his tire pressure, since his car was starting to drift slightly to the right. He pulled into a gas station on Fort Street and Schaefer Highway and checked the pressure on his front right tire, which was slightly low. As he began adding air, he heard the screeching of tires and the roar of car engines nearby. Three cars were drag racing southeast on Schaefer, just northwest of I-75. The cars were not visible yet, due to the obstruction of the freeway, but their arrival was imminent. Finally, the cars came bustling around the Marathon Petroleum refineries, barreling down the two-lane road. Suddenly a burgundy '78 Cadillac and two black Lincoln Continentals burst into view. None of the cars were built for racing, so this was not a race but rather a death pursuit. The police were unaware of the disturbance as the cars travelled under the I-75 overpass, crossed Fort Street, and blew by Michael.

He said, "I'd recognize that color Caddie anywhere. It's Busta's ass. They've got him hemmed in!"

Before he could get behind his wheel, Michael heard rapid gunfire, and one of the Continentals lost control and crashed into a nearby residential garage, just east of Fort Street. Michael anticipated Busta's next move and waited. As predicted, Busta made a hard U-turn, spinning almost out of control, and returned to drive directly in front of him. The other Continental attempted the same maneuver, with disastrous results. The car flipped over and tumbled several times before coming to rest against a large elm tree. As Busta crossed Fort Street he could hear sirens approaching from the north on Schaefer, so he had to slow down to make a right turn onto the northbound I-75 entrance.

As he slowed, he quickly glanced to his right, and thought, "*Shit. If I didn't know no better, I'd swear dat's Michael's ass over at dat gas station.*"

Michael only confirmed his suspicions as he pulled up behind the Cadillac. The two cars entered the northbound freeway with the downtown Detroit skyline in plain view. The police were not far behind.

. . . .

Busta reflected on his life over the past forty-seven years. He thought, "*Shit, dis is the end of da road fo me, but I'll be gotdamn if I don't take dat mothafucken Michael wit me. I had a great freakin' life, den this little prick enters it. I may be goin' out, but he's definitely goin' wit me. He thinks he's gots me cornered but I's got his ass as well. Da same punkass cops dat wants me, wants him too. Sumanski hates Michael and I'ma goin' ta make sho dis time dat Polock catches em.*"

Michael, gripping his steering wheel as their cars roar through traffic at over 95 mph, thought, *"This is probably it for me. I'm not following any of my survival strategies, leaving myself exposed by chasing this dickhead. But it'll be worth it to finally catch this bastard. My family will continue to be in danger as long as he lives.*

"I've been living this wild life for almost thirteen years. Most of the events are now just a blur. Hell, I barely remember anything during Robert's time in the service. We had never been separated before. I could always reach out for him, and he was always there. I don't understand it, but having him around kept me fresh, alert, and alive. When he was gone, I felt empty. If I survive this day, I promise I will spend more time with him. I never realized just how much I needed him."

Michael stumped on his accelerator as the cars completed crossing the two-mile long I-75 Rouge River bridge. He crashed into the Cadillac at Springwells Street, then again at Livernois Avenue. The impacts barely disturbed the heavy steal monster. The two cars approached the oncoming curve at the Interstate-96 entrance, but to Michael's surprise, Busta continued driving on the northbound I-75 split into downtown Detroit.

He said, "I can't believe he's going to enter the business district. He had an open road going out I-96."

Busta continued racing out I-75, passing Cass Tech and the old Motown recording studio on Woodward Avenue. He remained in the left lane, indicating he was exiting the freeway at Gratiot, which he did. Michael stopped bumping him since it served no purpose.

Busta came up onto Gratiot Avenue, turned left by Joe Muer's seafood restaurant, then turned right onto Vernor Highway, still traveling over 80 mph, only slowing down to make the turn. He continued down Vernor until he got to East Grand Boulevard, just south of the old Packard plant. Then to Michael's surprise, he made a hard right turn onto the Boulevard. Michael said, "This sucker is heading for Belle Isle! He's planning to commit suicide by driving into the river!" Michael floored his accelerator, trying to pass Busta, but the Cadillac weaved between lanes preventing Michael from getting by him. Southbound cars were forced off the road as the two cars roared by. Michael knew they were coming up to the tunnel under Jefferson Avenue, which led to the MacArthur Bridge, so he tried one more time to push Busta off the road. He crashed broadside into the right side of the Cadillac and Busta lost control of his car and drove into the oncoming traffic on the Boulevard, then the left side of the tunnel, crossing all lanes of Jefferson Avenue. He finally crashed into a large elm tree on the lawn of the Brodhead Naval Armory. Michael pulled up behind the Cadillac, just as Busta exited the car. Traffic from both directions of the nine-lane Jefferson Avenue was forced to halt. Customers in the nearby Big Boy restaurant poured into the street to marvel at the commotion. Naval personnel came out of the Armory. Police sirens could be heard blaring from the east, north and west.

Busta ran south toward the bridge with Michael in pursuit. Michael continued to ask himself, "Why are you chasing this man to both of your demise?" He would never know that he missed his two youngest brothers by a mere thirty minutes.

· · · · · · · · · ·

The two young couples settled on a picnic table, not far from MacArthur Bridge. After the long walk, the girls did not want to go any further into the park. That would extend their walk home.

Jessica thought, *"I love the view sitting here near the river and bridge. Just hate crossing that bridge. Really scary since it's so high over the water. These boys are really nice. Now Katherine and I have to decide who gets which one. Probably select by age. Horace is my age so..."*

She did not know that the decision had already been made.

Katherine said, "So you say you got these sandwiches from a lady on Iroquois? That's crazy. What were you doing over there anyway?"

Horace said, "Walking from the bus stop. We were just walking by, and Ervin offered the lady some assistance, so she gave us these sandwiches."

"Just what kind of assistance did you offer her?" Jessica replied, then laughed.

Katherine examined her sandwich, but Ervin noticed and said, "Don't worry. They're fine. She was a great old lady and would not hurt a flea."

Jessica said, "So I was right about you checking out other chicks, huh?" They all laughed.

They had been sitting at the picnic table for about twenty minutes when they heard the sirens. This was not an uncommon sound in the city, so neither of the teens looked up. The sound, however, began coming up the bridge and this alarmed all of them.

Horace said, "What the hell! Look! Those two men fighting on the bridge! Ervin, let's go get a closer look."

Ervin, however, had already jumped up and was starting to run to the bridge, shouting, "You girls stay here. We'll be back in a minute."

When they got to the bridge, they saw the police in the background. One of the men was huge compared to the other man. Both were seriously hurting each other. Both were exhausted but still throwing heavy blows. Then Horace yelled, "Oh... My... God!! That's Michael!"

He started to run toward the fight even though the police were opposite them with guns drawn.

Ervin forcefully grabbed his arm and yelled, "Horace, that big cop's going to shoot both of them. We've got to get back!"

Horace got ready to yell, but Ervin anticipated this and clamped his hand over his big brother's mouth.

He said, "No dummy. We can't distract him."

Horace said, "Isn't that Busta? Michael fighting Busta!? He can't beat him alone. He's too big. We've got to help! I'm going to kill Busta!"

Ervin, near tears, said, "No! We'll get shot too." The police officers saw the boys and directed them to get further back down their side of the bridge. Traffic was stopped in both directions. Ervin continued to try and pull Horace back, away from the fight, but was not having any success.

Horace said, "Let me go fool! That's my brother!"

Ervin finally lost his grip. By now, however, several police officers had reached them and pushed them and the other spectators away. Jessica and Katherine, having ignored Ervin's instructions to stay at the table, looked on in disbelief.

. . . .

Busta and Michael were throwing heavy blows at each other. Michael tagged Busta with several combinations, driving Busta backward toward the railing, but Busta recovered and landed a heavy blow to Michael's chest, dropping him to his knees. Michael had underestimated the speed of the old man and was getting his worst whooping ever. Busta tried to stomp Michael, but Michael rolled to his right, and was barely back on his feet when Busta pivoted and struck him again in the face. Michael's knees buckled and he fell backward and went down again. However, Busta could not move forward. He had gotten into great shape, but he was still a forty-seven-year-old big man, over 230 pounds, a lot of weight to lug around in a street fight with the likes of Michael.

Michael rose and moved to his left. He then squatted down, rushed in, and wrapped his arms around Busta's knees, pivoted behind Busta, lifted him an inch off the ground, then jerked Busta to his left. Busta lost his balance and crashed to the ground. Michael rolled away as the big man hit the hard concrete and howled in agony, the wind knocked out of him. Michael jumped to his feet but pulled back, uncertain of his next move. Busta lay on the hard concrete for a few seconds, then stood up. Michael moved in closer to take advantage of Busta's unsteady stance and paid dearly for it. Busta caught Michael with an uppercut hook to the jaw, which should have broken his entire face and knocked him unconscious. Instead, Michael partially blocked the blow. The impact still lifted him off his feet and down onto his back. Busta lifted his foot to stomp him, but Michael rolled away just as the size fourteens came crashing down. Busta was now exhausted. In seconds Michael was back on his feet, but his head was not clear, so he could not take advantage of the lull in Busta's attack. The men stood a yard apart. Busta was unable to lift his arms. Michael's vision was somewhat impaired. They continued circling one another, neither wanting to commit yet another attack.

Finally, Michael did something totally out of character. He charged Busta like a football linebacker, wrapped his arms around Busta's waist and drove him with all his might to the railing. Now Busta's 6'4" frame proved to be a disadvantage, as his back struck the railing, and he tipped over the side. Michael, suddenly thinking about Sammy the Pincer, grabbed Busta's size fourteens, preventing him from falling over the railing. When Busta's feet hit the ground, he reached down and grabbed Michael's 170 pounds, lifted him over his head, then began to turn to toss him over the rail. Then Lieutenant Sumanski emptied his .38, with four rounds hitting Busta in the chest. The impact of the bullets sent both men over the Belle Isle bridge's west railing.

. . . .

Lieutenant Sumanski heard on his radio that Busta had been sighted heading east on Vernor Highway. By the time he got from 1300 Beaubien to Vernor and Gratiot, the report had two men fighting on the bridge to Belle Isle. He radioed ahead that no one was to approach the suspects until he arrived, since they were probably armed and dangerous.

He drove east to East Grand Boulevard, then south on the Boulevard to Jefferson, going through the Jefferson tunnel to the bridge. When he drove out of the south end of the tunnel, the roads to the island, as well as East and West Jefferson, were cordoned off. Traffic on the eastbound side of Jefferson had backed up a mile because of the heavy traffic headed for the island. Sumanski parked his cruiser then proceeded onto the bridge, gun drawn.

. . . .

Busta's body began to flip over the railing, and he released his grip on Michael. As he grabbed Busta's body, Michael thought he heard a familiar voice of panic and shock from the crowd. He climbed the falling body, and just before Busta and he cleared the railing, Michael leaped to the outer railing. He grabbed the opening between the concrete rails, swung down to a small piece of protruding rebar, down to a second piece of exposed rebar, then a third, then under the bridge. He could now clearly hear familiar voices.

Busta flipped over twice before hitting the water.

His last thoughts were, *"I knows if I kilt the boss, they would be fishin me out da river."*

Sumanski heard the huge splash as he raced to the railing. He saw the water pool just before Busta's body surfaced for a moment, then disappeared under the blue-white waves.

Michael looked up and saw Sumanski peering over the railing, so he began making his way to the underside of the bridge. He could still feel Sumanski's presence just above him, so he climbed further upward to the undercarriage of the road. There he rested.

Sumanski checked his gun. It was empty, so he reloaded it. With a grin on his face, he thought, *"Nigga thought he owned me. Well, not anymore. Killed that little fucker from the alley as well. Now that's a two-fer! Ha!"*

The police struggled to hold the crowd back. There were shouts of "Cops killed Busta!", "Cops killed that young brotha!", "That pig shot those unarmed men!" The police, however, were able to push the crowd back to the island. The island was closed within the hour and evacuated. The shooting site was already taped off from the public and the southbound bridge traffic onto the island was redirected. Cars drove north off the bridge, only slowing down near the shooting site. The pedestrians, including four teenagers, were allowed to walk north over the east side of the bridge. The two dejected young males could not stop crying. Neither could the two girls.

. . . .

Michael had to wait until 7:00 p.m. before he could leave the bridge. Even then, the police coverage of the island was extremely heavy. He had to hold onto the outer side of the railings until he was pass the police directing traffic. He found a couple of men who were sleeping off the evening after a day of Boone's Farm wine. He encouraged them to join him for more wine, and the three of them walked to the bridge. The police were surprised to find anyone still on the island, and made them exit immediately.

"Hopefully they won't notice me if I stay with these two gentlemen." He had yet to realize that he did not need to be concerned about the police seeing him, since they presumed he was dead.

As he reached the north side of the bridge Michael began to realize just how badly injured he was. The beating he took from Busta was now kicking in. He knew he had to get home as soon as possible. However, he was confused where home was. Was it the carriage house on Iroquois or the frame house on Santa Rosa? He knew his family lived on Santa Rosa, a place he had not resided at for thirteen years. Regardless of the lengthy time, he did not want to be alone that evening, so he decided to head west to Santa Rosa.

Once off the bridge he looked for his car. The vehicle was missing, so he assumed the police had towed the car away. After giving his new friends a five-dollar bill, he caught the westbound Jefferson Avenue bus heading toward downtown. Then he transferred to the Fenkell Avenue bus at the downtown bus terminal at State Street, Shelby Street, and Griswold Street. Once he got on the bus, he lost consciousness.

. . . .

Ervin and Horace had arrived home an hour after Commander Cavaletti made his announcement. Their parents could tell that both boys already knew about the tragedy. Both crashed onto their beds and stayed there the rest of the evening. Neither told their parents what they had witnessed earlier that day. Jack stayed up with his parents, trying to console his mother. Mack, Richard, and Louis, extremely depressed after hearing the news, had already left for the evening with plans to return in the morning. Ervin wanted to call Robert, but assumed someone else had already made the call. He dreaded hearing the anguish of Robert's voice over the phone.

The following morning Ervin asked his father if Robert had been informed. His father could only return a blank stare. So, Ervin went upstairs to find Robert's Ann Arbor phone number, which Robert had written on paper for them and left in his old bedroom. He planned to call Robert at his apartment. What he found when he entered the room shocked him and he began to scream for his parents. Michael was lying in Robert's old bed!

He was unconscious, but alive. There was a blood streak in his short afro. The small crease across his scalp was obvious. He had been shot. His face was a mess with bruises and two black eyes. His lip was busted, and his chin was crusted with blood. His knuckles were busted and bloody, and his shirt was almost torn off his body. Bruises all over his chest told the rest of the story.

Ervin continued to yell for his parents, then he noticed Michael awakening. He said, "Michael, I thought the cops killed you! I thought you were dead! Horace and I saw them shoot you on the Belle Isle bridge! I saw you and Busta fall off the bridge! It was horrible!"

Ervin dropped to his knees and cried uncontrollably. Horace rushed up the stairs and stood behind him, also crying.

Then Horace said, "What happened to you Michael? How did you get here? Have you been shot?"

Horace sat on the side of the bed, next to Ervin, but was afraid to touch Michael. Frank rushed up the stairs and into the room, followed by Martha and Jack. Mack, Louis, and Richard were just pulling their cars into the driveway.

Martha saw Michael and burst into tears, her knees giving way. Jack reached out to her to prevent her from hitting the floor.

She blubbered, "Oh, thank you Jesus! God, thank you Jesus! Thank you, Grandmother!" Frank just stood there staring in amazement, like he was watching a miracle. Horace looked at his mother and said, "Mom, we saw them shoot Michael. How did he get here?"

Ervin looked up at his mother and said, "Ma, I saw them kill him! I saw him fall into the river! I've got to call Robert!" Ervin jumped up and grabbed the phone, but Jack gently took the phone from him and shook his head. Mack, Richard, and Louis climbed the stairs and stood in the doorway near Frank.

Then Michael stunned the room when he mumbled, "Dant Da Da Don!!!!!! I'm sup-er-man!!! I can fly just like Mighty Mouse!"

Only after Michael fell back unconscious did Ervin notice the old scar on Michael's shoulder. Jack smiled at his two younger brothers, then, still staring at Michael, said to them, "Ervin, you don't need to call Robert about Michael. All of us, except the two of you, and the rest of the family, have always known that Robert is Michael. They are one and the same."

The End

Epilogue

January 1958

A young mother enrolled her five-year-old son into the Royal Oak Township School District, a community just north of the city of Detroit. He would attend George Washington Carver Elementary, one block west of her home. She also requested if a school psychologist could interview her son. She was living in government housing and could not afford a private psychologist. The child attended school only half-days, so they arranged for the psychologist to see the boy during the school recess, just before his afternoon kindergarten class began. Only the principal would be aware of the sessions.

The boy walked the one block to school alone each day, crossing Wyoming Avenue. His mother watched him enter the building from the street corner, just outside their residence, since she had two smaller children in the home. He could walk home after school with his older brother, who was a first grader. After a while the mother did not bother to monitor the boy's progress once he was across Wyoming, since he was a responsible child and could be trusted to go straight into the building.

The mother introduced her son as Robert having an imaginary friend named Michael, the name of his twin brother who had died in childbirth. The psychologist, Dr. Elizabeth White, interviewed Robert for three months. Her findings were just as the mother feared. Robert suffered from a split personality disorder. He was Robert, and he was Michael.

After three months, Dr. White was reassigned to another school district, so the sessions had to end. However, her final report read as follows:

> Mrs. Martha McCants' son Robert, a mild mannered five-year-old, has an imaginary friend whom he believes is his actual twin brother Michael. Some days the child enters my office as Robert, clothing and all. On other days the child presents himself as the hyperactive, precocious Michael, with an entirely different wardrobe, voice cadence, and approach. Both personas seem to understand these sessions are specific for them and intended to deal with their individual personalities. They truly believe they are two different individuals.

> There have been days when Robert has excused himself for a moment, then returned to the room as Michael, with an excuse why Robert could not return. On other days Michael will attend the session, leave, and return as Robert, just to say hello, as if he had not seen me that day. Robert is unaware of discussions I have with Michael. However, Michael seems to be totally aware of all the discussions I have with Robert. One could very easily believe they are two different children!

> Michael has even managed to enroll himself into the morning kindergarten class. Apparently, he approached the teacher just after recess the first week of school, and not realizing it

was actually Robert and not a twin child, placed him into her morning session. The mother, with two smaller children at home, is afraid of the situation and does not interfere. She allows the child to leave in the morning, knowing he is not due in school until noon.

I have interviewed the teacher who works both sessions of kindergarten. She believes she has twins in her classes, one in the morning and one in the afternoon! Of course, I do not attempt to explain it to the teacher, and the child's mother, Mrs. McCants, only responds accordingly when discussing her 'two children' with the teacher. She is afraid that the authorities will attempt to take her child from her if the truth is revealed, so she goes along with the deception.

At no time do they attempt to switch personas in my presence. The child, however, will communicate with his alter-ego when left alone. I have witnessed this without his/their knowledge. I suspect that subconsciously the child's mind knows something is not right and therefore only attempts this communication when left alone. (Or perhaps he is tired of being reprimanded by his parents for doing this and therefore protects himself by not attempting this form of communication in other's presence?) They act as if they are sitting next to each other or that the other child is standing in the doorway, peeking into the room!

My conclusions are that it is very possible that the young child could be Robert imagining Michael, OR the child could actually be Michael imagining Robert! There is no way to conclude one way or the other. Robert and Michael are truly one and the same child. Which persona is the dominant personality is anyone's guess since neither persona attempts to dominate the other. I strongly recommend that further study be made with this marvel of psychosis. This young child could be headed for serious social problems if this issue is not addressed. His mother loves Robert dearly and hates the fact that this intruding persona named Michael is interfering in her son's development. She only wants Michael to go away. This could be very dangerous for the child if Michael is indeed the actual person.

. . . .

The head Psychiatrist of the Psychology and Psychiatric Division of Oakland County reviewed the report by the psychologist. He never wanted to send a resource to this community and only complied with the request to avoid any suggestions that he was neglecting the township, which was why he assigned an inexperienced, young, female doctor to the school.

He concluded the work by Dr. White was seriously flawed and therefore would not share the report with the parents. He had experience with Split Personality Disorder and did not believe this was a true case of it. Merely an imaginative child. There was no need to upset the parents of the child with such nonsense. Nor did his department have the budget for an extended assignment, especially in the tiny colored community of Royal Oak Township. This is why he reassigned the doctor to another school. With time, Dr. Karl Schutz believed, Robert would merely grow out of it.

. . . .

August 31, 1978

A middle-aged White woman walked up a block in Cooper Canyon, a neighborhood in the northeast corner of the city bordering the city of Harper Woods on the east and Eight Mile Rd to the north. The name suggested the community was heavily populated by Detroit police officers. She walked house to house on the block trying to sell various cosmetics with moderate success. She approached a home on Carlisle Street, just west of Kelly Road, knocked on the door but no one answered. She looked around, then walked around to the back of the house and returned a few minutes later, brushing dirt off her pink dress. She walked back to her car and drove away, tossing a small note into a trash container on her back seat. The note read,

"Send Unearned Money And Never Spend or Keep It.

Later that day, the Detroit Police Internal Affairs division at 1300 Beaubien in downtown Detroit received an anonymous call about a cop on the take. They were directed to a pink folder buried at the bottom of the inbox at the 12th Precinct's front desk. It had several pages torn from a small binder. The pages implied that a cop had been paid hundreds of thousands of dollars over the last decade. After getting a warrant from a judge, they search the home of the police officer in question and found $100,000 buried in his backyard rose garden. Lieutenant Sumanski was arrested later that day.

While Martha was on her knees, an elderly woman, having just turned 95, was sitting in her parlor in Wilmington, North Carolina, pondering the events as they unfolded hundreds of miles to her north. Her granddaughter, who recently contacted her, had her hands full and does not know it. She was concerned that Martha believed her problems were resolved. She spoke to no one in particular, especially since she was alone.

"My po Martha. Child dinks her matta is ober, but it ain't, no sir ree it ain't ober. She dinks dat because dat fool who fell into the drink is fish food her shit is ober. But it ain't ober. It jest beginnin. I guess I caint let dat dumb rule of mine, about jest one phone call, end my helpin my baby-gurl. Too bad she gots to ruin dat purty pink dress of hern.

"And dhoes two boys of hern, dhoes twins, day in fo mo fun and dance too! I gots to keep both eyes on dhem, one eye on Michael and one on Robert. Don't know how it happin but its got to be cause of me! Sometin I's done, I bet cha! Day was born in late 1951, and I was bad in late 1951, just weeks before day birth. So, I gots to see dis one through. Lordy-bee, I gots to see dis one through. What I shoulda-woulda-coulda ain't gon buy me a cup of coffee! What's don is don, so I gots to take it out of dee obin and stepup to it!

"My grandmammy didn't prepare me for dis. She ain't neber mention dis type of thang. Two-in-one! No-sir-ree-bob she aint! All I's kno, dis shit ain't no-wheres nar ober. No wheres indeed."

A Note about the Author

Omari Bayi, a 4th generation Detroiter, has been writing novels since 2019. *MICHAEL* is his third novel, but the first to be published. The manuscripts for *MICHAEL II* and *MICHAEL III* are completed and will soon follow.

www.bikobooks.com